Praise for
THE SOUND OF
BROKEN ABSOLUTES
from the epic fantasy series
THE VAULT OF HEAVEN

"*The Sound of Broken Absolutes* is one of the most beautiful stories I've ever read … stunningly gorgeous, painfully intimate, and magnificently epic. This is a story of war, music, loss, and restoration, and it will touch the hearts of its readers."

~The Ranting Dragon

"*The Sound of Broken Absolutes* offers a theme of rebuilding our broken selves. It resonates perfectly. Orullian pours love and dread into his rich novella about art, loss and reconstruction. His tale disturbs and ultimately uplifts with the authenticity only possible from a writer who looked life's hardship in the eye and shook its bony hand."

~PasteMagazine.com

Praise for
THE UNREMEMBERED
and
TRIAL OF INTENTIONS
BOOKS ONE & TWO of
THE VAULT OF HEAVEN

"Engaging characters and powerful storytelling in the tradition of Robert Jordan, Terry Goodkind, and Dennis L. McKiernan make this a top-notch fantasy by a new author to watch."

~ *Library Journal* (Starred review)

"A sprawling, complex tale of magic and destiny that won't disappoint its readers. This auspicious beginning for author Peter Orullian will have you looking forward to more." ~ Terry Brooks

"*The Vault of Heaven* is an ambitious story in the mold of Robert Jordan and Terry Goodkind. Peter Orullian is a name to watch in the field of epic fantasy." 〜 Kevin J. Anderson

"This is one huge, powerful, compelling, hard-hitting story . . . *The Vault of Heaven* is a major fantasy adventure." 〜 Piers Anthony

"A fine debut!" 〜 Brandon Sanderson

"Great fantasy tales plunge us into vivid new worlds, in the company of fascinating characters. The Vault of Heaven is great fantasy. It grips you and shows you true friendship, strange places, and heroes growing to confront world-shaking evil. Magnificent! I want more!" 〜 Ed Greenwood

"*The Vault of Heaven* by Peter Orullian is a vast canvas filled with thought-provoking ideas on the questions of good and evil that engage us all." 〜 Anne Perry

"Intricately crafted with its own distinct melody, *The Unremembered* is a groundbreaking work of epic fantasy." 〜 Bookwormblues.net

"Sometimes you just need a big, fat fantasy, and Peter Orullian's remastered edition of *The Unremembered* delivers everything you're looking for: a fascinating world, tense action, charismatic characters, and a magic system the like of which you've never imagined." 〜 Aidan Moher
A Dribble of Ink
Hugo Award Winner

"*The Unremembered* captures the unique essence and mystery of music, and weaves it into every line of a compelling and exciting world, while telling a character-driven story that resonates through the ages . . . a work of art on par with the masters of the genre, Jordan, Rothfuss, Tolkien, and more."

⌒ Elitistbookreviews.com
2013 & 2014 Hugo-nominated
for best review site

"Engaging characters, complex magic, and expertly written—a whole new kind of epic fantasy!" ⌒ Suvudu.com

"*Trial of Intentions* is a story of music and magic, of daring and sacrifice, in an intricate and believable world, where characters face difficult and heartbreaking choices. Orullian is doing things I haven't seen in other books, including an original system of magic. This tale will resonate with readers long after the cover is closed." ⌒ Robin Hobb

"Peter Orullian's *Trial of Intentions* is a book enormous in scope and in intricacy, with a welter of political, cultural, and magical intrigues, behind which lies the role of song in preserving a myriad of cultures, all of which disagree with each other to some extent, even as it becomes apparent to the reader that, without some degree of cooperation, all will suffer, if not perish. A challenging story about challenged cultures, and one well-told." ⌒ L. E. Modesitt, Jr.

"Peter Orullian is a master of dark chocolate fantasy; bitter, harsh and sweet at once. *Trial of Intentions* grabs us firmly by the breastplate and challenges us to face a world of moral contradictions, stunning characters and harsh choices. An unflinching fantasy." ⌒ Tracy Hickman

"*Trial of Intentions* is a grand novel, with strong worldbuilding and a sweeping cast of distinctive characters. Orullian is a promising writer, and I look forward to seeing where he takes us in the future." ⌒ Brandon Sanderson

Also by Peter Orullian

The Unremembered
Trial of Intentions
The Vault of Heaven, Story Volume One
The Sound of Broken Absolutes
At the Manger
Beats of Seven: A Collection
The Astonishing

BEATS
OF
SEVEN

A COLLECTION BY
PETER ORULLIAN

Publication History
"Lilith," first published in Hags, Sirens and Other Bad Girls of Fantasy,
2006, copyright Peter Orullian 2006
"In Thought," first published in Front Lines, 2008,
copyright Peter Orullian 2008
"RPG Reunion," first published in Crime Spells, 2009,
copyright Peter Orullian 2009
"Guilt by Association," first published in Intelligent Design, 2009,
copyright Peter Orullian 2009
"Don't Remember Me," copyright Peter Orullian 2019
"Canticle of Abraham and Issac," first published in Swordplay, 2009,
copyright Peter Orullian 2009
"God Uses a Dishrag," first published in Cosmic Cocktails, 2006,
copyright Peter Orullian 2006
"Last Ride of Johnny Fry," copyright Peter Orullian 2019
"Roxane," first published in The Trouble with Heroes, 2009,
copyright Peter Orullian 2009
"Beats of Seven," first published in Intergalactic Medicine Show, 2006,
copyright Peter Orullian 2006

Published by
Descant Publishing

10 9 8 7 6 5 4 3 2 1

To Stephen King

For reasons

ACKNOWLEDGMENTS

HE'LL NEVER READ this, but I'm going to acknowledge him anyway: Stephen King, this collection has everything to do with you, dear sir. The magic I found in your book *Night Shift*—at a rather tender age, I might add—pushed me to start writing some of my own short fiction. So, you're the man responsible. Thank you.

Many of the stories in *Night Shift* continue to take space in my mind. Stories like "The Last Rung on the Ladder," and "The Lawnmower Man." They're haunts in my brain that I'm happy to accommodate. They remain talismans for this road I walk.

I picked up *Night Shift* in an airport curio shop on Oahu. A friend said I might dig it. I'd never read King. But somewhere over the Pacific Ocean, in route back to the mainland, my life changed. Forever. I saw what fiction could be. I felt what stories could do. Much as I'd prized my canonized readings in high school . . . this was different. This was like getting into the cracked-leather passenger seat of a Camaro with a Chevy 350. It felt familiar—broken-in—but had a hum, an engine idle that fairly rocked as I sat awaiting the ride. And oh my lord, when the pedal went down.

I could thank a fat lot of other folks as I usually do.

But not this time.

I fell in love with short fiction because of Stephen King. I owe him.

BEATS
OF
SEVEN

TABLE OF CONTENTS

INTRODUCTION

I FONDLY RECALL MY years of reading nothing but collections and anthologies. For me, those books were mostly of the horror type. Initially, anyway. It began with *Night Shift* by Stephen King, and I never looked back.

These days, if I cared to count, I'd find that I read more novels than I do short fiction books. But I still get that familiar old thrill when I see a cover riddled with author names. And if I'm honest, I still buy just as many collections and anthologies as I ever did. They sit patiently in a to-be-read stack that will outlive me.

Why, you might ask? What's the attraction to collections and anthologies? The answer is: I love short stories. I don't love them because they're short and can be read in a few minutes. Though I love that part. And I don't love them because if I wind up not caring for a particular tale, the smorgasbord of the book will almost certainly still offer me something I'll dig. Though I love that part, too.

No, I love short stories because they're focused moments in time. They hit you hard and fast. They're train windows from which you glimpse some larger world as it rushes by.

i

They deliver they're freight—like all good trains do—and leave you with a sweet lingering feeling of *more*. More world beyond the window. More mystery behind those gut-punch endings. More stories in the universe you've just briefly, casually ridden through. Their brevity (*less*, you might say) is more. That's why I love them.

I have a host of short fiction writers that I absolutely adore. Writers who've taken the form to great heights. I won't name them all, but a few include: Harlan Ellison, Ted Chiang, Dan Simmons, and yes, Stephen King. Oh, and Charles Beaumont. These folks helped me fall in love with the short form. They've also made me work harder to try and use it well.

I started that journey in a Chevy Citation.

During my college years, I was a parking lot attendant on a lot with no booth. So, I sat in my car, all through the summer heat. The Citation didn't have air conditioning, but at least it provided some shade. Still, it was hot, and musty—I lived in the high desert, after all. Add to all this that business was slow. The days got hellishly long. But that left me time to write. I can still feel the runnels of sweat trickling down my back and finding their way into my ass crack as I began to scribble out stories.

First one I completed was entitled, "The Dark Child." I was flat proud. Never sold it. But that *completion* led to other stories that *did* sell. And now—these years later—it's led to a collection of my own. The book you're holding is a few handfuls of stories I got paid to write (plus some previously unpublished tales, for good measure).

So come along. Jump on this train and get a window seat. I think the things you'll see are worth the fare—moments in time that will by turns shock, unsettle, gladden, but mostly (with any luck) leave you with that sweet lingering feeling of *more*.

LILITH

EVE WASN'T FIRST.
 I was.

Eve ... mother of creation, my ass. I'm the one that gives the sons of men their first erection and the burning in their loins.

Lilith let the old thoughts simmer as she paused on the cool cement walk in the starlight shadow of a tall elm. Cricket-song filled the darkness with soft susurration. The dew had begun to gather in the recently mown grass, lifting a green smell tinged with the musk of loam. And beyond the grass rose up a two-story prefab home with beige vinyl siding, trimmed in white. In the upper window burned a light against the darkness. That room pulled her nearer, a feeling: One of her children was there, in this strange house, in that room, in danger.

Casting her gaze up the suburban street, she smiled bitterly. All these homes were so neatly tended, but they were all the same (as far as she was concerned). Mortals hemmed up in tidy quadrants trying to make meaning of their days—barbecuing in the evening, trimming their hedges on weekends. What was it about the sons and daughters of Eve that they all put their hands to horticulture, as if they might recreate Eden for themselves?

1

Peter Orullian

She shook her head and narrowed a scrutinizing gaze back on the lighted window. The pane of glass served as yet another reminder of the very long walk that had brought her here from her beginning.

If Eve had only listened.

She recalled going to visit the rib to try and talk some sense into her. She'd found Eve standing in a slow fall of sun not far from a small brook. Cottonseed drifted lazily in the light, stirring in Lilith's passage as she strode past several lilac bushes.

"He doesn't love you, Eve," Lilith had said. "He complained to Father because I chose to leave and he needed someone else to couple with."

"Sounds like jealousy," replied Eve.

Lilith shot out an exasperated breath, shook her head, then laughed. "You know why I left? Because he wouldn't let me be on top."

"What? On top of—"

"Sex, dear, sex. Your man, Adam, insisted that I always be in the recumbent position. To hell with that. I'm made of dust, just the same as he is. I'm not inferior to him."

It was Eve's turn to shake her head. "You were fashioned of filth and sediment."

Lilith folded her arms and paced to the edge of the small brook. Looking down, she said quite casually, "Yes, but you should know that Adam has sired several children for me already."

"That's a lie!" Eve's face had flushed.

"Now who's jealous?" Lilith had replied, showing a lopsided grin.

2

In the shadow of the elm thrown by starlight, Lilith held the same crooked grin she remembered from so long ago. Of course, Eve had stood by her man, had mothered many healthy mortal children. But Lilith hadn't exactly been celibate, either. The difference being that because she'd departed Eden before things got ugly, she'd avoided mortality. Which meant that the children she had by mortal men came into the world twisted and damned—demons they were called by some.

To her, they were her kids. Maybe with inclinations that often proved unhealthy to the children of Eve, but that didn't trouble Lilith much.

And now, she had the motherly sense that one of her kids needed her. Here in suburbia. In a second story room where a light burned and threw a soft green hue against the window glass.

So she started toward the front door, thinking of some words that had been ascribed to her over the years: *negotium perambulans in tenebris* . . . that which moves in the darkness.

⁓

THE HOME STOOD silent, the faint scent of lasagna just above the smells of leather sofas and Pledge furniture polish. Lilith imagined she could actually taste *mundane* on the air.

She truly had never felt apologetic for her part in harrowing the lives of men (by which she meant men and women). They just so deserved it. Stupid creatures. Stupid as their first mother and father. Lasagna. Furniture polish.

At the top of the stairs she turned left down a wide hall. She could already see the light beneath the last door on the left. If anything happened to one of her children, this family would earn more heartache than they ever dreamed.

At the bedroom door she paused, listening, sensing. No one rustled on the other side. Save the light, it seemed as empty and dead as the rest of the home.

Then she slowly pushed the door open, ready to shriek inside and cause men to cower.

Instead, she took two steps and saw an infant girl sleeping in a thick cherry wood crib on the right. The room smelled like a newborn, too: shampoo, scented diapers, and the smell of a child's skin. The walls had been painted in light green and trimmed with pink and purple pastels. The soft hum of a baby monitor came from a transmitter on the changing table.

To the left a man slept reclined in a rocker, his head lolling back at an uncomfortable angle. A dribble of drool seeped from one corner of his mouth.

He smelled . . . grown up.

Lilith drew near the man, bringing her mouth up to his, her lips trembling a finger's breadth away. He smelled of Ivory soap and dryer sheets. His face showed a day's growth of beard. But, ah, was he handsome.

And that age old feeling stirred between her legs. Lilith began to breathe deeply over the man's nose, taking in his breath when he exhaled. How sweet. Moist, slow suspiration. She drank it in like wine. Better was it, than any kiss. Then she parted her lips and let out her own slow exhalation, giving him the warm air of her lungs as he breathed in. This unconscious, intimate exchange exhilarated her.

Succubus, mortal men often called her in their myths. She rather liked the name. It rang with a hint of sensuality, which suited her fine. Better than hag or witch or sorceress. Though she liked the power implied by the last.

After a few moments, the man relaxed deeper into his chair with the swapping of breath. He wouldn't wake now until she'd finished.

Lilith mounted him, straddling his crotch and putting her lips to his ear. The soft, tenuous curves of the cartilage brought a needful groan from her throat and she pressed herself against him.

The man tensed in response, his biology predictable.

And she began to move, abandoning herself to the moment. In truth, it was the only time she completely forgot the beginning of it all.

Bliss . . .

A few minutes later, she was done, and she had coaxed from him his seed, the same way she had from countless men before him, and would from countless more. There would be another child, another demon, another one to harrow up the lives of men.

But a new feeling touched somewhere in the back of her mind, a feeling she'd had once before recently: She hated the life she consigned her children to. Disembodied, angry spirits who only wanted the same opportunity mortal children had—a body to feel and experience mortality.

Filth and sediment or not, she'd just wanted her turn on top, to be considered equal. Then all her wretched children would have had their chance.

To think a little pride had started it all.

She stood up from the man and watched as his body relaxed again into the rocker. He wore a peaceful expression that didn't seem right on his face for some reason. No matter. She turned to the infant.

This mortal child was female.

She was less than twenty days old.

And she'd been possessed by one of Lilith's own children.

"Aludon," she said softly, "Everything seems fine. Why did you call for me?"

"Because I asked him to," came a voice behind her.

Lilith whirled to see the man in the chair with bleary eyes staring up at her.

"Ah, hell. You guys are supposed stay asleep after sex." She raised her hands, readying herself for a fight.

"Give me a moment first," he said, holding his palms up in a gesture for her to relax.

She appraised him warily, keeping her hands in front of her.

The man retrieved a glass vial standing on a whitewashed bookshelf behind him. He pulled it around and gripped it in one fist. "Holy water," he said. "I'll tell you the truth. I didn't much believe in this stuff. But it's interesting what you'll try when the alternatives are gone."

"Exorcism," Lilith muttered, "great." She understood now why she'd been summoned. She gave the guy an exasperated look. "I hate this shit," she exclaimed, and stepped backward to a second rocker and took a hard seat.

"What?"

"The movies have made amateur exorcists of everybody. I swear I spend as much time rescuing tortured spirits as . . . never mind."

The man lowered the glass vile and stared. "Who are you?"

"I'm not having this conversation." She scrubbed her face and looked at the child through the crib bars. Aludon had a penchant for infants. She knew he secretly hoped that inhabiting one of their bodies might result in full assumption of the mortal frame. She didn't bother to try and convince him otherwise.

"I'm Paul—"

"I don't care for names," she cut in. She smiled a bit over the crestfallen look that replaced the hope in his eyes. "You haven't a clue, my friend." Then she shifted and gave him a wry look. "How were your dreams?"

Again Paul's face changed—embarrassment this time. He looked down at his crotch where she imagined she could see a wet spot.

"Spontaneous emission?" she quipped.

He lifted a puzzled expression toward her.

"Wet dream," she clarified. "Was I there?"

He nodded involuntarily.

"That's sweet," Lilith returned. "Now, are we really going to do this whole exorcist bit? Even Peter Blatty who wrote the damned book took a day off."

Paul's face changed yet again. This time, resolution set in, something unyielding that she found she admired.

"I'm not going to pretend to understand it all," Paul began. "It's been a long time since my own confirmation. But my little girl has been sick since the day we brought her home from the hospital. They can't find a thing wrong with her. But I've seen a glimmer in her eyes, intelligence, but in a way that isn't quite . . . human."

"Maybe she's advanced," Lilith opined glibly. "Don't most you folks think your kids are advanced?" She grinned.

Paul ignored that. "Then, sometimes, I get the feeling she can understand me. I mean really understand me. Like there's comprehension of the words I'm saying, but she either can't or won't reply."

"So you're bored of the one-sided conversations and have decided the girl can be healed with water." Lilith rested her head back against the rocker and began to rock. "I hate suburbia."

Paul stood up, keeping the water in hand, and went to the crib. He looked down at his daughter and pulled the blanket up over her shoulders. Without looking at Lilith, he spoke softly, "There's nothing a parent won't try when it comes to his child."

"Nice Hallmark sentiment. Now, look, let's not make a thing out of this. Let me collect my own and we'll get out of your hair."

Paul turned then, controlled fury in his face. "She's a child. Why would anyone do this to a child?"

"I'm not your Sunday school teacher. Do you want this to go hard?" Lilith stopped rocking.

"It's too late for that. I've been doing some reading—"

"Let me guess," Lilith cut in, "on the Internet."

Paul said nothing for a few moments. Then softly, "I don't think Ellen will survive the physical separation from the spirit inside her. She's too weak."

Neither of them spoke. The sound of the baby monitor grew loud in the silence. A white noise like static tuned low, far away, small waves of sound with no articulation, winking in and out with a frequency that left a low unassuming and yet ominous feeling in the nursery.

It reminded Lilith of a truth she tried daily to forget.

Then, she leveled her gaze on him. "Did your Internet reading reveal my name? Did it tell you that one hundred of my children die everyday as punishment for not returning to play servile housewife to some control freak. Don't expect me to fall all to pieces over the life of one mortal baby."

Paul opened his mouth to speak, and said nothing. He looked back at his daughter.

Lilith smiled. "Tell me. When you have sex, do you always assume the missionary position?"

The question achieved the desired effect; Paul's brow furrowed in surprise. "What?"

"I get the impression you're a guy who likes to be in control. You did quite the job of luring me here, didn't you? All ready with your holy water, too. But it's kind of a hollow threat, isn't it? I mean, you said it yourself; your daughter's too weak to suffer separation. You're not going to go splashing holy water on anybody."

Paul squared his shoulders to her, and Lilith saw that one thing she would never completely understand, that one something deep in the mortal race. Maybe it was love, maybe it was selflessness. Or maybe it was a desperation only a creature that dies can know.

His face softened, and Lilith thought she saw the truest part of the Fall of Adam in Paul's pleading expression. "Please don't do this. I took a chance that threatening an exorcism might flush you out. I'm glad it worked. And I can't imagine what it's like to live your life. But you came here to protect someone that means something to you. How is that different than what I want for Ellen?"

Lilith stood sharply from her rocker, sticking her face near Paul's. This time, though, she was inclined more to bite him than taste his sweet breath. "Don't you ever compare yourself to me! You have no idea what's it's like to be banished for simply not wanting to be thought inferior! You have no idea what's it's like to have your God condemn your children to death by the hundreds, thousands!" She showed him withering eyes, and lowered her voice to a husk. "You have no idea what it's like to live with the knowledge you were created from filth and meant only to serve."

Paul never dropped his eyes. And he lowered his hand holding the holy water. "You're right . . . but don't do this anyway."

Lilith had no words. Neither did she move.

Paul gave her a long look. Then he knelt, pleading, making himself subservient to her. His face shone with utter humility, and never, Lilith guessed, looked more beautiful. Anguished hope pulled at his eyes and mouth. "I love her more than anything," he whispered, emotion catching in his throat. "If there's any way to save your child and mine, I will do it . . . anything."

The sight of this simple mortal, kneeling in his daughter's nursery to plead for a single, fragile life, got inside her.

And something happened Lilith never expected. Not in all the years and miles she'd walked, nor all the men she'd hunched over to steal their seed. She voluntarily knelt with Paul, looking directly across at him, making them equal. She studied his pleading eyes, amazed, a little confused, but with a glorious wonder that filled her chest with a sweet ache like nothing she'd ever felt before.

But both children could not be saved. Lilith knew it as soon as she'd seen the infant. The trauma Aludon had imposed on Ellen by commandeering her body had left her at death's proverbial door. To save the mortal child . . .

Lilith remembered Eve and wondered for the first time if that stubborn bitch hadn't made the harder choice after all, going into the dark and dreary world to live and die with men, raising children, knowing the harshness they would surely face.

And then she looked again at Paul and thought that something finer had descended from the loins of the couple from Eden. Perhaps real strength had less to do with defiance, and more to do with sacrifice.

Reaching out with one hand, Lilith took Paul's hand, the one holding the vile. She squeezed once, and gently removed it from his fingers. She then leaned in and kissed him on the cheek with unfeigned affection. In all her dark years, it was the only kiss she'd offered in tenderness.

Rising, she removed the stopper from the vial and leaned in over the sleeping child. For the first time in millennia, she regarded a tranquil beauty in the babes of men. An innocence filled with promise that she would never truly touch. All the same, she smiled, and the sweet ache returned to her chest.

In a whisper, "I'm sorry, Aludon, but it must be this way. I do love you."

Then, with a softness she imagined a mother would show, she washed the child's head with the water, blocking from the world the shrieks that rose from her own child as the profane began to dissipate inside Ellen's body. The mortal child's hair matted in thin lines beneath Lilith's tender touch, while inside the little girl's body, another child who'd longed only for a mortal shell gave out a great cry that only its mother would ever hear. The sound of it tore at her heart. However vile the creature had been, however tormenting, he was her son.

The betrayal he must feel, being killed by his own mother, who he'd reached out to for redemption and safety from the very water she now used to destroy him . . . it touched her heart, too. Soft, gentle gestures had often been used to betray the beloved. This time, Lilith's hand turned the damnable deed. She would never be able to articulate the simultaneous calm in her heart that what she did was right but also terrible. Stony as her soul might be, this moment blighted a portion she knew she could never reclaim.

And then it was over.

Aludon's gasps faded to nothing. The thin, invisible substance of him evaporated forever.

Paul stood beside Lilith, watching as his daughter drew a long, shuddering breath, filling her lungs as though for the first time. Roses bloomed in her cheeks and she sighed against the blanket on her chest; the sound of it like all the hope the world would ever need.

Lilith handed Paul the vial. "Your daughter will live," she said.

Tears swelled in the young father's eyes. Gratitude beamed from his face as a smile spread on his lips that would live in her memory as brightly as anything she knew. Then Paul spontaneously hugged her, squeezing her with tight affection.

"I will never forget what you have done," he managed in her ear as they embraced. "And I won't let Ellen forget either."

She gave Paul a genuine smile, no regret turning down corners of her mouth, and took herself back to the stair, the door, and the cool walk beneath the starlight and elm trees. All the while, she held on to the foolish hope that the child conceived tonight inside her, Paul's child, might be changed from those that had come before. That perhaps what they'd shared could overcome the damnation of being the first.

It proved a beautiful thought to stroll by as she moved slowly up the street, abiding somewhat better the neatly tended grass and hedges.

IN THOUGHT

JOHN SMITH STARED into the dawn from the glassed-in breakfast nook . . . and trembled. In the warm light of the sun through the window, with a hot cup of coffee cradled in his palms, the shivers caught his lips and cascaded down his back. Even in the comfort and soft chatter of his wife and daughter as they took their morning toast together, the anticipation of another day *in thought* stole the safety and pleasance of family.

In thought. John smiled wanly over the euphemism. *War, they mean.*

He looked over his left shoulder, down the hall toward what he deliberately called his "war room." Bile rose at the sight of the closed door. He sipped again at his coffee to wash the sour taste from his tongue.

From far away, he heard his little girl, Katy, talking to him, but could tell nothing of her words (the war room in his head). Then came Cathryn's soothing voice with soft, remonstrating tones for their daughter—ever keeping things on an even keel.

Especially during times of *thought.*

But for the third time, Katy poked John's arm with some craft or assignment she meant him to look at. "See, Daddy. See!"

14

As flashes of yesterday's hours spent in his war room coursed behind his eyes, the cocoon of anxiety and cold broke and the warm chatter of morning sizzled hot on his reserve. Without thinking, John seized the item Katy brandished and twisted it in his angry fist. "Not now! I don't have time for this!"

A horrible silence stole over the sunny nook. Something was broken.

Probably me.

With the ache of dismissal hanging still on the air, John stood, his chair's legs loud in the hushed morning sun. His eyes had not left the door down the hall.

Soon, his body followed. Another day *in thought . . .*

He paused at the door, taking a deep, steadying breath. No use. Filling his lungs with air only made the thrum of his heart more noticeable in his chest.

I can't keep doing this.

And with that thought, he pushed the door open and went to war.

The room beyond lay mostly bare. No windows. No art upon the walls. Certainly no entertainment devices of any kind. Few distractions. There was a small table just inside the door with a pitcher of water and a glass.

John gave his wan smile again. The space was remarkable for only two things: deep, plush carpet with the thickest pad underneath that could be bought; and the chair.

Closing the door behind him, John eyed the device. Simple in form, elegant maybe, the chair appeared essentially as a sleek, stylish recliner. Rather, it was the weapon of a new age of war-mongers.

I'm the new weapon, the chair just enables me.

He was splitting hairs.

And stalling.

But that was part of the routine. He had need to trace the evolution of it all (every morning) to try to make sense of his place in the machine, the device.

John had chosen the military early, age ten actually. To be more accurate, it had chosen him. Career soldiers for Earth's Confederation were identified young and for one reason: a genetic predisposition for resistance to the side-effects of the chair.

Stepping toward the instrument, John's feet sank into the soft carpeting. He circled the simple object as a combatant might his opponent, when in truth they were dangerous only when partnered against the enemy.

He reached out and touched the head rest, another part of his ritual of preparation. The padded semi-circular extension where John's head would recline appeared little more than a comfortable place to lay back his head. *Ingenious bastards.* The headrest was really an amplifier and conduit.

Science had shown late in the 21st century that space didn't really exist. That what they'd believed to be dark matter was really the connective tissue of the universe. And more importantly, *thought* was the universal mechanism for communication which could move along the pathways of *all* matter. But like the radio or any other communication vehicle, it needed a transmitter.

The chair.

John climbed in, not yet reclining back, not yet ready to fight.

Initially intended as a communication device, the technology that allowed thought projection was co-opted by the military. Good thing, too. In those first years of off-world exploration, Earth's Confederation woke a slumbering neighbor that brought the first inter-galactic conflict in Earth history.

Conventional weapons were useless.

The intrusion on the mind, the wounds of memory, were not.

And once that enemy lay in metal ruin, expansion had begun.

But by then, John had sewn his career too deeply . . . No other appreciable skills. A family to support.

He rested back his head and the almost imperceptible hum of the chair began. With his eyes still open, John watched as orders flared across his vision. There was little need to read them; the commands entered his consciousness regardless.

He felt himself offer another wan smile toward the ceiling.

The new military. No uniforms. No salutes. Even orders were offered in conversational language. All to cloak the stultifying effects of their business, their trade, their assault upon the minds of an enemy so far away that starships wouldn't reach the defeated world for thirty years.

Clean. Efficient. *Thought.*

And so he went.

A black vortex opened up in his mind's eye, swirling, crackling with energy. John gave himself to it, and hardened his mind. The blackness rushed past him at dizzying speeds. He passed waves of light as he rushed headlong mentally toward a battlefield that existed only in the subconscious of his foe.

The travel across space and time always left him exhilarated, despite his purposes. He reveled in it briefly, being one of those who could use the chair without losing themselves (losing their minds) completely in its use.

That was his genetic fortune.

For him, the effect of thought transfer was to cleanse the mind, filter out the noise and superfluous information. It was like a cleansing diet that left the mind trim and fit and more vigorous. Where for others, it was cerebral death. And he couldn't deny that it filled him with a sense of power—moving at will across a wide expanse, outstretching colonization.

He felt a touch of immortality in those moments, omnipotence, omnipresence.

And often he saw in the memories of his enemies a beautiful world he would have liked to have known better.

But only as a traveler, not a warrior.

And that's how it always ended—in some construct of mind where he sought to tear down a stranger from the inside.

Like now.

The black vortex fell back as John cascaded down toward a remote planet called Gellania. That was the name the Confederation had given it. Human language couldn't simulate the indigent name.

Like a rush of dark wind, John swept through clouds, seeking the surface. His orders took him automatically to the place and person. Terrain blurred past like trees through wet, steamy glass.

Then came the shrieking.

The pitch rose as he narrowed in, drawn to a set of memories and persona. The sound of entry into the enemy's mind changed with each new race they fought. Today, and for weeks now on this world, the entry came with a fading whistle, like a train disappearing up a stretch of tracks.

John caught a glimpse at the individual's face as he entered *in thought*—a handsome, proud face.

Then, inside that mind, millions of miles from his chair, John felt new panic. Something was different this time: awareness, preparation.

As he occupied the space of memory and cognition, John suddenly found himself standing on a broad, darkened plain. Overhead, heavy clouds moved fast, threatening storm. Shale covered the land beneath.

And standing opposite him twenty yards distant was a figure whose loose clothes furled in the wind sweeping across them both.

It reminded him of any number of baneful scenes told by fantasists in the books he liked to read for escape when he wasn't *in thought*.

Oh my God. He knows—

Before John could finish his thought, he felt the probing of his own subconscious begin. It came like the pressure of being deep underwater, completely enveloping him, finding his soft spots, compressing his ability to breath (think).

He stared across the barren plain at the figure watching him and pushed back. With a brightness of hope sprung from his own memories—holding Katy as a newborn, passionate love with Cathryn—he erected a bulwark to stave off discovery of memory wounds his enemy might exploit.

Even as he did so, he shot a communication back to the Leadership about what he'd encountered. If this world was as well-informed as it now seemed, their objectives would be difficult to maintain.

Worse. If they had counter-intelligence . . .

Light years away, John felt his face smile at the term—*counter-intelligence*—nothing could have been more apt given the circumstance.

With his slight distraction came another surge from the mind who'd created this scene to define their battle. He knew John all right. But now it was time for John to do what he'd been trained for.

Like the taking of a great inward breath, John set himself mentally and focused on the individual *consciousness*—not simply the ominous figure standing in a field of badlands. He reached out, seeking the blind spots in an infinite matrix so connected that it often folded on itself to make connections. It was the world of a life's experience held private in the mind of its owner.

The universal truth the new military banked on with each new conflict and race was the sublimation of personal tragedy.

A soldier's task was to root out those moments and expose them in awful cruelty.

If enough of these were brought to light, the individual consciousness could not suffer it . . . and would die.

Or be rendered inoperable.

Either way set the stage for adoption into the Confederation, or perhaps colonization. It all depended on the world and its population. Really, it amounted to the old adage: The only defense is a good offense.

Earth would not be conquered, so they chose to conquer. John was at the front of that.

And at its core, it was moments like this, where he sought the hidden griefs of another with the hope that enough of them would collapse the matrix.

Probing, John identified one of those blind spots, a patch of experience somehow muted in the collection of conscious moments. Immediately, he channeled himself into it, drawing out the scene from behind repression.

A great shock of darkness erupted, followed by a wail of regret that filled John's mind.

And the memory began.

∼

JENTAL STRODE QUICKLY toward the hospital. Under a pair of bright suns, one more red than white, he noted thick foliage encircling the place in shocks of yellow and orange and green. About him, others moved more slowly, recuperating, lost in worry, enjoying the warmth on the courtyard. Jental hurried past them all toward a set of doors.

John felt the reluctance to follow this memory, but easily forced its continuation.

Inside, Jental bore right, passing the areas for disease and convalescence. Today his visit held a happier aim: the maternity center.

A comfortable feeling settled over him as he rushed through soft lighting and familial décor. *Welcoming.* This place gave the sense of deep familiarity and casualness, as though birth were such a part of life that it might happen anyplace.

A powerful tug threatened to distort or change the scene. A mind willing the memory down.

John tightened his grip.

Jental didn't stop when he asked directions to his wife's room, giving Honna's name as he but slowed his step toward the delivery rooms. After a mild remonstration to be careful not to rush, a young birth assistant offered Honna's room number and pointed. Jental turned and ran, his heart pounding not from exertion but sheer excitement.

A host of images coursed though his mind—all the things he meant to do with his child, the things he wanted to share, teach. The sight of new parents here and there gently stroking the small features of their babies got inside him.

It had finally happened for them.

He could think of nothing else but holding his child, perhaps offering the soft songs of his ancestors to the infant, telling her the stories he'd grown fond of in his own youth.

And Jental wished to kiss his wife. Thank her. Share the knowing smiles that would fill the room after the long wait.

At the door, John felt hatred and sadness scream for him to release this memory.

Jental pushed open the door and stopped. The anticipation compressed suddenly into a painful look. On the bed lay Honna cradling a bundle with small, delicate hands. She sobbed low, shaking her head in denial.

He went in, noting a hard fall of light in perfect squares on the floor underfoot from windows opposite him. On the other side of the bed stood a biology attendant gently reassuring Honna as he measured her wellness with a small handheld device.

"What's the matter?"

When his love looked up, her face showed utter despair.

Jental stopped short. Could he know this? Bear it? Was the child ill? Was Honna?

His body tightened, but he finally forced himself to her side and sat on the edge of the bed. He could not help the leap in his heart as he looked down at his . . . daughter. "I'm a daddy," he said.

Looking back at the face of the child, Honna whispered, "No."

"But . . ." And it hit him. Slowly Jental inclined, the sorrow descending upon him as each moment passed and yet his little girl had not taken a breath.

Her small, perfect features sat still, tranquil. But forever quieted. When he touched her soft cheek, he thought he might die. The great hope and love in his chest battled with the swell of mourning and regret.

And hatred. John felt fury from his enemy for the vivid remembrance of this moment.

"She lived only a few hours." Honna's words trembled from her lips. "If you could only have been here to see her, Jental. She was so sweet. Is so sweet . . ."

The violence of his grief sought release, but he did not want to remove his fingers from the fresh, clean skin of his little girl. Some moments later, he crawled onto Honna's bed and gently took the child into his arms. They would come soon to remove the dead, any moment perhaps, and he wanted to know the feel of cradling her against his chest.

The hardest thing he ever did in his life was release the child when an attendant reached to take her from his arms.

~

THE MEMORY SNAPPED back, complete.

For an instant, he stood again on the endless, blackened plain where forever winds coursed around the figure wearing loose, tattered garments. The clouds had bruised further. The shale tinkling occasionally as thought light pieces were being lifted by gusts.

And the figure (Jental) stood now closer to John.

Then blackness took all. Streaks of light. A vortex of sound and emotion and clouds.

And John fell from the chair to the soft carpeting in his war room.

He lay there, breathing hard, his skin slicked with sweat. He felt shame, as he always did, for shining a light on the dark places of another's heart. He pounded a fist into the plush padding. "Damn!"

The worst part for him was that calling these things to mind meant he had to experience them himself. Sharing the cognitive space of another man's mind literally meant *being* that person when the memories came back.

No, the worst part is retrieving these memories at all. No one should have to relive them.

When his breathing had normalized, he pushed himself to his knees beside the chair. He didn't yet trust his legs, so he crawled to the table beside the door and carefully poured himself a drink of water. He slopped most of it onto himself trying to take it in, but that wasn't so bad either.

Then he collapsed against the rear wall of his war room and tried to forget what he'd seen. All of it.

When he felt he'd come fully back to his own mind and life, he struggled to his feet and went out, shutting and locking the door.

~

THE CHIEF DIRECTOR of Military Leadership welcomed John with a firm handshake. "Have a seat, John. May I call you John?"

"Of course, sir." John pumped the man's hand once.

"No *sirs* here. Just Sherman." He motioned for John to sit. "What we do is a long ways from boot camp and regimentation."

"I guess."

The Director then pulled up a second chair and they both sat.

This "war room" stood in sharp contrast to John's. The walls had been pained a subtle shade of brown, beige maybe. Narrow lamps on finely carved bases glowed in the corners. Reprints of master paintings hung museum style on every wall—Bosche, Dali, Klimt, Rubens. Bookshelves teemed with books that appeared to have actually been read. And dark-wood furniture, elegant but not ornate, set an informal, studious air to the place.

This was a room mean for *thought* John imagined. Each man had his own way.

After a long, thoughtful pause, the Director began in a soothing tone. "We got your communication, John. To say the least, we're concerned. What else can you tell us?"

John related the scene with his enemy on the endless darkened plain. "I usually drop directly into their minds. We don't go to a place like that. We don't go *anywhere*. We fall to consciousness and feel for the *undisclosed*. When I saw the figure with ragged clothes fluttering in the wind, I knew he knew me."

"Knew you?" The Director focused his stare on John.

"I was taken into the military because of my aptitude to resist the chair, but the side effects . . . I read to escape."

The Director nodded. "And you read about the kind of place and person you saw *in thought* today."

"It's escapism. Stories with relatively clear lines of right and wrong."

"And material weapons," the Director finished in a knowing tone.

John said nothing.

"An age ago, they said the second fatality of war was fidelity. Today it may well be sanity." He offered John a shallow, reassuring smile. "What I mean is, I understand an escape where there is less moral ambiguity and the weapons are something you have to aim."

Having heard little, John nevertheless nodded and cut to the point. "If he knew me well enough to construct that scenario, then he has an advantage I can't risk."

"You think he's got advanced intel on who you are, is that it?" The Director sat back, steepling his fingers beneath his chin.

"Yes. And I may not be so fortunate next time I go *in thought* to him."

The man named Sherman stared for several moments. "How old is your daughter, John?"

"She's eight, why?"

"It's natural for a soldier to have doubts when he's a family man. To be honest, I'd be scared if you didn't—"

"It's not just about this one man," John interrupted.

They sat a few moments before the Director answered. "We know, John. The nature of today's mode of engagement itself allows us to monitor our men and women and how they're holding up."

"Then you know I can't keep doing this."

The Sherman look of concern and ready explanation rose on the man's cheeks and brow. "You can, John. And you must. I understand it's difficult. But the truth is, that your empathy and reluctance are precisely why you're so insightful when you go *in thought*."

John opened his mouth to refute.

The Director held up a hand. "I know. Dark irony. Unfair. Exploitive. And a thousand more colorful ways to describe it. But it is war, after all, John. Cleaner in some ways. But more painful in many others.

"You can question our moral authority and expansionistic plans, but I'll tell you what I've seen, hand to God." The Director lifted his right arm, palm up, in imitation of the old sign—a token of honesty before the All Mighty. "Since finding the ability to reach beyond our own cluster of planets, the races we've encountered in deep reconnaissance make me fear for our future, the future of our *eight-year-olds*, and that's no lie. We've woken the sleeping dragon with our galactic mobility. All we're trying to do now is secure our future before it's taken from us."

John laughed. "I'd expect you to say the same thing even if our moral ground were unstable."

"I know. And our people at the front are right to question. But . . ."

"You're sending me back."

"First thing tomorrow. Same mind."

"And if he gets the better of me?"

Ignoring the question, the Director went on, "For the very reason you came here it's imperative you confront him. We think he's an isolated empath, in which case we need to eliminate him as soon as possible. If he's not the only one, then we need to escalate our offensive, remove the broader threat. And you, John, are one of our best."

"Then you'll personally explain it to my eight-year-old if her dad dies in the chair."

It was Sherman's turn to say nothing.

John got up and crossed to the door without so much as a wave goodbye, let alone a salute. Reaching for the door-handle, he paused, caught by something the Director had said: *We think he's an isolated empath.*

John turned.

"You *knew* Jental possessed foreknowledge about me." And saying it out loud brought a cascading recollection of other assignments, in the minds of other combatants worlds over, where the contest of *thought* with another proved damaging for John.

So that I sit in the sun with hot coffee in my hands and shiver.

"Come sit down, John. There's much we should discuss." The Director's face showed equal parts reassurance and (something new) authority—flexing his military muscle.

Not that he'd have accepted Sherman's invitation anyway, but John felt suddenly powerless with the revelation: In stage after stage of conflict and expansion, he was being targeted at those whose natural gift wasn't simply resistance to a device (like John's immunity to the chair) but rather the ability to connect with the one great matrix.

John thought he might be sick.

The unifying theory of dark matter had given rise to a new age of thought on the topics of both the paranormal and the divine. For instance, the understanding of dark matter proved the interconnectedness of all things—one great matrix; it made possible thought transfer for war (among other things). Imagine then a being with the capacity to tap that matrix: omniscience, omnipresence . . . God.

Not unlike the reconnaissance the new military did to draft assignments for John and all the others *in thought*, except on a different scale and with different intentions than a creator.

An alternate theory held that the aggregate thought of intuitives shared across the great matrix *was* God. Whatever the case, John began to sense a dark purpose in the plans of the new military.

They were raging war on heaven.

One mind at a time.

The Director shattered the silence. "Remember, John, that your family is a courtesy we allow. Your career takes its toll on you, but it also makes your family possible in the first place. Don't jeopardize it. Do your job." He gave a smile to relax the tension. "Come. Sit down. Let's clear the air a bit."

John gave Sherman a last look and pulled the door closed on his way out.

~

WITHOUT THE LIGHTS, his clothes still on, John crept to bed.

He lay down beside Cathryn, the gentle musk of body-warmed bedsheets a familiar, welcome smell. In the dark, his breathing slowed, but sleep wouldn't come.

And listening to the shallow rhythm of his wife's respiration, he knew neither was she asleep.

"You okay," she said. Her voice carried low in the dark.

"No. How about you?"

"I'll be fine. It's your daughter you should think about, John. You're so distant lately. Even when you're in the room, you're not with us. Some ways, that's worse." Cathryn rolled over to face him, though they couldn't really see each other—she liked it pitch black to sleep.

"These *thoughts* lately. They're . . . I don't know. Heavy. It's always been hard. But now . . ."

"What can I do?" Her hand stole out to find his.

John made no reply. Had none.

But in the next moments they touched, caressed, kissed. And found each other's love again in a sweet, slow union where neither of them could see but knew each other more completely for that.

Later, when the silence of the night came loudest, Cathryn's breathing fell to long, restful pulls, and John got up, still unable to sleep.

He wandered the house, stood in front of windows looking out on vistas he only imagined beneath the dark of night. Distant lights flickered miles out over the bluff and lake—someone moving to some intention in the wee hours.

Like John.

Who ambled, but knew he meant to go back *in thought* while his heart felt calm.

He passed Katy's door on his way and paused, thinking he might check in on her the way he had when her bed had been a crib. Worried he might wake her, he chose not to go in. He may not be at the top of her invitation list, in any case.

At his war room, John went in without hesitation, leaving the lights off. Not seeing the chair helped him ease toward *thought*. From great familiarity, he poured a glass of room-temperature water and drank deeply. Then he walked a circle in the windowless room, sensing the presence of the chair, more aware now that it not only pushed his mind out to battle, but carried information back to the Leadership.

Nothing for that now.

He put out a hand in the dark, touched the headrest, took hold, drew himself in.

Sat down.

Laid back.

Humming. Louder in the small hours of night.

And the black vortex opened, less noticeable.

And the rushing began. Streaks of dark and bright. Exhileration.

Clouds. Shrieking.

And a fading whistle, like a train moving on to some distant, unknown stop. Perhaps an endless, darkened plain . . . where John again now stood, looking at the figure whose tattered garments fluttered in a desolate wind charged with the immanence of storm. John thought of his fantasy books, of moral certainty, of wood and steel used to make war.

Then he pushed his consciousness forward. Because he knew the Director's threat on his family was real. Because he needed to know what it meant for this *Intuitive* to have fore-knowledge of John's appearance.

As he occupied the figure's same space of mind, the question came: *Do you know where this leads?*

At first, John imagined he hadn't heard the query at all.

Then it came again.

John did not attempt a reply.

A powerful mental shove from his enemy rocked John's soundness, instilling a flood of doubt and fear behind which a wall of his own hidden memories waited to break free. With the simple thought of he and Cathryn's tenderness in the night, he framed a defense. *God, what would I do without her love for me? Or mine for her?*

Before another question could weaken his resolve, John laid hold to the matrix. This time, Jental's mind came more readily, and he scoured quickly to a memory buried deeper than the first. Collapsing the fold of two disparate points of time, John opened another window onto Jental's past.

A flash of darkness.

JENTAL CURSED MILDLY. He was late.

His son Malus' theater performance—if it were on time—had already started. And Jental hadn't even had time to go home and change into proper attire.

But he wasn't missing this for anything. It was part of the reason he worked a second shift in maintenance. And Honna would be saving him a seat.

He pushed his rover madly through the thick evening congestion and came quickly to his son's school. White chiseled marble rose skyward in straight lines, spires crowning several points across the face—each glowed in a cone of light shining up from the school rooftop, giving the place a majestic appearance.

Theater night.

Ducking inside the auditorium, Jental met the expectant quiet of the crowd who focused on the stage where a single voice spoke with gentle authority into the hush.

It was Malus.

Pride rushed up through Jental's body, that warmth and sweet adoration only a father feels for a son he hopes will know fewer pains and greater joy. He then scanned the rows for Honna, finding her near the front on the left. It was only then, standing still in the rear of the hall that Jental realized he carried the scent of his day's labor.

Others would have to pardon him this one time.

John felt a pull—Jental trying to shut down the memory. But he handled it, kept the wound in place.

That's when John wondered: Am I controlling this too easily, especially if he's an empath?

Bent over, Jental crept down the far left aisle to the third row, then excused himself as he cut across to the empty seat beside his mate. She patted his leg and pointed to Malus, as if Jental hadn't already noticed their son on stage.

Jental nodded and folded his fingers in her hand. He heard her sniff once. "I know," he whispered. "Still in my one-suit. I had to get leniency to get here this fast."

She smiled without looking over, and they settled in to watch the performance.

Each line, each movement, felt like success to Jental—Malus' and his own.

And the night swept by sweetly.

When it ended, the crowd stood and bowed their heads in deference and congratulation. It was a unanimous and compelling ovation that brought emotion thick into Jental's face and shoulders. He grinned pleasantly through it all, wanting now nothing more than to find his boy and take him in his arms.

Not long after, the crowd began to dissipate and Jental gave Honna a squeeze before shooting to the side door of the auditorium. He burst into the hall and wove through those filing out into the mild evening air. Not far ahead he turned right into the anterooms, where performers prepared and retreated.

The area teemed with parents and children congratulating one another, laughing, comparing notes, and making late evening plans.

And there was Malus, among them all, taking his adulation in stride and thanking each kind word.

The crowd prevented Jental from getting closer. "Malus. Son. Son!"

Some few looked up at Jental, who tried to pry his way forward to his boy.

He called again, "Malus. Malus!" His voice resounded over the masses, perhaps the one physical gift he'd bestowed on his child. And Malus' eyes darted his direction . . . then quickly away. Perhaps Malus hadn't really seen him.

A painful wave hit John's psyche—something he could only describe as profound regret. It pressed heavy upon him as if to say: 'You may know this, but it comes with a price.'

As if Jental weren't going to resist the exposure of this dark, hidden secret, after all.

"Malus!" Jental shouted. "I'm here! I made it!"

At that, a fellow dressed in resplendent robes turned. "Who, Malus, is this—in the uniform of maintenance, no less—that is making such a nuisance of himself to get your attention?"

A few nearby Jental backed away, eyeing him up and down critically, one woman covering her nose.

Finally, Malus' attention could not be easily diverted, and the rear staging area grew quiet as the night's lead character was given a second stage and audience.

Jental became acutely aware how out of place he looked in the cramped quarters where parents wore the clothing of tier one accreditation. He was out of his class, here at all simply because he'd been willing to go overtime to make the costs for Malus to attend. His one-suit seemed to reek in his own nose as he looked to his son for acknowledgment.

Malus stared back, unspeaking, his eyes uncertain.

And Jental's heart broke.

The child that had come and lived after his daughter had died in her mother's arms. The child that he'd cradled and hefted and tickled. Who'd laughed in his ears and cuddled close when frightened. Who had once stood on his feet when he wanted some bit of advice, and they'd walk and talk and end up on the long grasses beyond their home to stare nightward and talk about things.

His son, with his silence, denied knowing him.

The embarrassment Jental must have been on the verge of causing his boy . . . He, a menial worker in the ranks of the martial forces, come to this eminent affair in his one-suit, and claiming the time of the evening's celebrity.

Jental looked down at the hands he used to make Malus' schooling possible, and saw his fingers rimmed with soot and soil.

When he looked back at his son, it was through eyes glazed with tears that he managed to say: "Sorry to have bothered you. I don't really know the boy. I'm just looking for the maintenance office."

As laughter erupted around them at the fool interrupting their celebration to find a mop, Jental showed his son a sad smile. He'd saved his boy from the embarrassment of his father. And in doing so, he'd lost some part of their relationship that he would never reclaim.

He nodded once and shuffled back through the crowd toward he knew not what.

~

DARKNESS FLARED AGAIN, dropping John back on the plain of shale, where now the figure stood just inches away.

Again the question came in his mind: *Do you know where this leads?*

In the shadows, he could not see the face in the cowl until he reached and pushed the hood back.

It was not Jental's face he saw, but his father's.

The shrieking of minds converging.

A whistle.

And two points of time previously collapsed together unfolding to show a memory wound John had not imagined . . . his own.

~

THE KNOCK ON the door filled John with dread. His father strode passed him where he sat in the bay window, his bag at his feet. He thought he could still smell cake on the air from the celebration of his tenth birthday the day before.

As the front door opened, bright light spilled in around the tall, lean figure of a man dressed not in a uniform, but in shorts and a shirt with no collar. This was the military recruiter?

Panic set in, and John desperately looked about the room. He wasn't searching for an escape route. He was gathering memories, recalling the instances of his life that had taken place in this very spot—rainy days caught inside, standing on the bay window seat and reciting pirate poetry by Robert Burns and Robert Louis Stevenson, holding his big sister when she was sad about having to go away to school two years before.

Like John now.

Except *he* had somehow qualified for military training.

Still, being identified didn't mean he *had* to go.

I can't do this again! Stop! Please. I don't want to remember . . .

But Jental, or whoever it was, wasn't listening. Turnabout, it seemed, was fair play.

He turned to make his last plea to his dad—he'd worked it all out ahead of time—when mom came to the entryway from the kitchen. His little sister, Anoria, stood clutching mom's leg.

"Dad?"

His father rounded and brought up his hands on his hips the way he always did. "Yes, John."

"I know you think this is the best thing for me. But please let me stay. I promise to keep my room clean and help out around the yard. You don't have to worry about school either, because I'll study all the time."

"John, we've already—"

"No, dad, I mean it." He stopped, choking back the emotion. He needed to show his dad he could be grown up. "You can ask mom, I told her, too. No more fighting with Anoria. No more sneaking downstairs at night for extra cake."

His father's eyebrows went up. And he looked over to mom.

John looked at the man in the door, who seemed to be measuring his father's reaction to all this.

Then his dad brought his heavy glare back to rest on John. "It's not about your behavior, John. You're a good boy. But this is an honor, son. Do you know how many even get this chance?"

John said nothing.

"Less than one thousandth of one percent. You've got an opportunity here, John. I can't let you waste it. You'll thank me one day, even if it's hard for you to understand now." He held out a hand for John to come forward and get going.

And John began to weep. Not cry. He kept it quiet, so that it would be dignified if nothing else (just the way dad had taught him). But there was no help for it. The decision had been made. No appeal would help. So he wept.

On the endless plain of shale, John pleaded: I'm sorry! Stop it! Please! Don't make me relive this! I can't!

But the face of his father remained implacable in the watery light.

John picked up his bag and stepped slowly to his father's feet. Mom came up beside them and hunkered down. She kissed his cheek and hugged him tight. Anoria did the same. John felt mom's own tears when they embraced. Anoria sniffled the whole time.

His dad stood tall, sharing a look with the man in the doorway. John looked up. "Dad?"

"Yes, John."

"Please . . . let me stay." He had to ask one last time. He said it with all the hope left in him. "I love you. I don't want to go." The tears ran freely to his chin and dropped.

His father simply patted his shoulder. "We better get that bag into the truck, huh?" And he walked out with the military recruiter, leaving John to follow behind.

Leaving the only home he would ever really know, until he had a family of his own . . .

~

THE DARKNESS DESCENDED again, brilliant, complete. All John felt was the rushing of wind. All he heard was the tinkling of shale and the whip of loose, tattered fabric—the shadowed, ominous figure (his father) stood a breath away, but the clouds had finally occluded all light from the sky on this astral plain.

Out of the darkness—maybe in his mind, perhaps from the mouth of the figure resembling his father—came the simple phrase: *It is thought that no man may know the mind of God . . .*

The wind stopped.

The silence suddenly as ominous as the dark.

And connections formed in John's mind: To lose a child; to be denied, considered a shame; and (from John's own life) to have a plea go unanswered. These were wounds of memory; these were tales of holy writ since time immemorial.

My God . . . is this what it feels like to be in the mind of . . . Have I found the ultimate target in the plans of the new military . . .

Was Jental . . .

But all that crumbled suddenly beneath the onslaught of the memory returned to him of the day his father pushed him away for good and sent him far from home.

All the way to the minds of beings a universe away, where he surfaced their own private hells to torment and destroy them.

John began to tremble in the isolation of the far away plain and consciousness, and turned the pain of it all to a great, loud yawp that broke the darkness and sent him spiraling back through the vortex to his chair.

He tumbled to the carpet, burying his face in the softness, the roar from his own lips muffled in the deep fibers.

He lay a long time before his strength returned enough to kneel. The fever in his body continued to burn, his hair and shirt drenched. But the heat cleansed him. And when he crawled to the door and pulled it back, he delighted in the draft of cool air that hit his chest, chilling his nipples. Delighted more in the small craft tucked just under the door and now visible in the light of dusk—he must have been *in thought* all day.

He cupped and raised it up with tremulous fingers: a snowflake cut from white paper.

Katy's craft.

John smiled. Stood. And found his daughter's door—late a second night in a row. But this time, the hour wouldn't deter him from going in.

He sat at her bedside and gently stroked her hair until she woke. "Hi, sweetie."

"Hi, daddy."

He held up her snowflake. "Thank you. It's the best present I ever got."

She smiled, proud.

"And I'm sorry I've been grumpy lately. But that's over." Because he knew now where it all lead—the memory wounds, the stranger on the darkened plain—back home, to his family, to his daughter, where he needed to be *present*.

"Good, I'm glad. Let's get mom and go make some toast."

Nothing in the world sounded better.

RPG REUNION

I LEARNED MAGIC was possible the day I toured Old Ironsides in Boston Harbor.

Ten years before I get this stupid-shit invite to see the old gang. Came by currier. As if that harkened back to medieval communication or something.

I was on my graduation trip. I think mostly we were in Boston because we thought the bar for Cheers was a real damn place. That, and Salem sat just up the road a piece. Easy drive to where they hanged and pressed some nice folks because they wanted their land. No magic going on there—I did the research.

Anyway, I'm on the underside of Old Ironsides (the oldest commissioned ship in this the United States Navy), and the tour guide tells us that the ship used to carry the wives of officers, and that when they were in battle and shooting off their cannons, the pregnant ones sometimes went into labor. Thus, "son of a gun," as the saying goes.

At the time, I was mostly doing sessions of Traveler. (After it all went down with the old gang, I couldn't even do speed sessions of D&D. Too much baggage.) But when I heard the term "son of a gun", something got in me. Like, kernels of truth live inside the old sayings. Made me think that the notion of magic was just too pervasive to be passed off as a geeky game played by pasty face youths when they'd finished their calculus assignments.

So, I went to Rome.

Took me four years of non-stop study to ferret out the real stuff on magic. Bypassed college and all that nonsense in favor of a parking job that gave me hours to read (if no real compensation).

Turns out magic, for the most part, descends from things religious. Not in the way you're thinking though. Not like transubstantiation to feed the masses or the regeneration of cells to wake the dead. It's more like Lucas's Force. Kind of sapping the inert life in things, calling forth the idea from the form. You could say Aristotle was on to something.

Point is, a group calling themselves Assinians professed to teach from texts the true method of drawing the idea from the form and using that "energy" (for want of another term) on the next guy.

They're a cultish bunch, the Assinians. More like gypsies than ecclesiastics, roaming the dark hills north of Rome some eighty miles. Lots of lamps at night and star-charting.

I spent six months with them. Cashed in my trust; gave half to the Primero (he liked to call himself that) that led the tribe, and used the rest to eat and get laid. ('Fraid I haven't gotten better looking since the old days, either.)

But I don't regret it.

Not a minute.

I learned real magic. God's honest truth.

Problem was, turns out magic is mostly about offense. It's not meditation for self-improvement, it's not defensive bullshit like karate. It's commanding *things* to inflict damage. I suppose it would require a revision of all editions of D&D.

But that's just a game.

And then I get this invitation: "RPG Reunion" it says.

Like they've forgotten what the hell happened. How the Saturday Night sessions came to an end. Friggin' idiots.

Though, to be fair, that night was what sent me on the quest for the real thing.

So, there was just one thing to do: Get my artefacts.

The reunion was being held in Cedar City, Utah. Our old dungeon master wound up doing stage combat choreography and a few creative writing workshops out of CSU (Central Southern University), renown for its Shakespeare festival every summer.

Just like him to make us all travel to where *he* lives.

And it left me just a few weeks to conceive my spells and determine what physical items I needed in order to give those spells life. You see, the whole idea of *combat spells* is bunk. Every spell requires a material component. And as I've said, the whole notion of innocuous spells just doesn't exist in the real world. I think their fanciful ideas: read languages, purify water, shield. Why bother? Really?

So, in the end, it wasn't hard to figure out what I needed. I hit a deli, a candy shop, and the maple tree behind my house. I figured that would do it.

~

GARY LOOKED THE same. Opened the door with a big-ass grin tucked into his neatly trimmed beard—now spotted with silver. Still looked like he polished his head. He took me into a bear hug, which I thought kind of weird, given how it all ended. But I could bide my time.

"Good to see you, man." He took my coat and dropped it on the sofa beside the door. "Damn, you haven't aged a bit."

"I know." I nodded, distracted already by three cardboard tables laid end to end and strewn with all the fixin's for a night of gaming. Asshole meant to actually have us play.

I wheeled around to lay into him, when the screen pulled wide again and let in Trent and Daryl. Fine sons-a-bitches both. Fighter and thief who managed to vanish when shit started hitting fans twenty years gone now.

Everybody was hugging, and I turned to look back at the table, which (by God) had not just dice, but chits. Can you believe it? Original box chits—you pick one and turn it to get your number.

I wanted to vomit.

Last to come was Floyd. I could smell the bakery on him from the door. Loser had been working nights scrubbing pans, prepping trays, and kifing croissants for twenty years now. I hope he had a union, otherwise his career path could surely be mapped to minimum wage increases.

They all passed by, giving me firm handshakes and half-shoulder hugs. I kept the grimace off my face, I think.

That's when Gary formally announced the reunion: "Gentleman," he said, trying to sound cute and semi-formal, "It's been twenty years. And I think a trip down memory lane is in order before we get to the food and beer."

He then swept an arm at his cardboard tables, complete with a DM screen at one end.

"Aren't we going to wait for Dave?" Floyd asked.

"He's on his way," Gary replied. "And if memory serves, his character was asleep for the first part of the battle anyway."

Sage nods went around the group.

"And Brian?" I asked this one. I wanted that dick there . . . for sure.

Gary smiled. "In the bathroom. You know how he likes to wash his hands before handling the dice."

Everyone laughed like it was the fond in-joke they all remembered with teary eyes when they consider their misspent youth.

I'm not sure I kept the grimace back that time. So, I pretended to cough so I could cover my face.

And then the damndest thing happened. Trent and Daryl took their seats at the table, and produced character sheets (yellowed and smudged (with twenty year old erase marks)) stuffed inside protective plastic paper holders made for 3-ring binders.

"You still have them?" I could feel heat rising in my cheeks.

"Yup," they said in unison.

The characters had been drawn on legal pads. The yellow, lined paper took the hue of canary piss now, but the sheets had been well-preserved. And from the looks of it, the stats had been lovingly retraced often enough that the lead hadn't faded.

Doesn't surprise me.

Brian entered the room, his shoulders almost too wide for the bathroom doorjamb. "Let's go to town first and get some wenches."

Everyone laughed and got up for more hugs.

All this goddamn hugging. I made a quick finger survey and found rings on the left hand of each man. Then the hugging made sense, or at least could be explained.

I could practically hear them saying that gaming was the process, the journey, not the prize at the end.

Gentrification. That was the word that came to my mind. Don't know why. But I wanted to slap some gentrification off some faces.

But I kept my cool and gave Brian one of those half-hug things. His back mooshed in when I squeezed him. I used to be afraid of him. Man do things change.

"Everyone sit," Gary called. "Let's see if we can recreate it all. How many of you remember the sequence?"

"Are you kidding?" Daryl asked, flipping his character sheet over. "It's still here."

Everyone inclined close to look. In all caps, he'd scrawled it at the top of his weapons list: Stormbringer. Elric's sword. A nightmare of a weapon if you came up against it in battle. A relic, really. And a preposterous thing for a few fools to game for.

But we had, and of course Gary had seen to it that we defeated Elric and took his blade. The start of an auspicious quest for everyone to hunt down their favorite special item or weapon. Manipulating the dice. Neglecting the actual mechanics of the world we were playing in. Tromping around like demigods when we were really just 9th level hack-and-slash artists.

Except for me.

I read those manuals over and over, creating authenticity to my play. I built new spells with logic and study (even then), that Gary mostly laughed about before pulling a chit and telling me the whole thing failed.

"Your ship is coming into the harbor," Gary said, setting the stage. "A black ship is moored to a dock. It looks . . . otherworldy."

I have to admit some tingling crept up my back. I loved this shit.

"We're going to board," Daryl called.

"Of course, this is *your* quest." I tried to play down the bitterness with a smile.

"Don't join in if you don't want to," Daryl shot back. "For Chrissakes, we're just having a little fun."

"Is that what we're doing . . ."

No one responded to that; Gary was already calling out the opposing layout. "Two men arrears." (Like that meant any fuckin' thing.) "Two in the nest above. Six on the deck. And a man clad in black at the bow. His sword is glinting in the moonlight."

"Stormbringer." They all said it like a Greek chorus whispering the name Oedipus.

"We need light to battle, none of us are elves," Floyd called. "Quick." He pointed at me. "Light spell."

I rolled the dice and failed, but Gary allowed the light anyway . . . in the interest of the recreation.

"The deck flashes, streaks of light illuminating the decks and the ready faces of your foe."

Who talks like that . . .

"And one whose begun an incantation near the mast."

"Silence spell, man, now!"

I rolled again. Ironically, this time I made the roll. But again, in the interest of recreation, Gary kept things historically accurate.

"You've just pissed off an 18th level magic user, dude." And he giggled. "His hands are rising in the light of your spell."

"Guys, hit him with something, fail out his spell!"

Their silence came the same way it had twenty years ago. I stood on that black deck in the dark night under a moon and the light of my own goddamn spell . . . alone.

"You're going to let me fight alone?"

"It's the quest that matters," Daryl replied. "While you distract him, we're boarding in the dark up the ship, closer to Elric. We made our stealth rolls."

And that's when eighteen months of roll playing Gareth the Young, my first serious character, came to an end. Storm clouds gathered above the mast and lighting flared down out of the sky as the mutterings of the wizard I'd failed to lock began to end.

"Hold it! I have a new spell," I yelled, before Gary could call my damage.

Confused expressions lit the faces of my party. I paused long enough to enjoy that before proceeding.

"How about this?" I said, and pulled some twigs from my bag.

"I don't remember this being part of it," Gary said.

I smiled at that and tossed the sticks at Daryl and Trent. As they tumbled in the air, I muttered a few things and watched the sticks lengthen, fatten, and begin to writhe . . . and rattle.

Slack jaws and wide eyes grew as hands and arms shot up to protect their faces. It happened pretty fast, but I think they each took four or five bites. "It's a fucking game!" they were yelling, as they scrambled out the door.

I never heard their motors start, so I'm thinking good thoughts there.

Brian, of course, wasted little time coming right through the table at me. "You're an asshole!" he shouted. "Just a cry-baby pouter over a stupid magic user character. Did you ever wonder why we let you take the fall for Stormbringer . . ." A shit-eating grin curled in the pinched face barreling down on me.

As my chair began to topple back, I fished the fireball jaw-breaker from my bag and made one easy motion toward Brian's chest. Heat scorched out from my palm in a blast, singeing the hair on my knuckles and wrist and venting in a lateral geyser, slamming Brian back against the far wall. I hadn't planned it, but Floyd got caught in the blast. Good fortune.

Their bodies dropped in a flaming heap; the smell of burning flesh already thick in the small room. I took a bit of delight in seeing Daryl and Trent's character sheets as so much melted plastic and ash.

That's when I looked over at Gary, hiding behind his Dungeon Master screen. There emblazoned on the two tri-folds were matrixes for hits and damage and terrain movement, and they quaked with the fear of a bald DM. The guy who hadn't had the balls to call his players on their ethics when they'd left me to die twenty years ago so they could take possession of a fucking sword.

I mean, for godssakes, Gary was a school counselor, even then. He should have known better, right? The whole idea of roll-playing is to better the self. To rise to heroic action you can't sustain in real life. Didn't they get that? Even now. Didn't they just fucking get it?

I did.

I spent a lifetime making it real.

And someone had to be accountable.

Someone had to do the accounting.

Reunion, indeed. Everyone just the same as twenty years ago . . . until I was through with them.

I pushed the screens down and caught a sheen off Gary's sweaty forehead. "Ain't so funny this time, is it, pal? I mean, what the hell was that, you having a character in the damn party. Everyone knew you were angling for Mourne Blade, sister sword to Stormbringer. You can't do both, man! You can't play and DM. You're either in or out. You're either playing or making it happen!"

"You're not talking about a game anymore, are you? We can talk about that."

"Save the counsel, Gary. The semester of psych won't work on me. Maybe your twelfth graders, but I graduated that business twenty years ago . . ."

Gary sat frozen for a long time, his eyes darting back and forth like a rabbit in a trap. Loved that. Then he asked, "What do you want?"

I knew he was stalling, but I also wanted to tell him. And besides Brian's burning body, there wasn't anything else to be distracted by, so I let it out. "I wanted you to take it serious, man! No bullshit pacts with members of the party. You were supposed to be above that!"

"But—"

"You sold me out!"

That's when I pulled the deli toothpicks from my bag. The ones with the little frayed ends, used to hold large sandwiches in place.

Like little arrows, they are.

I didn't really notice Gary's pleas. That's typical, I imagine, of those receiving a reckoning, right: pleas. I'm pretty sure the Assinians told me that, too. The power of God manifest to men in the flesh was about reckoning—thus sinners wanting restitution when they think God's a wink away.

So, he was blubbering something, his eyes diverting again and again. And in the end, just as I called forth the most inane spell imaginable to put an end to the miserable son-of-a-bitch, I think his face was less concerned about dying and more about something he was looking at.

Magic missile.

Three arrow "ideas" pulled from smaller forms lit the room and air and dove into Gary's face and chest. He gurgled a bit as he fell to the floor. I believe he flopped once or twice with indignity.

Liked that, too.

And that's when the last of two things happened.

As I stood and looked down at Gary's body, feeling vindication at last, I felt my vision tugged around to the place he'd been spying as he prepared to die.

Peering around the entry to the kitchen were two small faces, both agonized and wanting to run to their father, both afraid to enter the room, frozen in their pain and fear.

I hadn't known Gary was a dad.

I felt the pain of it hit me. A goddamn game. Old Ironsides. Revenge pushing me to Rome and a hundred nights in a dark forest reading and studying the ancient ritual for calling the form from the artifact to impose my will on another.

Lusts in the body and the blood that might have lain dormant until this friggin reunion.

It was just a stupid sword.

Why did I care?

Before I could answer, the second thing (the last thing) happened that night.

Dave showed up.

The screen opened slowly—he must have seen Daryl and Trent out on the lawn somewhere—screeching on its hinge. And when he stepped inside, I smiled in spite of myself.

Seeing me standing over Gary's body, he asked in a calm voice, "What the hell happened here?"

"A bit of vengeance a long time in the coming."

Dave looked down at the two kids, who immediately ran for the safety of his strong legs.

It took him only a moment to put it together. "All because of a sword?"

"Your character was asleep, but I think you'd have stopped it. Paladin's are Lawful Good."

Which was why I smiled, and what made it so ironic that Dave should come late again, tonight. Somewhere along the way, he'd made his own transition from fantasy to reality in the form of a Utah State Patrolman.

And me without anything to do a Wizard Lock as Dave pulled his cuffs.

GUILT BY ASSOCIATION

EDMOND WHYTE STRODE the marble floor of the High Kirk of Scotland. His footfalls echoed against the high gothic ceiling of the cathedral. Night held beyond the windows. It was well passed close. But he had a standing appointment, and today of all days he wouldn't be late. Passing through the warm light of candles, he arrived at the confessional, set in a remote alcove beyond the Thistle Chapel. A bit of excitement caught in his chest as he went in, sat down, and held a cashed check up against the confessional screen. "Father Michael," he said, "God is dead."

Wood creaked as Pastor Michael (Edmond still couldn't shake his Catholic roots) sat forward from his seat on the other side of the panel. "It's good to see you, too, brother. What am I looking at?" He put on his glasses.

"My research grant." Edmond's breath rasped through his throat from his rush to get here and share the news.

"That's to be the tack today, is it, brother? The funding of science demonstrates the lack of societal faith?"

Edmond laughed. "No such thing. I stopped arguing with you about faith months ago."

Pastor Michael observed the bank processing text through the face of the check. "I see you've deposited the money. A princely sum, too. And now with your new research money, you believe you can prove God is dead." He smiled.

"No, Father, I didn't cash this check. You did."

The wood creaked again, as the Pastor's quizzical face drew near the confessional screen. "After all this time, you're tithing, Edmond? I don't understand. Did you make some sort of bargain with God? A test? That if you paid, he'd grant you some request?"

Again Edmund laughed. "I haven't prayed or bargained in years, Father. Much less ask God for anything. Don't you see? The money may be mine to spend, but only if it goes toward my research . . ."

Edmund turned the check around, where the church endorsement had been stamped prior to deposit. "Oh, Edmund. You've stolen this money and given it to the church. Why?"

"Like you said, I'm not exactly a regular tithe payer, am I. And maybe, in a strange way, this is research after all." Edmund now sat forward, bringing the two men's faces inches from each other through the privacy screen.

"Why, Edmund? How does this prove God's death? Interesting choice of words, though, isn't it, since you've come here for the better part of six years now trying to convince me God was never alive to begin with." It was Michael's turn to laugh.

Edmund stared back at Father Michael until the silence had stretched a good long time. He wanted this alleged man of God to feel the full gravity of what Edmund was about to say. He needed him feel it in his soul. Finally, he spoke. "Because, Michael, I feel no guilt."

The words hung in the air between them.

It felt like the preannouncement of death, leaving heavy, mournful thoughts on the very air. And to his credit, Father Michael did not rush to proverb or explanation.

After some time, Edmund went on. "No guilt. And not because I believe the money will profit the needy or build the kingdom of God. I'm no Robin Hood."

Father Michael stared long. "Why then, Edmund? If nothing else, stealing is a crime. Have you regard for your freedom?"

"To prove a thesis. To prove to you, finally."

"Edmund, you shouldn't—"

"If we were all here at God's wish," Edmund interrupted, "to fulfill some divine mission or plan, then this guilt your so fond of would make total sense. Guilt is a fine way of maintaining a penitent, maintaining control." Edmund put down the check and whispered. "But what does it mean, Michael, when a man feels no guilt for breaking one of God's great commandments? And not because he's stealing bread for the poor, or wealth from a tyrant."

"Sounds like you have your answer already." Father Michael scrubbed weary eyes. These *confessionals* with Edmund came late after a day's work.

"Indeed I do. It means guilt is a construct of evolution that is no longer being selected for. Do you understand? It is an oddity with no evolutionary benefit, no clear purpose. It is the oddest thing in your creationist view, Michael, that you teach guilt as the consequence of sin . . . if the natural process of evolution can undo a man's conscience . . . undo the work of God."

$\sim$

MICHAEL HAD MOSTLY listened after that. Listened for an hour, the night waning, as Edmund kept repeating his epiphany. Committing sin should cause guilt. If it did not, then either God did not exist, or He no longer had control of the natural processes that scientific creationists claimed He used to direct the evolution of life.

Either way, true ingenuity belonged not to the heavens but the world of men.

And while Michael might have argued. He no longer had the heart (*or faith, Michael, if you're honest*) to do so.

Edmund said farewell, asking Michael to prepare a rebuttal for the following day's *confession*. Promising, himself, to come armed with another sin and a clear conscience.

When the young scientist's footsteps had echoed their last, Michael slumped from his side of the booth, and retreated to his office. He did only two things: He left a note for Mary to reverse the tithing deposit to Edmund's bank; and he booked a flight to Rome.

The General Assembly ruled the Church of Scotland. And the Diaconate had many wise men. But the kinds of questions Michael meant to ask were at best symptoms of apostasy, at worst heresy. He didn't mean to leave God over a few questions.

But he must ask someone.

Even before Edmund and his scientific philosophy had begun to come to the High Kirk, Edmund had felt like a house built on sand. And he'd reached some kind of spiritual border he must either cross or forsake.

Gathering some texts he thought he might need, he caught the last flight out of Edinburgh for Aeroporti di Roma. An evening later, he trod the slick backstreets of Vatican City.

Wet cobblestones up a narrow alley west of Viale Vaticano brought him to the door of an improbably friend, Signor Viscenza. Michael had begun to exchange letters with the man after a visit he'd paid Edinburgh two decades since. In that time, Nicolo had ascended to become Archbishop and chief ethicist to the Holy See. He had the quiet passion for rightness any ethicist must. A few years back, unpopular stances on key political questions had seen him remanded to retirement.

He now worked in a public library, running fund raisers and occasionally doing readings out of translated American fiction. He was a hit with the kids.

Tonight, Michael called on the man for what he had been.

He shivered once, steeling himself. Then knocked.

Shuffling steps came slow. Nicolo pulled open the door, but did not register surprise to see Michael. "Come in," he said, waving a cheese knife with gnarled fingers.

Michael stepped in, finding the home ripe with the smell of age. In the back somewhere, music played, Sinatra. The sound of it came in rolls, with static like a record player stylus thick with dust. Michael collapsed into an old couch and spread his books on the coffee table set in the center of the room.

Nicolo disappeared into the kitchen, and returned with coffee. The old man set a cup in front of Michael. He then sat himself, sipped thoughtfully from his own café, and observed. Moments on, he said simply, "These are things you have to decide for yourself, Michael."

Michael nodded. "I know. But please can we talk."

The other man took some more coffee, wiping a few drips that got away onto his chin. "Of course. This I have plenty of time for. What today?"

Michael thought. He had much to ask, but landed on, "Guilt. Does this belong to God?"

"It is all God's, Michael. Refine your question."

Michael looked down at the books on the table. Not scripture, not hymns. Novels, stories: Fyodor Dostoevsky's *Crime and Punishment*; Edgar Allen Poe's "The Tell-Tale Heart;" William Shakespeare's *Macbeth*; John Steinbeck's *East of Eden*. And many from Nathaniel Hawthorne.

This had been part of the simpatico he and Nicolo had found. They both often turned to literature, much of it Western, to find commentary on things of the spirit. It had made neither of them popular.

"I see you brought your friends," Nicolo said. He did not show his humor, but the smile was in the words.

Michael only nodded, refining. "What is the purpose of guilt? And what does it mean when man no longer feels guilt for sin?"

Wrinkles turned up the corners around the man's cloudy eyes. And he let out one hoarse bark. "Fantastic, Michael! Let's follow it through."

Michael grabbed his notepad as Nicolo squared around on the edge of his chair, cradling his café under his chin.

"Your question presupposes something more fundamental, doesn't it? That is, how God went about the business of creation. I suspect you've been talking with your scientist friend of late, hmmm? No matter. Keep your head, my boy, and remember that even the scientific evidence for evolution is a leap of faith. Those lab boys have yet to duplicate one single left-sided amino acid. And the odds on it happening by chance are 10 to the 123rd power. That's 123 zeroes, if you remember your math. Then it would have to happen no less than 500 times to create life . . . you get the point." He barked another laugh.

"But what about guilt?" Michael said again.

Nicolo leveled his milky stare. "For a moment forget guilt as a means to cause repentance. Instead, consider that guilt and shame help us maintain proper relationships, even reciprocal altruism. When you feel guilt for harming someone or even failing to reciprocate kindness, what are you avoiding?"

"Selfishness."

"Right, which increases ones ability to survive, doesn't it. Since such a person will avoid retaliations. No one likes a selfish man."

"But couldn't this just as easily be the evolutionist's argument? That guilt is a trait which would win out in society?" Michael picked up *Crime and Punishment*, feeling its well-worn cover.

"But recall your second question, Michael: What does it mean when man no longer feels guilt for sin?"

Michael did not see.

Sinatra scratched out *Fly Me to the Moon* from beyond the hall.

Nicolo took the Dostoyevsky book from Michael's hands. "These stories, all of them, come to what end? Confession. Some as they sleepwalk, others as they lay dying. But however it happens, these people," he tapped the book, "kings, scholars, clergy, all bow to conscience in the end."

Michael still did not see.

"You are lagging the jet," Nicolo said. "Your scientist friend cannot eat his cake and have it, too. Guilt is part of life, always it is this way. The capacity for guilt is innate, absolutely. It may simply be that what we feel guilty about is learned."

Michael felt as though he'd been hit by a hammer in the chest. "You're saying that our moral compass is individual, not universal."

"Why do you think we're drinking instant café? These opinions were not popular at the Vatican."

Which left Michael with only one question. "What we feel guilty about . . . can it be *unlearned*?"

Nicolo considered. When the old man's eyes turned back on him, Michael saw the weight of a lifetime in his face. "That would be an interesting trick. How does one unlearn a thing?"

Michael wondered if the lifetime priest spoke also of himself. "Do you believe it possible?"

The old man put the book down and took up his café. He sat back, drank a mouthful of instant, and swallowed loudly. "Which brings us back to where we began—these are things you have to decide for yourself."

Michael picked up *Crime and Punishment* and worried the cover until he knew what he must do.

⌇

EDMUND PICKED UP Patricia's third grocery bag, heaving it like a gallant. "Who are you cooking for, my goodness. You could feed an army."

His neighbor laughed, the flirt audible.

Edmund had seen Patricia looking his way for months. Ever since she'd moved in across the street. Her husband, John, was a sea-floor surveyor, spending weeks at a stretch on a boat in remote parts of the world. This time it was the Mid-Atlantic Ridge off West Africa. Patricia was lonely.

And Edmund needed to sin.

It was practically a science experiment.

He carried two sacks of food into her kitchen and set them down, deliberately lingering as she began to stow the perishables.

"John's away?" he asked.

"For another week." Patricia gave him a look out of the corner of her eye. "And Isabel?"

"She's in Aberdeen with her family."

Later, he lay on his back with the warm smell of her close as she curled up beside him. He watched the light of passing headlights track their lines across the ceiling of her apartment. The clock read 2:50 a.m. He'd almost expected to be fraught with guilt, betrayal, a tortured soul for his adultery. Isabel was a good woman. Kind. Beautiful.

Edmund smiled for himself when he thought of returning to the High Kirk to share this with Father Michael. He wished in some ways he could go back to his youth, and play through the sins he'd agonized over before he'd learned the folly of guilt.

"You're awake," she said, interrupting the silence.

"So are you."

"Feeling an adulterer's shame?" She traced a circle around his nipple.

"I could ask the same of you."

"God's sake, no. I never said I loved you. We had a simple transmission of fluids and bit of pleasure besides. I think of it like using the loo, but a hell of a lot more fun." She laughed at her own joke. "But there's something more serious in *your* face. Do tell."

"Let me ask you something. Will you tell your husband what we did?" Edmund shifted his head on the pillow to see her when she answered.

The smile on her face dried up. And she said nothing.

"I didn't think so. I'm not sure I'll tell Isabel, either. And that's something I hadn't thought about before. But it doesn't change a thing. It's fascinating, don't you think."

She propped herself up on one elbow, her breasts exposed. "What doesn't change?"

"That I feel no remorse. I realize I won't tell my wife because it would hurt her. Some small bit of nobility in that, if it's not too crass to suggest it. But I don't feel the part of a sinner. I honestly think it's passing out of the genome."

"You won't tell John, will you?" his neighbor said, pulling the sheet up to cover herself.

But Edmund didn't hear her. He was watching the lights on the ceiling and thinking about his next visit with Father Michael. Morality was number two on the Hit Parade the priest called the commandments of God.

Oh yes, things were evolving.

~

IN THE OFFICES deep in the bowels of the High Kirk, Michael pulled a worn corner of carpet up and fetched the rusted box from its hiding place in the earth. In some ways, he reflected, this was their true sacristy. Under the pale glow of bare bulbs, he pushed back and lid on the few items the Church held some shame to own: birth records sealed from genealogists for wealthy Church patrons, an exorcism kit, land deeds secured in less than holy ways, and a revolver loaded with silver bullets.

Michael had never found an answer for the silver rounds. Perhaps in a period of the Church's history, it had believed in man's ability to change shape. Michael gripped the gun by its wooden handle, feeling its heft. The barrel glinted dully in the basement light.

He concealed the weapon in his vestments. Returned the box to its grave. And went up to take a seat in the first pew.

He hadn't been sitting long before the confident steps of his scientist friend came strident on the marbled floor. Michael lifted his eyes to the cross and spoke a silent prayer. A prayer for himself. A prayer that some things don't change. (*That silver bullets were never needed, right Michael. Not then. Not now.*)

Edmund came full into view, standing before the altar, and lifted his hands. "Here I am, Father, ready to confess my sins. And today, I think you'll confess something, too. Am I right?"

Michael made no move to stand. "Not today, Edmund."

Confusion and some panic, Michael, thought, pulled his friend's face taut. "I don't understand. Are you giving up? Have I at last convinced you?" Edmund's face relaxed, and a smile began to show.

"A lot of years, Edmund. A lot of years we've done this dance together in the quiet abandon of this holy place. For my part, I foolishly assumed that over time I'd win you back for God. I also assumed you were here each night because you meant to disabuse me of my faith."

Edmund pointed at Michael. "I want you to acknowledge the truth. That's all. It's never been malicious, Michael."

"I know. I know. But the truth is . . ." Michael looked around the nave and up the vaults before finishing. "The truth is I struggled with the truth long before you walked into my confessional. Suffering has a way making a man question if mercy is real or imagined. And the one thing I've held on to all my life in the Church is my ability to relieve some small portion of suffering by absolving the sinner of his guilt."

Edmund's smile widened. "Then we're competing for the same goal."

"I don't think so," Michael replied.

"Come, let's go into the confessional and discuss it." Edmund started toward the Thistle Chapel.

"Not today," Michael repeated.

Edmund stopped dead. Again panic rose in the man's face. "I have things to share, Father—"

"To confess, you mean," Michael cut in.

"I don't need your absolution. I told you. Guilt is no longer relevant." Edmund started again toward the confessional.

Michael sat still. "Edmund."

The man of science continued.

With gravity, "Edmund."

The only man Michael could call friend, stopped. But didn't look back.

"I won't hear any more. If guilt has gone out of you. Then there's nothing for me to do anyway, is there? In any case, I am finished taking your confessions."

65

Edmund whirled. "You can't do that! I want to tell you what I did! With no guilt!"

"What you want," Michael paused, "is to sin with no consequence. And I can't be a party to that anymore. I just realized, Edmund, the charade you and I have played now for six years. My part in that is over."

Edmund stalked toward Michael, looming over him where he sat. "I would never have thought this!"

"Thought what, Edmund?"

"That you would hide behind your cross in the face of reason and science! You're twisting the open dialogue we've had to examine important questions—"

"Ask yourself why you're so angry. What is it that twists in your own heart at the prospect that I won't follow you into that box and listen to whatever sin you've committed?"

Edmund's eyes filled with hate and anger. "There is no torment in my heart. I am free. We are evolving beyond the need for your archaic methods of control. So either God in his wisdom is directing change into an enlightened place, or God is dead and the human animal no longer needs to be bound by feelings of inferiority and shame."

With that, Michael stood. "Then let us test this new enlightenment." He drew out the gun, causing Edmund to shuffle back several paces.

"Don't be alarmed. This is for you." Michael held the revolver by its barrel and extended it toward his friend. "If remorse is passing from this world, either by God's hand or the natural processes you study in your lab, then I don't want any part of it."

"What?" Edmund took another step back.

"Take this," Michael closed the distance between them. "I cannot unlearn what I know, and believe, and feel. As my friend . . . as a man who can act with no guilt . . . I ask you to kill me."

Edmund shoved the gun away. "You're insane!"

"No. I've never thought more clearly. If you're right about all this, Edmund, then I don't want to live such a world. I wouldn't survive it. And if it is true, then taking my life will cause you no remorse."

The silences of the High Kirk stole over them as the men stared at one another for a very long time. Then in a whisper, Edmund spoke. "What if I am wrong?"

Michael gave a wan smile. "Then your guilt will be my best eulogy. Since then I'll have proved you were wrong after all."

Again the silence stretched. Edmund cast a longing gaze at the confessional, then looked back Michael . . . and took the gun.

The scientist's hand trembled, the pistol's barrel casting its shivering shadow on the stone floor. With apologetic eyes, Edmund said, "I should have called you pastor. Not father."

"Our rearing runs deep," Michael answered.

Edmund nodded, heaved a breath, and raised the gun.

Michael looked down the barrel. "The oddity of creation was never guilt, Edmund. The oddity is the world you imagine without it."

The tremors in Edmund's hand shook the gun in wild arcs. "My thesis is true," he rasped. "It's true!"

The gun fired.

Michael dropped to the floor, clutching at his chest. A few moments more, and he realized he had not been hit. Edmund stood over him, the gun smoking in his hand, his aim high and to the right. He had shot into the vaults above.

Angry, silent tears rolled down his face. He looked down at Michael, mouthing something. *You bastard.*

Then the young scientist dropped the pistol and walked softly up the nave.

Michael followed a minute later and found Edmund on the cold stone steps out front of St. Giles. The man sat with his head in his hands. Michael took a seat beside him.

Muffled through his hands, Edmund asked, "Why do you think your God plagued us with guilt? Is it his own dark joke?"

If Michael had had the answer he would have given it.

The empty streets left them in a bigger silence than the church behind them. And Edmund interrupted it again to ask, "Can we go in to the booth . . . and talk?"

Michael looked up at the stretches of dark night, the stars high in the sky, and felt the touch of cool air on his face. It left a calm in him that he hadn't known in a long time.

"I think we can talk right here." He nodded. "Yes, this'll do nicely."

DON'T REMEMBER ME

IS YOUR NAME Rumpelstiltskin?"

The queen smiled. It was not a question.

And Rumpelstiltskin fell hard on his knees to the marble floor of her private reception room. Panic seized his chest and he gasped breaths, clutching at his throat as man hung for theft.

How did she know? No one could have told her.

"In all the world only my wife knows my name!" Anger began to rise in him. "What deviltry is this? You are a witch!"

The queen smiled thinly, and rose from her velvet, high-backed chair and strode casually to the opposite side of the room, where she poured chill water from a decanter and drank.

All unhurried.

Then she leveled Rumpelstiltskin a stare. "It's not important how I know these things. Only that our bargain is met. The child will remain with me."

He bit back his wrath and threw his head back to stave off the slander he meant to spew. Politics. Think. But he could not summon a clever thought or stratagem. He saw only the sure hand of an artist in great murals on the vaulted ceilings above. Maidens depicted there, walking the bulrushes, the gowns of the gentry, of civility.

And the bitter taste of his stomach rose into his throat at the sight.

His gift, turning plain things precious, had served lords and ladies who claimed the need to serve the people they stood protectorate for; just as his gift had fed the hungry, clothed the naked, and freed the debtor.

His gift had also saved the queen's father.

Three times.

Straw to gold for trinkets in the prison cells far beneath the castle courts.

A year since, when this peasant-queen had been only a peasant imprisoned for her father's boastful tongue.

Yet, for his kindness, for all his kindnesses, his gift could never be used to shape gold for himself. And as if exchange for the alchemic power, he never been able to give Em, his wife, a child. The family they'd set out to have had been denied them. A quiet home ever the reminder.

Gods be damned! Gods be dead! I will use my skill for dark instead!

A refrain he railed into the heavens again and again for the unfair exchange heaped upon him to ever only give. Never to receive.

So he'd made his bargain with the peasant girl whom the king had asked to spin straw to gold to prove her father's lie.

Her first child in payment.

And when she'd begged him not to take the child, he'd granted a reprieve—guess his name and she could keep the child. He'd taken pity on the young mother, who looked so like Em, though taller.

And by the damned she'd discovered his name. Some magic. Some seer. She'd twisted his pity, unfairly robbing him (and Em) of the family he had fairly earned. Not by gold, but by the rescue of this peasant-queen's life.

They could not keep taking and never give! Rumpelstiltskin slammed his fists into the marble and screamed, railing at the gods again. "Gods be damned! Gods be dead! I will use my skill for dark instead!"

He rose and whirled to face her. "NO! I came into the stink and mire of your dungeons and found you mourning a father soon to lose his head for his lies, because you knew not how to spin straw to gold. Pathetic young girl. And now look at you, your chin raised high in the company of others like a swan who does not see the shit lying in the murky pool beneath its plumage. You stuff yourself here on roast hen, take warm baths with attendants who scent your water with rose petals, and you adorn your peasant flesh with fine-twilled silk purchased with the blood of men bearing spoils from the wars your king declares.

"NO! The child is rightly mine!"

The queen's stony face betrayed no fear or intent to acquiesce. She sipped her chilled water again, then pointed a finger at him. "Chose carefully how you speak to the queen. We struck a bargain and I have kept my end. If you break our trust, you risk prison or death."

And that he did. Because the greater trust lay with Em, whose cries in the heart of night when she thought he was asleep and could not hear her seared him to bone and accused his philanthropy of never returning the simple pleasures he'd promised her the day she given him her hand in marriage.

So he squared his shoulder to her and let it out like Gabriel's horn, calling all to Christ to war on the legions of the adversary. This was his stand, and the hate and need drove chills over his flesh in waves as his accusing words blared.

"Then death it be! But not before the king will know that yours is not the skilled hand that spun straw to gold. And then what do you think he will do, my queen. Will he forget that yours are thread-bear shoes lately through the shit of a horse's ass, or that your raiment hung like gossamer over nubile teats that showed every blemish when the rain soaked them through?"

"I warn you," she said.

"WHY DO YOU THINK HE MARRIED YOU?"

She might have been preparing to say love, when Rumpelstiltskin silenced her with his next barrage. A torrent of anger come from a thousand unrepaid kindnesses where his gift had liberated others who never asked after his own need, or Ems.

"You are his war machine, peasant queen. A mill of gold to buy ships and soldiers and metal to build an army to march against the eastern prince. The king holds no special place in his heart for your father. He was a token to induce your compliance. Only you had no gift to meet his demand. And so I did it for you. And when he learns you are incapable—"

"Guards!" the queen called out.

"—you will go back to the fields where your fingers will rub and burn as mine do from serving the ungrateful."

Rumpelstiltskin spun a tight circle pointing at every finery in the room: the grand tapestries, paintings the height of three men, statuary quarried deep in the east where marble ran the colors of royalty—crimson, drake, honey—and great sconces flaming from the walls to lend everything the glow of civility.

This was her condemnation. He would see to it.

By his blood and sweat. Come the guards, come the king, come the gods themselves. No more! The refrain of his wife's suffering, of his endless march of sacrifices repaid if ever by nothing more than a weak smile.

"COME THEN! Let them come! I will denounce you as an imposter. I will speak the truth of your skill. And the king will usher me into his court to hear a full accounting. And do you know what will happen then, my peasant-queen?"

Her lip trembled ever so slightly.

"You will be lucky to be returned to the fields where your horse pulls a plow through the manure to sew your pumpkin seeds. More surely you will find the stocks. And your father . . ." he shook his head ". . . his tongue cut out before he is hanged for lying to the king."

The queen touched her belly, betraying her greatest concern.

Rumpelstiltskin smiled darkly. "And your son will remain here, a bastard heir, until the king finds a proper sire for his progeny.

Fear crept into her face. "Why?" she asked. "Why would you do undo all you have done . . . for a child that is not your own."

Rumpelstiltskin rushed to her, glaring up into her peasant face. "Because of your ingratitude. Because there are better arms to hold the babe and give it a home, not of war and lineage and lies, but happiness," his voice softened momentarily, "and giving."

An awful silence stretched in the queen's reception room, as he stared up at her and the queen stared back. He believed she was considering all he said, giving him the child; considered her misfortune in crossing him, ever meeting him, perhaps; considered the life of her father, who she could save a fourth time.

Then again her hands stroked her belly, so recently full with a child. And with that, determination set her brow. Her stare hardened and she trumpeted into his whiskered face, "GUARDS!"

The clamber of booted feet, scabbards, gauntlets as men rushed the stone stairs toward them from beyond the door.

But not once did he drop her stare. He looked back the look of the damned, for in his failure that was all he could hope to be. And he would go there hardly.

Then he smiled again the blackness he could feel inside. "Beware, my peasant-queen. I look delicate, but I am long-lived in this world. And I am no longer intolerant of unpaid balances."

Looking more a queen than any moment before, she held his gaze. "Your threats have the consequence of spilled water." And she poured her chalice at his feet.

"I want you to hear me," Rumpelstiltskin said, as men began pounding on the door he'd locked to the queen's reception room. "Your selfishness is going to bring a world of grief to someone I love. When I settle the account on that, my queen, the payment will be dire." He raised a finger and pointed at her. "I will ask one last time: Trust the child into my care. Balance the accounts for yourself before they are balanced for you. Think on your home, your husband, your kingdom. Think on your father, who lives and furrows the earth to draw forth fruit.

"I will give the child a happy life. You may trust my word on it.

"Then you and I are paid." Rumpelstiltskin finished, awaiting her response.

But before either could say a word more, the men-at-arms crashed the door and made for him.

Rumpelstiltskin leapt the window, glanced back once to find the conflicted face of the peasant-queen, and then disappeared into the night to the calls of the guard.

He would return here, bearing ill news when he came.

But now he had a long, dark walk ahead. Home. To tell the good woman he'd promised a child to, that there would be none. Her barren womb would remain a scourge and pity to her.

Unless . . .

~

RUMPELSTILTSKIN WALKED HALF the night to his home deep in the balsamwood glen at the reaches beyond the castle's protectorate. There, in the moonlight, outside his mossy door, he paused. And breathed. Taking in the evergreen scent and stealing himself for what he must now do.

He had tried so many times before to find a way to give Em a child. And this last time, he'd succeeded; until he'd given the queen the opportunity of a reprieve.

And he knew why he had done so.

He'd seen the dread in the peasant-queen's eyes when he'd come to collect his due (her first born). And so when she'd asked him to reconsider, he'd offered a single chance: Guess his true name.

Because the look of grief on a woman's face when she thinks of her family . . . was hard to deny.

Just as it was when he looked at Em and saw the mother inside her pine to share that love with a child.

And now he must tell Em. Tell her that a child would already be snuggled close in her arms, but for the pity he'd taken on another woman over the child he'd promised his wife. Forgetting the pity of Em's life—years of barrenness and sadness. Where had his loyalty fallen?

Or had it been sheer stupidity.

He wanted to scream again! Hit something! Lay his desecration on the Heavens and invoke the wrath of the gods to lay him down. Put him under. End him.

But in the quiet he knew two very quiet truths: his gift had descended from the gods themselves and his rebuke would mean nothing; and just maybe—though this new despair was his own doing—he might be the only one in the world who could comfort her.

Rumpelstiltskin heaved a great sigh and pushed into their hidden cottage.

And found Em waiting, her face lit in amber hues, expectant in the dim light of the hearth.

The immediacy of her pain shot through his heart when she saw his empty arms. He went to her and took her in his gentle embrace. "I'm so sorry, Em."

She wept for a very long time, while Rumpelstiltskin held her. And in those long moment, he spied something more that tore his heart. In the corner she'd put up a crib, laid in with fine blue quilts wrought in her own strong needle.

She had made preparations while he had been off to the castle, ready to receive the child and rest it comfortably for its first night in their home.

He also caught a whiff of warm milk in a pot set near the fire—a baby's first meal.

And as they hold one another, he began to rock side to side to sooth her, the floorboards beneath them creaking in time.

Sometime later she ceased to weep and sat again.

He girded himself emotionally and knelt beside her in her rocker (where she had intended to rock the child).

It was time.

"Em, I need to tell you something."

She looked at him through wet eyes.

And so he explained it all, and watched his loved ones face shift from surprise to shock to horror to anger. Through an awful scowl she stared a fiery disappointment that he hoped never to see again.

"You traded our chance at a family to this peasant-queen on a game of luck? Rum, you fool! You fool! Why would you do it? Why?"

He had no excuse and merely shook his head. "I'm so sorry. I looked at this young mother's face, and I had to give her hope."

"You're so weak, Rum. And—"

77

"But how did she get my name? It's not possible unless you told her. You and I are the only ones who even know my real name. Forever, to those who know me, I'm only Rum. Have you told anyone? Even in confidence?"

She shook her head. And then the look of disappointment in her face shifted one last time. And what he saw there was a real kind of fear. But not for herself.

"Rum, do you know what this means?"

"Yes, Em, I'm sorry. But I was thinking I might still win the child back. The king is sure to want more gold, and when he finds out that his queen can't—"

She put her hand on his lips, silencing him. "You have forgotten. Rum, your name is the source of your gift. It bears a unique power that gives you the ability to make plain things precious."

Rumpelstiltskin nodded. "I haven't forgotten, Em. The gift was handed down—"

"Unless," she cut in, "It is revealed to another."

The cottage fell heavy and silent like a death shroud. They stared at one another, clasping hands to keep from falling with the one simple caution and condition of his gift.

Ed only knew his name because their marriage, sealed in the bonds of matrimony, made them one flesh in the sight of the gods. And he'd shared the conditions of his life with her on their wedding night, including his name. And his people, gone now for so long into the long narrows of the world, had taken her aside and taught her the ways of the life that would ever live.

And she'd remembered.

Better than he.

But this must be a mistake.

No! It can't be!

He rushed to the barn. There he grabbed handfuls of straw and jumped into the seat behind the spindle and began to spin. Straw to gold. Straw to gold.

Except that what came out was only straw.

It was true. He had forgotten the law governing his gift. He could no longer make plain things precious. No longer help the poor or prisoner out of their shackles.

He could no longer look for that opportunity to trade a great favor for the life of a child, as he'd tried to do with the peasant-queen. And without his gift, there was no chance to return to her with the ill-news he'd promised to settle the account that left his wife bereft.

But this time he did cry up, rattling the rafters of the barn and shouting his wrath until his throat fell raw and ravaged.

And when the chaff had finally stopped falling from the loft, leaving the barn silent and still and empty of all sound, Rumpelstiltskin thought of one place he might go that might help him get that child back, even without his gift.

~

"I KNOW THEE, and I want thee off my land. No good comes of your unhallowed magicks, feline. Get thee out!" The peasant-queen's father jabbed his pitchfork at Rumpelstiltskin to goad him back toward the road.

Rum didn't move.

"You'll want to listen to me, you old dodger, or else you and that daughter of yours are going to climb the gallows together and not a one will care. You'll fall to the cheers of children and I will have myself a drink to the sound of your snapping neck." Rum knocked the pitchfork out of his face and glowered at the old man.

Eyes milky with age stared back in a glaze. The old sot wore three days of beard and smelled as if he hadn't bathed in as long. They stood together in his corn fields (green to the knee just yet), locusts jumping around their feet and landing with unhappy thuds on the dry ground.

"Nonsense. Get thee behind me. Or I'll call for my daughter the queen and we'll see how the royals will deal with thee. I'm not afraid. Thou dost stink, my boy. Not like work. Thou smells hateful. Got some pride wounded, I'll wager. That about the size of it?"

Rum stepped in close, catching breath rank with rotting teeth. "Oh, it's hate, old dodger. But I think you better know why." And so he told the entire story, sparing not jot or tittle.

The queen's father slowly lowered his pitchfork as the tale unfolded.

When Rum finished he stared the man straight. "I saved your life three times. Saved the life of your daughter three times. I gave her a husband, a kingdom. And now all I ask is my due. Since your daughter's trickery has stolen the skill I might have used to look elsewhere for a child. Will you talk to her?"

The old man looked away with his milky eyes, his forehead wrinkling in concentration. "Thou art asking me to go against the queen, then, aren't you? And to send along mine own grandson, the heir to the throne."

"In payment of your lives and prosperity, which I have given." Rum felt dread stir in his chest.

"And this gift of straw to gold. It's gone now, because someone else knows your name. And you'll only ever get that back if those who know come to their end one way or another, is that the truth?"

Rum nodded.

The old dodger thought a moment more then said, "Come with me."

They followed the rows of corn toward the farmhouse, walking under a high blue sky filled with promise. Perhaps this man could help as Rum had hoped. But they wound around the house toward the barn, and once inside the old dodger picked up a handful of straw and held it out to him.

"Make it gold."

Confusion bloomed in Rum's head, his anger beginning to simmer. "I told you I cannot."

"Try."

Rum took it, turned his thoughts and ran his fingers along the stalks. He concentrated. Closed his eyes a moment.

Nothing.

He dropped the hay. "I told you. Now, will you help me? Or—"

The old dodger nodded. "Had to try one last time. Be sure of things. This way." And he went to the middle of the barn, which lay thick with the scent of unshoveled horse manure and the nests of doves. The man bent over and found a ring-handle in the floor. He pulled up a large hatch, hinges screeching in protest as it came. The door pulled free though, whoofing the scent of old earth as it opened a dark square in the floor of the barn.

"What is this?" Rum peered down the stairs.

"I've known some bits of magic in my time, lad. Kept them secret. Kept them safe." He pointed into the cellar. "Let's go down."

Internal warning flared in Rum at the idea. But the thought of Em got him moving. His feet bowed the wood steps as he descended into the dark. Dead roots extending from the walls like long, thin fingers, scraped at his arms and cheeks. A hand shovel and some gloves sat on one of the top steps, neglected. Then, just as he turned to ask something more, the light from the barn winked out, the hatch door slamming shut, the sound of bolts being thrown.

Rum rushed up the steps and pounded on the hatch. "What is this? Let me out of here!"

From just the other side of the wood that separated them, the old dodger spoke, his voice falling down through the cracks like a ghost. "My boy, asking for my grandson is one thing, the future king, another. But any man who can make gold from a stone or twig is bound, in time, to miss that ability. Even if he's found himself a family." He paused, as if thinking. "No, boy, thou wouldst eventually seek to take my daughter's life to restore what thou hast lost. I cannot have that."

"Honor what I have given! Make it right! Or I will bring the hate I bear for your daughter against you as well!" Rum pound-ed at the hatch. Fine dirt falling into his face with each strike.

"This cage will not hold me, old man! I will find a way—" The sound of retreating steps across the barn floor.

"—out of here! Listen to me!" Rum pounded a few moments more until the sound of another hatch screeching open somewhere down and to the left in this blackened cellar.

And something more.

Growing louder.

Growling.

Feral.

And the distant voice of the old man cursing, kicking, and then slamming another hatch-door shut.

Then the padding of feet. Animal feet. And the use of noses to sniff the air and ground.

And then silence.

Rum stood alone on those steps in the pitch dark with something, maybe several somethings, out in the blackness waiting, alert to sound, movement, smell.

The darkness and awful expectancy gripped him in shivering panic. A man of normal height and stature could maybe contend with these beasts. Rum . . . was small—a lineage of alchemists.

And the moments drew out, waiting, his muscles beginning to ache for need of movement.

As quietly as he could, Rum reached for the hand shovel he'd seen, moving his hand lightly over the stairs until he felt something.

Just then, the beasts in the dark began to move, their feet hurried in the cellar darkness. Getting closer. Their throats roughing out snarls of wanton hunger.

Rum reached faster, and knocked the handshovel away, hearing it fall to the floor beneath the cellar stairs.

By the gods! This is insanity!

But he moved then, scrambling down the stairs. His only chance to have something in hand when the beasts came.

He didn't make it.

Unable to see, Rum came to the bottom of the stair but did not know it. He tumbled forward hitting his head hard on something metal. And the next moment the beasts were upon him.

Their teeth tore at his shirt and sleeves. One taking his arm in its snarling maw and shaking its head violently, tearing his flesh like so much fabric. The other snapped at Rum's flailing hand, as he tried to ward it off.

He couldn't see a thing.

He would die here. The truth of it constricted his breathing again, the way he'd felt when the queen revealed his name.

Then he thought of Em.

And he surged up from the floor, his arm's flesh ripping in the jaws of one beasts. He rushed blind in the dark feeling for the stairs, when the other creature caught his hand and snapped two fingers in its teeth, ripping them from his hand with one great jerk of its head.

Exquisite pain shot up Rum's hand and elbow and shoulder and he howled into the blackness. But the beasts did not relent and grew more frenzied.

Rum struggled to where he thought the handshovel had fallen and fell forward himself to the ground, his free hand swiping in broad arcs, searching for the tool. As he did, the other beast took hold of his ankle and clamped down hard. Warm blood bubbled up to the skin, exciting and maddening the dog like a berserker.

Just as his hand hit the handshovel.

Rum grasped it and swung it around in a vicious arc at the darkness where one beast still held his arm. The blunt arrowed tip must have hit the dog in the ear, from the angle. And Rum felt it bury itself in the dog's head. A yelp sounded in the cellar, a final feral cry, and its jaws relaxed on Rum's arms.

Blood flowed from gashes above his elbow, running in rivulets like small streams down his arm. The scent of his own blood now thick in his own nose.

As his companion's yelp faded, the other beast let go Rum's ankle and leapt. Rum guessed it came for his throat and brought the handshovel up defensively to ward off the attack.

He guessed right.

And the creature's gaping maw took the tool in and down the throat, sprays of blood erupting from its mouth and coating Rum's face.

The beast scrambled off him, crying around the thing stuck in the soft tissue behind its razor teeth. Gagging, coughing, gnashing teeth receded in the darkness, until the sounds stopped completely.

Rum lay beneath the stairs panting, the shock of it all fading, replaced by the awful sting of the bites in his flesh, and the ache of two missing fingers.

But he did not move just yet. Gathering his senses, his eyes adjusting to the darkness.

Hours later, he sat in a far corner of the cellar, thinking.

The old dodger had, in fact, a shelf of arcane objects. Small skulls and short sticks and vials and books and other trash buried in a blanket of dust. The props of a pageant man. No wonder, Rum could see, that the old dodger spoke so fantastically about spinning straw to gold so long ago in the presence of the king—the bark of a confidence man.

But these things wouldn't help Rum out of his cellar-cage; he was looking for a hidden key or tool to win his escape. He found nothing.

So he sat near the far hatch, where the beasts had entered, considering what came next. He'd decided that there was nothing more to do but kill the queen. Take back his name and find a way to turn a profit by his gift.

Damn the service!

Damn the ingratitude!

As his scorn settled in his heart, he lifted his ruined hand and studied the place where his fingers had been. He wiggled each of the others, having the strange sensation that he moved those not there as well.

And as he did, a thought occurred to him.

A way to remove a part without destroying the whole.

Oh yes, he would visit the queen. But his revenge would come a far bit sweeter than murder. And he'd get his name back, to boot.

And Rum felt that dark smile again touch his face. Like had come when he'd argued with the queen.

In the blackness of the cellar (which he would escape when the old man came to check his dead beasts) that dark smile wouldn't be seen. But the intentions it carried would most definitely be felt.

~

RUM STOLE INTO the queen's reception chamber the same way he had come before. At night. Up the wall. Through the window. His ire boiled near the surface as he dropped to the floor and looked up at the peasant girl come lately to grace.

She did not notice him.

She sat folded into her chair this night. Crying. Her body shook with each new sob. And though he made no effort to mask his approach, she never looked up. Still she spoke when he stopped before her.

"The king has asked me to spin more gold from straw. These last few days I have found excuses. But his patience wears thin. And this last hour he accused me of duplicity. He promises to keep his word to execute my father if I cannot produce the gold." Her voice broke down again into sobs.

Rum's ire fell off. He was looking again at the peasant girl he'd first found in the deeps, who'd needed a miracle to save her family. The girl he'd helped in exchange for trinkets, until their bargain for her first born.

A needy girl.

At the end, one not so different from himself, Rum thought.

One in grief, who will deal however she must to save the life of one she loves. That was the tie that binds. And in the moment he thought it, she asked him.

"Can you spin it for me? Would you? Despite our quarrel, to save my father's life . . . to save me?" She held a lace handkerchief under her nose, catching the tears as they fell.

This close, Rum could smell the salty tang. A familiar scent. Em wore it all the time these days.

"My queen," Rum said softly, "In discovering my name, you have unmagicked me. I no longer can make the plain precious. No longer spin straw to gold."

At which, the queen's sobs wracked her body and she collapsed back into her chair. Rum could feel the darkest irony in it, that in solving his riddle she'd saved her child's life, but undone herself now when she needed Rum's gift again.

The reception room echoed with her cries. The murals above uncaring, the painted ladies still walking the bulrushes.

Far away, another lady walked a mossy glen, losing faith her husband and in the hope of that simplest desire: a family. The thought of Em (as it did so often) stirred him to action.

Rum drew from his tunic pocket a small vile, taken from the cellar shelf of the peasant-queen's father—a strange man whose boasts of alchemy had started this entire affair.

"My queen, listen to me." Rum placed his diminished hand over her own. "This elixir I found in the cellar of your girlhood home, where your father tried to kill me. Its label reads: *forgetting*. I know this magic, my Lady. To drink it is to lose all memory. To become as a babe in understanding."

She looked up at Rum, the questions clear on her face.

"If you drink it," Rum said, "You will no longer recall my name. And I may spin the straw to gold for you."

Understanding lit in her eyes, hope following close on.

"But I have a condition . . ."

She withdrew her hand. The smile that had teased at her lips falling to a frown of awful expectation.

Rum nodded. "You must give me the child."

Tears fell again, that she bothered not to catch. Some small ire of her own lifted in her eyes and mouth. "It is my baby, you monster. What man blackmails a woman with the life of her father to take her child?"

Rum might have been angered and shot back at her. But he'd thought this through. He had a ready answer. "My queen, if you drink the elixir, it is not only my name that you will forget, but everything . . . including your son. As dismal as that sounds, once you've consumed the vile, you would have no grief because you would not remember your baby."

The mere suggestion of it brought hateful sobs afresh to the peasant queen. It was the sound of despair.

A sound Rum knew.

"My queen, listen to me. It is an awful choice to make. And had I the power to undo it, I would. But let me tell you one thing more." Rum drew a very long breath and gathered the queen's fretful eyes. "I came to you in the castle deeps that distant day to help you bear a burden. To help you save your father's life. And all was well. But the king's greed and our game lost control, and we each looked after our own interests, didn't we?"

The peasant-queen nodded. "I *am* grateful for what you did."

Rum smiled at that. "Thank you, my queen. But what remains a mystery to you is why I would have your child. And it's a story you should hear."

So Rum explained it, talking mostly of Em and how good and gentle a heart she possessed. How she ached to hold a child, but could not bear one. Rum related a great many small kindnesses to the queen to share Em's heart and mind.

"It is awful for you, my queen," Rum concluded, "but all this venom between us comes to a light end. The child will know happiness. Mayhaps greater even than in the court of the king, where he will scant have a boyhood before he is training for war."

In the great reception hall another long silence stretched. But unlike his last visit, there came no threat of guards or destructive glare. The peasant queen sat in her highback velvet chair beneath her painted maidens, holding hands with Rum, and surely wondered if this was the right choice.

Somewhere beyond the window, a gathering storm brought thunder to the hills, like a voice out of heaven. What did it say, Rum thought. Did its peal mean anything more today, this moment?

When its roll had echoes its last, the queen, tears running free and silent, nodded. "I will drink."

~

RUM WALKED THE road, tired from a long night of spinning gold from straw. The rain fell, making his way slow through the mud. But he drew a small cart, tightly covered, filled with silken sheets, brightly-painted toys, and a small bassinet where the child lay sleeping.

He thought back on the queen's great resolve. Sending forth her guard to kill the ranger who had discovered Rum's name; writing a last letter to her father before she lost his memory forever; calling on the healers in advance to make preparations for her departure (the king would lose interest in an ignorant woman after some time); and putting together all her baby's needful things, then holding him for a long while to say goodbye.

Rum walked in the downpour, regretting some of what had recently come. His anger and hate. His misguided intention to take his skill back only for personal gain.

But that was over. He could no longer hear Em's cries in the back of his mind. He plodded slowly to bring her the family she'd hoped for across so many years. And he'd give her a kiss when they met. The same tender, grateful kiss he'd given the queen before she'd given her all away.

CANTICLE OF ABRAHAM
AND
ISAAC

Isaac: Father, I am sore affeared
To see you bear that drawne sword.
Abraham: Isaac, son, peace, I pray,
Thou breakest my heart . . .

SIMON DONNE RAISED the short blade high into the morning air and looked down at his son William, bound and pleading, and waited to be stopped. The chirrup of birds in the cool dawn belied the horrific tableau Simon held for his audience, who watched with memory the reenactment of Abraham's heavenly commission. And again, for the hundredth time or more, Simon trembled with real fear at the God who'd asked a father to kill his own child.

Simon's face grew slick with sweat. His eyes blurred with the sting of his own tears. He blinked them away, and held his pose. *To teach and entertain.* But not for the onlookers here in Wakefield, or in any town the troupe came to.

He needed to know.

Needed to understand the test that forged the infamy of the weapon he now held up in mock of death. *The blade of faith.*

Would Father Abraham have gone through with it?

Simon's fingers cramped on the hilt, and the small sword began to shake. He stared down at William, seeking the answer in the twelve-year-old's face. But the boy showed back only the panic and fear of a good thespian. Playing his part. Unafraid beneath the drama. *Had Isaac remained even so? Sure his father would do no harm?*

Simon raised the blade higher, preparing to plunge it into the sacrifice.

Some few groans escaped the crowd. A gasp. Others were silent, either deeply reflecting or still half-asleep.

And then the sun rose up, piercing the morning chill. Its light cast over the mass a long shadow of Simon's up-stretched arm, like the shadow of a spear quaking in its master's grip.

The unexpected poignancy caught William's attention, too. The boy shifted, looking up to see the ominous silhouette weave like a lance raised heavenward.

Simon grabbed hold of the blade with both hands, his breath ragged in his throat. How much now is fancy, he thought, of this thing I (Abraham) would do.

To teach and entertain.

The pageant wagon had started the play cycle with the benevolence of Creation in the pre-dawn light, just as it had since Simon had joined them in 1554—twenty-two years ago.

But the killing had soon come. Cain had killed Able, God had killed everybody with Noah's flood, and now Simon as Abraham meant to kill his son. Thirty-two pageant plays, telling the biblical tales (mostly): Conspiracy, Scourging, Hanging, Expulsion, Sacrifice, Slaughter, Mortification, Harrowing . . .

Bad business so early in the morning.

Even with the sun dawning in the east.

It is only a mystery play. To share the scriptural stories.

But it all rattled in Simon's chest. He wanted to scream. To destroy the tranquility of this mild summer morn in which townspeople now calmly continued eating their warm breakfast bread while watching him relive the nightmare.

A great sob burst uncontrolled from his lips. A yawp out of his heart as the moment drew out with excruciating lethargy. The grief in the sound caused even passersby to pause and look.

The noise also startled Robert Fuller, a guildsman playing the angel today in Wakefield. Bob (as he'd asked to be called), was a parchment maker—a craft with no urgency. But at Simon's wail, he hurried onstage to stay Simon's murderous hand.

Simon sighed relief. And together, he and William pulled James Faust (dressed in a ram's outfit) from a twist of willow branches stage left. James would be God's sacrifice—a local bookbinder already smelling of the sweaty wool in his costume.

The laughter came with the braying and bucking of the ram. James put his ass into it.

But Simon did not laugh.

~

IN THE PUB across the commons from the pageant wagon, Simon sat sipping his ale. The quiet, empty room (dawn being early for a pint) suited his nerves after the play. To his back a small fire burned, chasing away the chills—those that came from the cold anyway. And the bite of the ale felt good on his throat, which had grown raw from so many performances. He was not a good singer, but canticle was the playwright's form. So he and William had traded snippets of song every morning (weather permitting) for years now. Telling the old story.

His boy sat pleasantly at his side, writing on some parchment Bob had given him. And through the door, the melodies of Adoration came distant and mellow. The three kings come to see the child in the manger, and his mother mild. It always reminded Simon of William's mother, Isabel, who'd died giving their son life.

He could still see the peace in her face, feel the touch of her skin. The day she'd told him she was pregnant, she'd had one simple request: a home.

She'd known what she was asking. Leave the pageant wagons, the play cycle, the role of Abraham. And the initial shock and panic of the request had stolen his breath. But with the thought he'd also felt some ease of his life-long question about Abraham and his sacrificial sword.

God, he missed her.

The gentle strains of Adoration went on. The cycle would continue all day and well into the night, until the sketch of Judgment played out on the decorated cart in the glare of torchlight.

Such was a sight.

Celebrants at the cycle of Corpus Christi here seated in the dark with the cast of flames on their faces.

Damn fools!

All of them, this seed of Abraham . . .

Like me. Literally.

Simon turned the blade over in his hands, running his finger over the Hebrew inscription. It read simply: blade of faith. But faith in what?

Someone sat heavily beside him. "The cycles are coming to an end." It was Bob—his angel. "The clergy don't care for your *embellishments* to the liturgical dramas. And a new kind of entertainment is said to be replacing us."

"Is that right?" Simon returned his attention to the short weapon in his hand.

"Professional theaters are opening in many towns these days. And people want more to laugh about, with fewer *lessons* in their entertainment."

Simon just nodded his head as another patron entered the pub. The fellow guided himself with a staff, steering his ponderous belly between the tables. The man fell twice as he wove his way toward them. Probably drunk already.

Bob tapped the sword in Simon's hands. "By 'is wounds its strange how you lord over a simple stage prop. What meaning is there in it?"

Simon considered telling him. Why should he care what others thought of his story? But before he could begin, the great big bumbling man ambled up to their table.

"Well met." Simon raised his mug of ale.

"We haven't met," the other said. "I'm Tinker."

"Then, well met, Tinker. I'm Simon."

Tinker bowed. "Pleased to meet you. You gave a stirring performance this morning. But now, I'd like to hear an answer to this man's question. A pub's the place for stories."

Tinker leaned in, resting on elbow on Robert's shoulder. He was ready for the tale.

"It's a family heirloom," Simon began. "Passed down for more generations than anyone bothers to count."

"A relic, then!" Tinker boomed. "I'm a relic, too. More ale!"

Mugs were shortly set before them, as though the barmaid had begun to pour upon seeing Tinker enter. And Tinker's was gone before anyone could lift their drink. "Proceed, young master," Tinker said, settling in again.

Simon found his start. "Did you ever wonder what happened to the sword Abraham raised to kill Isaac?"

"Bloody hell, no. Who cares about such things? It's the moral of the story that counts. Morals must be understood, else there's no fun in breaking them." Tinker boomed more laughter.

"Isaac might have cared," Simon replied. "As have all those descended from this blade." He ran a finger over the Hebrew inscription again.

"You think this belonged to Abraham? My, you're deeper in the cups than I am." Tinker hefted Bob's mug and quaffed it in a few large gulps.

"Every father passes it to his son with the charge to remember. Remember faith before life. Heaven before mortality." Simon looked into the meaty features of the man. "Our remembrance is our wound. But history has forgotten."

Tinker started to fall again, but propped himself with his staff.

"Are you all right?" Simon asked.

"Ah, bloody day, yes. Something in my ears since birth. Makes me dizzy." Tinker closed his eyes, smiled, then laughed out loud. "I should drink more."

Simon finished. "I do the play . . . I need to understand."

"And this is your lad?" Tinker asked. He reached across and tussled William's hair. "What do you think of all this, my young man?"

William looked up at his father, then across to the men. "Makes one hell of a story."

Tinker reared back and bawled laughter into the pub rafters, not realizing William meant his comment literally.

"Wakefield has a vicar, Bob." Simon stood. "I was told yesterday by a grieving widow that he's the best man south of Edinburgh and north of London. A man who reads in Hebrew, understands Isaiah, and can prophesy out of Revelations. You're going to take me to him."

"What good—"

"Hold on there!" Tinker interrupted. "I like your story, Mr. Simon, and would defend your right to tell it. Bloody hell, I've probably told that story myself at some point. But a vicar? He's no help to you. He's going to talk, and smile, and put his hand out for a little something."

Simon kicked Tinker's staff, nearly causing him to fall. "Sounds a bit like you."

"A vicar!" the man cried, undaunted. "You're a silly person. Let me make you wise." He paused, gathered their attention. "Forget it all."

"Lets go," Simon said, tapping William to stand.

"Truly," Tinker continued. "You've a stripling lad there, who bears a good sense of humor. Likes to use his hands, too. Not embarrassed by a father taking his drink while the cock still makes his noise. And you," he lifted his staff and tapped

Simon's shin, "you make a damn fine Abraham. Very poetic. And it's summer. A good time to be riding a wagon, and receiving the congratulations of a crowd. What right have you got to be miserable?"

"Let's go," Simon said again, this time motioning Bob to stand.

Tinker stood erect, like a thespian delivering a prologue, and chuffed in and out before pronouncing, "You need to abandon this impractical quest. Learn to have a jot of fun. Here, watch." He called the barmaid over, and dove in face first to her bosom before she could react.

"Come now." Simon grabbed Bob and pulled him out of the pub and up the road, while his son laughed and laughed at the antics of a stranger who couldn't stand up straight, and was already drinking Simon's second, untouched mug.

～

WAKEFIELD CHANTRY CHAPEL squatted beside the River Calder in the late-morning light. The chantry served a practical purpose, besides its spiritual one, as part of the bridge itself—support on its northern bank. Drawing near, Simon saw along its west front, five ornately carved panels containing depictions of the Annunciation, the Nativity, the Resurrection, Ascension and the Coronation of the Virgin Mary.

Simon had little use for such places.

His church and worship belonged to the pageant wagon, where he saw an angel everyday come to stop his burnt offering.

Bob pointed at one of three doors. "Our vicar serves here."

Inside, the smell of spent candle wax lingered on the still air. Watery light leaked through windows to the right. And together he and Bob approached the head of the chantry (William behind). At the far end, they found a modest alter backed by stained glass more ornate than Simon might have imagined. Muted red and blue and aqua shone on the white alter linens.

Bob dropped to a knee and genuflected. Simon looked about at empty chairs and a portal in the left corner, where a man dressed in a dark grey robe emerged from the shadow.

"Vicar Michael," Bob spoke with haste. "We need your help."

The fellow nodded as he came, unhurried, and sat on a chair in the first row even before greeting them. He motioned for them to sit beside him. Simon eased onto a chair. William sat beside him, immediately setting to his parchment again.

Bob reached across and took the vicar by the hand, gathering his full attention. "I'm going to leave Simon to your care, father. I'll be in the back if I'm needed."

Then the man who'd played Abraham's angel that morning stood, offered Simon a squeeze of the hand, and withdrew.

"Well, what's this all about?" the Vicar asked.

Simon stared. The priest had a kind face, made softer somehow by successive folds about his eyes and mouth. His skin had spotted, too, though the effect came more like a child's freckles than the blotch of time. And he peered out under wooly brows, made bigger by the absence of hair on his crown. This was every man's good father.

Simon simply pulled the short blade from his belt and handed it to the man.

The vicar's brow knitted with some confusion before he raised the weapon for examination. The light was not good, but after several moments, the man found the inscription and shortly looked up with knowing eyes.

Simon and the vicar shared a long companionable silence, accompanied only by the scribbling of his son. Then the man's face softened, and he placed the sword on the seat between them.

"Do you know what I do here?" Vicar Michael asked.

"It's a chantry. You chant dirges for the souls of the dead."

The man nodded, smiling. "Most of whose lineage belongs to the great patriarch, Father Abraham."

"You don't believe the sword belonged to him, do you?"

"Do you?" The vicar priest held the same unassuming smile.

Simon paused at the question, his hand reflexively touching the weapon. But he did not drop the man's easy gaze. "My father told me the story with details not found in the holy book. He passed the gift to me as a legacy of faith unbroken from the Mount of Moriah."

"You're here with the traveling cycle. I saw your performance yesterday."

Simon said nothing.

"Was your father a storyteller?" the priest asked.

Simon smiled bitterly. "I see. A family of fantasists, that's what you think, telling each other stories for generations . . ."

"What *I* think is impertinent, Simon. Tell me why you're here."

"Maybe I should go."

"You're welcome to leave." The priest still sat, relaxed, friendly, somehow assured in a way that left Simon unsettled.

But he did not get up. Instead, he placed his other arm around William's shoulders, now touching the two things he held most dear. And the irony of it struck him: hope on the one hand, helplessness on the other.

"Simon," the priest began, his voice just above a whisper, "you and I are very much the same. I stand in this place," he lifted his hand toward the altar, "and I sing the praises of the dead, because we should not forget. Because their lives mattered. And because we learn from their passing and our own devotion to their memory.

"While you," he gestured at Simon's chest. "travel from village to village, town to town, proclaiming the stories of the dead to teach and remind us of plain and precious truths. The truth of faith. And of the great promise Abraham earned in Genesis: for his obedience, numerous seed and abundant prosperity."

"I know the promise." Simon's voice edged with impatience.

The vicar priest stared a long moment. "I do not think you do. Come."

The man stood and retreated toward the darkened portal from which he'd entered. Simon debated whether to follow, the gall of bitterness spreading in his chest. He hated to be patronized.

"Stay here," he said to William. "I'll be right back."

And he followed.

In the northeast corner of the chantry, a staircase wound up to some chambers and down into blackness. Simon descended slowly behind the priest into a small crypt. The scent of sweating stone and unswept floors filled his nose. The darkness was near complete, when the man lit a small torch. The room brightened in flickering orange hues, revealing a short line of chiseled caskets.

The vicar walked past the queue to the end, where a shortened tomb sat huddled in the shadows. Their footsteps echoed with hollow refrain off the hard, dark surfaces.

Simon came to stand at the caskets end. "A child," he deduced.

"My daughter," the Vicar replied.

His face, in the hellish glow of the flame, reminded Simon of the crowd's awful stares when night fell on the cycle and the play of Judgment was offered. Except, fear and bitterness did not live in the man's countenance. Loss, yes. But not anger.

They stood together for a long time in the flutter and hiss of the torch, in the company of death and granite and silt . . . and said nothing.

Then finally, "The promise, Simon, isn't wealth or grand-children." The vicar moved the torch near the tomb of his own child, illuminating the graven stone: Emily Gardner. "The promise is reunion with those we love. Endless seed and prosperity mean only that our family bonds will survive death. That is the faith of Abraham in sacrificing Isaac. God tested him, and he proved faithful."

Simon glared through the darkness. "Then what of Isaac's test?"

Confusion stole into the priest's eyes and brow.

"When Isaac went to Moriah he was not a boy as you all believe. He was a man, full grown, twenty-five years and able to prevent his own binding if he'd wished."

"You don't know that . . ."

Simon ignored the vicar. "He went as a lamb to the slaughter."

Then the familiar smile returned to the priest's face. "Simon, you only prove what I brought you here to share. Don't you see?"

Simon did not see.

The priest seemed to refocus, looking deep into Simon's soul. "I think, my son, your struggle is that every day you re-live that moment, but you've no need of faith to do it, because you are not truly planning to sacrifice your son. God is not testing you. It is not your story. Despite your ancestry. Despite the sword heirloom you carry."

He came near Simon, placing a kind hand on his back. "We don't remember or honor the instrument of death. We remember and honor the virtue and faith of he who wielded it. You should throw it away, Simon. Be rid of it."

But Simon did not here the admonition.

In his mind, the vicar's words resounded: ". . . *you've no need of faith to do it, because you are not truly planning to sac-rifice your son. God is not testing you . . .*"

Perhaps Simon now knew how to have, at last, the answer to his question.

~

WHEN THE FIRST charcoal shades bloomed in the east, Simon sat up. He hadn't slept. A black night had passed in the small tent he shared with William, whose mother had died in childbirth. It was a memory he could not shake. Her hand growing limp in his. The baby still stuck inside her. The quick action of the physician with a knife. Opening the body up to pull the baby free.

Simon hadn't known how to feel.

A birth. A funeral.

And when it grew quiet and dark each night, and he could hear William breathing in his sleep, Simon thought about sacrifice and injustice. But mostly he saw in his mind the pallor of skin . . . and red.

He drew the short sword to his chest, then. Hugging it tight. *I will have my answer today.*

Sometime later William awoke, and they went to the fire and took bacon and biscuits for breakfast. They hadn't finished eating when the tones of the canticles began: Creation.

"You seem more at peace," William observed. "The vicar must have helped."

Simon looked down at his son. "Helped?"

"You're not usually happy, papa."

"And when did you become so keen to my feelings?" Simon half-smiled.

His boy shrugged.

"I've had need of faith, that's all. Things are better now."

William smiled in return and the two went to prepare for their scene. They changed in the cold of morning, pulling on the rough costumes. William cheerfully hummed the tunes of his lines as he readied himself. And it wasn't until they were about to enter the stage that Simon knelt to look his son straight. "Do you believe Abraham would have killed Isaac, William? If the angel hadn't come, I mean?"

A curious look entered the child's face. "He loved God. And he loved Isaac. That's why it was a test. God was asking Abraham who he loved the most. I don't know what Abraham would have done. But I think it would be hard to love someone more than your family. Most people can't even get that right."

Then his boy spontaneously hugged him. Simon wrapped his arms around the lad, feeling his sword pressed against his hip.

The blade of faith.

Then they were called into their cycle. Simon heard the voice of God instruct him on the sacrifice. He gathered the child, and father and son trudged together up an imaginary Mount Moriah.

And they sang.

Their voices joined together in a harmony meant to be the voice and will of the eternal father. They soon reached their pretended summit, and Simon bound William in a ritual they'd performed a thousand times.

The crowd watched, rapt in a way Simon hadn't seen before.

To teach and entertain.

But his fingers quaked long before he drew the blade of faith, trembling with a different intention today. Simon paused to look up, to assure God that this was real. Black and bloody, but real. His eyes found only grey skies—the windows of heaven shut to him.

He sang:

O Isaac, son, I say to thee
God hath today commanded me

A sacrifice, of thee to make

And let the creatures be

Simon pulled his sword. His heart slammed in his chest. *Don't let me do it, my Lord! Don't let me do it!*

William's antiphonic song rose from the altar:

Is this God's will?

"Yes, son," Simon/Abraham sang. And he raised the blade of faith high against the grayish light. "My blessing I give you, and your mother's too. And God's."

"I pray," sang William/Issac, "turn down my face. For I am sore afraid."

Then Simon raised the sword, his entire body wracked with fear and trembling. For today, no guildsman would come. Not Robert Fuller. Not anyone. The angel costume lay empty in the changing area behind the pageant wagon. That had been easy to manage in the night and dark when a man can't sleep . . .

Simon/Abraham pitched forward, canting, "Jesu! Have pity on me, for what I have in mind."

And that's when Simon saw it. A look in his son's eyes. Understanding.

The look of it broke something in Simon that he knew could never be mended. Even if he had his answer to the question of Abraham's resolve to kill his own son, it may not be worth the price.

Because for Simon, none of this was God's test for Abraham. Nor God's test for Simon.

It was Simon's test for God.

"Stay my hand for once and all!" Simon screamed, breaking the rote canticle. "Or don't! And prove you are not the God of Abraham!"

Simon felt nothing. Saw nothing. Save the look of horror on William's face.

But this was the price. The answer must be had. "If you're there, smite me down and spare my child! Because know this: If you let me murder my son—the last good thing in my life after Isabel died—then you and I are done! Do you understand?"

Simon's voice carried long at that windless hour, shuttled along under the lowering clouds like a damnation running to its maledict.

Then the blade of faith was at its peak, and could only be brought down. William lay frozen, looking at Simon, his face screwed tight in a plea. "No, papa. Please. No. We're going to be all right."

In memory, Simon saw his wife's cut and bloodied body. He saw his father handing him the sword he'd worn all his life and asking him to carry it with pride. He saw drunken bouts, and nights when William slept alone in their cold tent.

It was all a bloody business. This life! This tragedy!

Simon quivered like a drawn bowstring over William's body.

His son looked up, as he did every time, and watched the silhouette of his father's arm and blade describe nothing so much as a long spear jabbing the sky, and trembling from the furor of the moment.

But Simon stood oblivious. To the crowd. To his son. To himself. He listened only for the voice of Heaven. *You are not God if you can let me do this to an innocent! My faith can't be blind! It must be the faith that you will stop me from this vile deed!*

Simon wailed at the sky, "This is *your* test! YOURS!"

The skies remained mute.

"Do you hear me!" Simon screamed. "*I* am testing *you*!"

And he brought the blade of faith down toward his son in a great hammerfall stroke.

But as the sword's edge arced, a massive blur from the rear of the pageant wagon caught him and tackled him violently to the boards.

The blade of faith skittered across the cart and fell to the ground, leaving Simon pinned and panting beneath a hulking frame.

Tinker.

"You," Tinker huffed, "are a silly person."

The crowd stirred at the abruption. It was not the traditional story of Abraham and Isaac. This angel had stopped Abraham by force. But they sat and waited, eating their warm morning bread.

Simon began to weep.

Tinker did not move, holding Simon safe, immovable. "I think I know what's going on here, my friend. And I can only ask you this once: Have you grown any wiser? Or will I be taking you to the King's guard?"

His cheek pressed to the wagon, Simon could barely nod. "I am a fool."

"No argument there," Tinker replied, and let him sit up.

What did I almost do?

It wasn't until William drew near that the weight of Simon's sin truly fell upon him. It came like the crush of sadness he'd felt when his wife had slipped away. So much so that he struggled to breathe. Shame and fright ripped through him, as did gratitude—his son was alive. But William did not show Simon sad or angry eyes. He simply stood, waiting, as if for an indication of who sat before him: his father . . . or Abraham.

But he did not wait long.

Simon wrapped his boy into his embrace, squeezing him tight. William squeezed back. And they held that embrace blessedly long.

Then William sat beside his father and pulled a bit of parchment from beneath his tunic, handing it to Simon.

"What is this?"

"Open it.

Simon carefully unrolled the parchment. And something bright and new stirred inside him.

"It's for us, papa." William beamed with pride.

Simon looked down at the page to see the lines of a new play, something they could do . . . stationary. Not on the wagon. Not a mystery. Not liturgy. But something they'd need to find a home for—the timing propitious if Bob's rumors about the cycles were true.

And by God if it wasn't good.

Very good.

Simon swept his son into his arms again, which drew applause from the audience. And that sounded mighty right, too.

"We're putting it all behind us, William, every last bit of it. Perhaps even our names we'll leave upon the wagon. Genealogy has not been kind to us anyway." Simon smiled with growing enthusiasm for the idea. "What name shall we take?"

His son had only one thought. It didn't leave the past entirely behind, but it was the very thing that had made him decide to write he and his father off this wagon. It was the image he'd seen every morning when he lay upon the alter ready to taste the blade of faith, if only for pretend. He'd find a name in that silhouette, so like a spear raised high to deal death, but shaky with doubt.

"We'll think of something," his son finally said.

Simon, Tinker, and William stood.

"How about an ale?" Tinker asked, taking up his walking stick once they'd climbed off the wagon stage.

Simon noted the gimp in the man's stride again. Had God answered Simon's test with a dizzy, drunken buffoon? Or was that just luck and life? He decided maybe an *angel* can take many forms. Maybe help comes from the least likely source. Regardless, he learned that whether Abraham would have gone through with it wasn't the question at all. Simon's only real question was: Do I love my son more than bitter legacy of a damned sword? More than the bitter memory of a lost love?

The answer, he now knew, was *yes*.

Still, he had to ask, "How did you fall on me without use of your staff?"

Tinker hunched his shoulders. "I had the right motivation." He winked at William. "So, Master William, what's this new drama you're writing."

William's face lit up as he started to speak. "It's about betrayal and getting a knife in the back."

"No, no." Tinker scrunched his face. "Write about comical things, about things you actually know . . ." He stopped,

111

catching the irony. "Well, never mind. What do you call this new play?"

"Right now, I'm just calling it Rome."

"All well and good, but don't forget people like to laugh." Tinker gimped toward the pub. "However, Rome is quite lovely."

"Have you been there?" William asked, seeming ready to ask Tinker for details.

"Well, no," the lummox chuffed, "but I've a right to my opinion. Enough with all the questions. What time is it? Are we going to drink or talk? Who's buying the ale?"

Then Simon hunkered down again to look his son straight. "What do you think of Wakefield, William? Do you think you'd like to stay? Maybe find a cottage to call home?"

His son beamed. "I think mama would have liked that."

Simon nodded. "Me too, son. Me too." And he left the blade of faith where it lay as the three crossed the commons to share their *own* songs and company.

God Uses
a Dish Rag

T HE GUY ACTUALLY wore a fedora. No one did that anymore. Oh, a few throwbacks tried putting them on early in the 21st century, but they possessed none of the class of a Sinatra or Crosby. And in the year of our Lord 2248, the marvel was that a fedora existed at all. Of course, I see all kinds come into my bar. But something about the way that hat sliced through the haze of smoke and caught table-glow on its brim got my attention. This guy was unique, all right. Familiar, even. But was it enough to make him the Son of God?

He took a seat at a far booth, a quiet corner. Good. Even though I hoped he proved more social in the long run, I wanted our first conversation to be private. I adopted the persona of a server, complete with apron (another throwback I thought he might appreciate) and navigated through the late night crowd toward him.

"Get you something?" I asked.

"Beer."

How delightful, hardly anyone brewed beer anymore. "I don't think you came here to drink," I said. "May I sit down?"

The man buried his face in his hands as if my impertinence were the last straw in a long day of disappointments. I took that as an invitation and sat opposite him.

"I think I know what will help you."

His face still in his hands, the guy chuckled tiredly into his palms and said, "Really."

"You need to serve someone else. It eases one's own burdens. Intoxication isn't even smart escapism."

He finally glanced up at me and I got my first good look at my successor. Dark brown eyes sunken deep under a strong but gentle brow. Creases in every corner of his face, telling stories of intense worry and gladness. And a shag of black, uncombed hair that seemed more natural than messy. Thirty-five standard solar years in that face—plenty wise to see the value of what I was prepared to offer him.

"You think I'm trying to escape to someplace?"

"With that hat . . . yes." I folded my hands on the table between us. "Do you know where you are?"

"I know where I'm not. I'm *not* in a bar that serves beer. And I'm *not* in the mood for meaningful conversation with a stranger." He sighed. "I'm here to celebrate two years without a job, and I don't want company."

I smiled. Could I pick 'em, or what?

"What do you do? Maybe I can help?" And I meant it.

For the first time, I saw earnestness touch the creases in his face. It's a familiar look, close cousin to desperation; I call it the 'bar face.'

"I'm John Cahan," he replied, and offered his hand.

If I'd had a corporeal body, I think I would have shat my-self. No one shook hands anymore. The simple, genuine ges-ture had become archaic long ago. That, and I knew the name. I decided the fedora had been a sign.

"Call me Ubi," I replied and took his hand.

"Ubi? That a nickname?"

"Indeed it is. Now, about your occupation."

"I was an Intelligence Engineer. Spent eleven years with the Civil Corp working on planet-side infrastructure: housing, transportation, like that."

"Two years without work," I mused aloud. "About the time the Feds licensed the intelligence software to the private sector—"

"That's right."

"—and about the time this establishment came into be-ing." I gestured grandly at the bar. "Seven Gables we call it be-cause when we launched we had jump access to seven worlds."

John's brows went up. "You've got jump access here in the bar?"

"Better than that, my friend. The bar itself is laid out to service unique off-world spaces . . . and drinks. It's as easy as walking from one room to another."

"I can visit seven other worlds without visa credentials?" He sat back, interest lighting his face.

"Seven worlds when we started serving drinks two years ago. Over a hundred worlds now. We get around visa cred by allow-ing only indigenous customers to exit the bar." I pointed across the room at a diminutive, hairless fellow drinking alone. "That little guy is Auralian. He comes here for French Chablis. He's welcome anytime, but he has to go right back where he came from or to an-other world-room to drink. He can't exit the bar from here, only from his home world. Make sense?"

"Hell of a system. Nice use of the technology, too," John complimented. Then his eyes started to grow distant again as though consumed with his own concerns. It was time to get at it.

"Do you want a job?"

Puzzlement folded John's brow. "Here?"

"Well, here . . . and on a hundred other worlds."

"Doing what?"

I sat back, appraising him, taking a moment to be sure I really wanted to do this. Was this guy in the fedora the right one to take the reins? Did I care? The burden of it weighed on me: all the people, all the problems. For the most part, happy people don't come to the Seven Gables. Every damned one of them had a story . . . and a need.

Yeah, I wanted out. Fedora was it.

"My job," I answered.

"Serving drinks?" John's puzzlement twisted into amuse-ment. "I don't think so."

"Beneath you?" I shot back.

"It's not that—"

"Take a walk with me." I stood, but John remained seated. "Please," I asked.

He looked up from beneath the brim of his hat, searching my face for guile. He found none, and followed.

UBI LED JOHN from his secluded booth past a few tables. The guy struck John a little presumptuous, but somehow, he trusted him—there was something familiar about the man. Waiting tables didn't hold much interest for John, but he guessed Ubi planned to try and sell him on it by taking him around to some of the great off-world establishments to which the bar had jump access. Worth the price of admission, John thought.

They hooked left toward a wide doorway over which an unlit sign read: Palasia. He'd heard of the world; it had been in the news a lot lately. The Catholic Lobby had tried to block Palasia's inclusion in authorized trade routes. John couldn't remember why.

Looking into the room that existed just a few steps away on a different planet, he decided he knew.

Stepping into the room, he'd expected to feel some change as a result of the jump across space. But he transitioned seamlessly, feeling only a slight change in gravity.

Low-slung chairs sat grouped around projection tables where holographic women did a thousand lewd things as they removed their clothing. Music pulsed in the dim chamber as though setting a rhythm to have sex by. No talk, or low talk. Men and women here were preoccupied with other things. A sour smell tinged the air, like burnt oranges, leaving John light-headed and . . . acquiescent. He wondered if he were breathing a Palasian equivalent of second-hand opium.

Ubi led him deeper into the Palasian room, and somewhere along the way, the women became real, the holograms left behind. Clothing at first grew more extravagant—silks, gilded velvet, vests embroidered with rich shades of crimson and jade—then the colors changed as clothes lay piled on the floor exposing flesh tones.

Palasians didn't appear biologically much different from humans. They were generally shorter, and almost universally light in complexion. Translucent eyes made it clear you were talking to a Palasian, as did the fact that they were lean to a person. The only fat people in the Palasian room were off-worlders.

A race evolved for sex, John considered.

At the far end of the room, Ubi gestured to a seat at an empty table set before a sunken stage. John sat, still craning his neck at the sight of men and women doing things in public that would have earned them a fine in the next room.

"Surprise you?" Ubi asked.

"Yeah, a little," John replied. "I get that it's a different world with different customs and laws, but if you don't know that coming in . . ."

Ubi smiled. "Does it make the job more appealing?"

"Because I could watch alien sex habits while serving a drink? Not really. You'll have to do better than that."

Ubi's smiled widened, and he turned his attention to the stage, where dim red lights illuminated a very private stage— one hidden to all but Ubi and John.

A few moments later, two Palasian males dragged a woman onto the stage and shoved her to the floor. A spark of anger lit in John's chest and he turned to see Ubi's response.

The waiter sat unmoved, looking at the girl.

With the music pulsing around them and the smell of burnt oranges in his nose, John watched as the two men circled behind the girl and two more Palasian males emerged from a rear curtain onto the stage.

John's gut churned at the thought of what was about to happen.

The men regarded the girl for a few moments; blank, uncaring expressions staring down at her, illuminated by the red baleful lights.

Between two of the men, John could see the girl and thought her face battled horror and the same acquiescence that had gotten inside him.

It wasn't until the men began to circle in on the girl that John realized she wore no clothes.

"What the hell is this?" John said, pointing.

"It's Palasia, one of our more frequented affiliates." Ubi's face showed a kind of resigned regret at the scene before them, but he sat still as the private show rolled on.

"But it's your bar, right? Don't you have some provisional authority here?" John twitched in his chair.

Ubi looked away at a window against the wall to his right. Beyond it, the night lay interrupted by vertical columns of light in an alien skyline. "It's a condition of inclusion that the room be governed by the host-world's law."

John looked back at the sunken stage and saw terror clear in the young woman's eyes. She began to scramble to avoid the clutching hands of the men, who tightened their circle, their faces now taut with expectation and savage delight.

"Then turn this damn room off," John yelled over the din of the music. "All you're doing is creating a venue for this bullshit." John's voice quavered in sympathy for the young woman.

This touched a nerve he didn't want exposed.

Ubi said nothing.

John rubbed his eyes, which were stinging now from the heavy smoke. Did they release this opiate to encourage customers to partake?

The rapists had teased at the girl long enough. With an uncanny synergy, they lunged in on her and pinned her arms and legs down. Well sculpted muscles danced in the light, a horrific ballet of flesh as four males prepared to take something that didn't belong to them.

"God damn it!" John pounded an open palm on the table beside him, sending shards of pain up his forearm.

The men either didn't hear him, or ignored his indignation.

Tears came to the girl's eyes as she screamed and thrashed to preserve something others were content to watch have taken from her.

Leers grew in the faces of her attackers, excitement, shit-eating grins that John had seen aplenty in the world a room away.

He didn't so much stand as launch himself from his chair. He threw the full force of his weight into the Palasian who'd deemed himself first to violate the girl. They went over into the curtains behind the stage, and John lost his fedora. As they tumbled, he caught a look at Ubi's face. John had hoped, maybe expected, the waiter would throw in with him to stop this thing.

The Seven Gables employee hadn't left his seat.

A heavy fist buried itself in John's chest, driving out all his air. The Palasian then hauled John to his feet and put iron-like fingers around his throat. Behind the beast, the other three closed their circle, preparing to continue their "show."

The nonchalance of it brought new fire to John's disgust. With all his strength, he drove one knee up into the exposed genitals of the guy holding him. A look of surprise spread on the Palasian's face, as if John had transgressed some strict taboo on this freakin' planet.

But it worked.

The Palasian's grip loosened, encouraging John to strike again. This time, he took hold of the guy's shoulders for leverage and put his hips behind his strike. The Palasian collapsed to the floor.

John whirled at the sound of the girl's screams and saw one of the remaining three kneeling, preparing himself for access to the girl's womanhood. His head bounced to the beat of the music infusing the room. The others swayed to the sounds, too. Happily, the rapists were too caught up in their doings to be bothered with John.

So this time, John calculated his attack. Taking two running strides, he kicked the sonofabitch from behind, catching him where he lives. Number two slumped forward onto the girl, moaning. She shoved him aside.

The remaining two shared a look of bewilderment and walked off the stage, disappearing behind the curtains.

John chuffed from exertion. He extended a hand to the girl, intending to help her up. She shrunk from him, easing herself toward the same curtains the men had just used to exit.

"I'm not going to hurt you," he said, sparing a look at the two Palasians clutching their goods.

She shook her head. Did she distrust him? Did she not understand English?

"Come, John, we should go." It was Ubi, standing now, disappointment clear upon his face.

John let a bitter smile touch one corner of his mouth. "What the hell is going on?"

Ubi pushed in his chair, pivoted on one foot, and started back through the bar. John gathered his hat and went after the waiter. When he caught up to him, John reached out to pull the man around face to face.

John's hand landed heavily on the waiter's shoulder . . . and Ubi flickered.

"Oh my God, you're Artificial Intelligence." John looked at his hand and chuckled.

"I'm a good deal more than that, sonny. And you just stopped the conception of this world's next great senator."

John scrubbed his face. "Wait a minute. Are you telling me that was consensual?"

"No such thing," Ubi answered. "But Seven Gables is not a place to make assumptions based on what you see."

"What did you expect me to do back there?" John leaned in close, challenging the waiter.

Ubi didn't reply.

"Never mind. Goodbye." John started to leave.

"I can help you forget your own worries," Ubi said, stopping John. "I'm not just some sophisticated AI who keeps accounts and serves drinks. You need a job. You need to feel *wanted*. That's why people come to a bar. Even one as elaborate as Seven Gables."

"What makes you think I would want a job in a pit like this?"

"Trust me, John. You just need more information."

John paused and looked around him at the various sexual appetites being sated in this corner of the universe. He wasn't about to bite on the whole "need" line Ubi was selling. He needed a job, to be sure, but when it came down to it, he meant to stick around a while longer for only one reason: Ubi was one hell of an AI—it was a matter of professional curiosity. At least, that's what he told himself. After all, in his former life, he'd been an intelligence engineer building dumbed-down versions of Ubi for the state.

"Where next?" John asked.

～

I CAN'T SAY I was surprised when John tackled the Palasian consummator. He couldn't have known what was happening. I'd set him up, sure. But having this job meant understanding a greater good. Sometimes God says no, right? To stand at the head of the Seven Gables, one has to take the long view.

That's why I was so damned tired. Why I needed out. And on some level, John's reaction showed a decency that confirmed my original assessment that he was the right guy to take the reins. He'd grow tired, too, in time. But that was his problem.

Still, I needed to know he could show temperance. Even good bartenders possess the skill. And what I intended to offer him far exceeded slopping drinks.

"Why did you jump to that girl's defense?" I asked as I led John from Palasia and deeper into the bar.

"She didn't look like she was having any fun?" John smiled to himself.

"Really. Are you an expert on the customs of Palasia? Or anyplace besides your own world for that matter?" I needed John to start accepting that he couldn't save everyone. Very important for this job.

He ignored my question completely. "You're not biological, but you seem to have mass."

"A design of energy," I answered. "And really, all mass is, is energy."

John nodded. I could virtually see his mind racing behind his eyes. "So the bar is 'intelligent'?"

"Why thank you," I answered, bowing as we went.

John smiled more genuinely. "I'm guessing that was some kind of test. Either that, or you take me for a letch."

"We're all letches, John. Even me. It's just a matter of *appetite*."

John nodded, and seemed to get that I didn't plan to admit I was testing him.

"Where are we going now?" John asked.

"To gamble," I replied.

We climbed four short stairs and pushed through a set of double doors into the Cumulous Casino.

~

JOHN HATED TO gamble. His dislike for the pastime probably stemmed from his statistical work and pattern theory when he'd been studying for an engineering career. But that very coursework had made of him an exceptional gambler, or more accurately, an exceptional identifier of cheaters, which sometimes meant the same thing.

As they entered the casino, John found his preconceptions challenged and defeated.

The expansive room lay bathed in bright but soothing light that fell from great skylights. In this world it was clearly daytime. Completely absent were the garish lights, the bells and chimes. Instead of ashtrays, plants and small trees (real ones) stood here and there.

As they surveyed the many games underway, John was struck that it appeared like nothing so much as a civil mid-morning tea. He couldn't call out one working girl or desperate laborer throwing away his check on payday. Rather, people either strolled or sat calmly as though the axis of the place weren't money, but polite interchange in modest, neatly pressed clothes.

"You're kidding me, right?" John said without thinking.

"Refined, isn't it?" Ubi led on to the right where the games ran to interesting variations of chess and other strategy entertainments.

Passing several tables, John distilled the difference between this place and Palasia: Here, the men and women crossed their legs when they sat to table.

Deeper into the room, John marveled at the white, stucco walls, which scaled a hundred feet to great, clear domes. Underfoot, he noted that his shoes didn't grind on the red, marble tile.

"Someone spends a lot of time sweeping," he muttered.

"What's that?" Ubi asked over his shoulder.

"Nothing. Anyway, this is a waste. I'm not much of a gambler, and I don't have any money. I'm out of work, remember? That's why you're trying to pawn your job off on me."

"I'll stake you," Ubi answered.

John expected as much and laughed. "What's the buy in?"

"Just play your best."

Ubi drew up at a short distance from a table where two men sat engaged in a game of cards. He bowed and approached a man in an oversized white robe. The garment looked comfortable, perfect for the stress of—

"Poker," Ubi said, turning to John. "You're in." On the table before an empty seat, he placed twelve small white figures that resembled chess pawns. "The difference here, John, is that there's no ante, and each raise is limited to one."

"One what?"

Ubi placed his index finger on one of the pawns.

"Standard deck?" John asked.

"Yes. Have a seat and wait for the next deal."

John shook his head and planted himself. At the highest level, he knew real players played people, not cards. That was out the window with these two.

"Who am I playing?" he asked.

"Cumulous Casino belongs to the world of Rowls. These distinguished competitors are Rowlian." Ubi bowed again to each of the others at the table.

John appraised his competition. The two aliens (who he guessed were male) each wore a similar robe, sashed at the waist and chest. Superfluous buttons, also white, had been sewn in simple lines at the hems and cuffs. Burnished skin spoke of much time in their system's sun. And long hair woven in an intricate queue lay draped across their shoulders like a snake. A third Rowlian (with a much shorter braid) dealt and gathered cards, setting them in piles at the edge of the table.

John gathered his cards on the next hand and began to do the math and probabilities as the table cards turned up.

Really, it all seemed rather banal. Why did Ubi want him playing poker with a couple of aliens in an antiseptic casino that looked like it fell out of a cloud?

Several hands later, he thought he knew.

Despite the superior play of the Rowlian on John's right, the guy had been losing.

The player on John's left was cheating.

The shark had a superb gift in manipulation of the cards, and had clearly inserted winners to bolster his hand when he needed something to take a pot. John hadn't seen it, but he'd swear to it based on the probabilities he'd calculated over a few dozen games.

There was something else.

When he'd been introduced, John thought the two strangers appeared virtually identical. A couple of hours of poker made them as distinct as any two humans John had ever met. It wasn't their clothes or hair, but something in their faces, in their eyes.

The Rowlian to John's right (who hadn't shared a word the entire morning) never flinched, never showed any animation over a win or his many losses. His manner was easy and aloof.

By contrast, the fellow on his left (the man cheating his ass off) showed a quiet desperation to win. Once or twice, a note of glee escaped his lipless mouth over a particularly large pot. Yet, for these spates of emotion, he never struck John as a gambling addict or even a poker player with bad manners.

Perhaps his nerves bothered him; he *was* cheating after all. And that pissed John off.

It may not have been his stake that got him in the game. But the player on his right continued to give up his cache and did so without a word of remorse or bitterness. Meanwhile, the increasingly sweaty player on John's left gathered in pawns like a miser, smiling over each figurine.

If anything bothered him more than bad intelligence work, it was the frustration of loss when others didn't play by the rules. In a significant respect, it was the human element, the one thing that could never be coded for by an intelligence engineer.

And the one thing John was often grateful he'd never been able to replicate.

Part of him wanted to slap the pawns out of the swindler's clutches and call him out for what he was right here in front of Ubi and everybody.

No tact there.

He didn't mean to earn the waiter's job, but he didn't want to make a mistake here like he apparently had in Palasia.

"Sir," John said, shifting in his seat to address the cheating Rowlian.

"John," Ubi said softly behind him.

John held up a finger without looking back again at his guide. "Hold on, I've got this under control."

The Rowlian narrowed his eyes and pulled his arms tighter around his bounty.

"My friend, while I'm new to your world, and unfamiliar with your customs, poker is poker. And I can't sit here and watch you steal the rightful winnings of this gentleman." He gestured to the other Rowlian without lifting his gaze from the first.

A series of ticks and vowels escaped the dealer's mouth as he interpreted what John said.

"He says," the dealer returned, "he has done nothing wrong, and he withdraws from further play."

John focused on the dealer. "Then he won't mind if we check him for cards, will he?"

When the dealer spoke back to the cheater, a look of anger passed quickly over the tanned skin, but soon turned to despair.

Some poker face.

It took only a few moments for the dealer to stand, draw back the other's long robe sleeves, and reveal the instruments of the Rowlian's deceit. To his credit, he stood still, accepting that he'd been caught red-handed.

What happened next would live with John for the rest of his life.

∼

I WANTED TO warn him. In some ways because I needed him to replace me, but more importantly because I didn't think I could stand it if John ratted the poor father out.

I may have been wrong to hold my tongue. But in the end, I knew John really needed to have this lesson driven home.

The outed Rowlian broke down, the grief as human as anything I've ever seen or felt. Through his sobs, he clucked and cawed, slumping back to his seat.

I spared a glance at the upper caste Rowlian as he accepted the lion's share of the table pawns, not once thanking John.

Impassive, the sonofabitch gathered the markers and left the table.

"Ubi, you better tell me what the hell just happened? I'm getting tired of all the shadow and mirrors bullshit."

"Not now, John," I said.

"Now!" he yelled back. The echo of it lifted up the sheer walls and resounded against the domed skylights. Gamblers paused to look over at the humans, then returned to their civil games.

I sat across from the still weeping Rowlian and gave John a regretful look.

"The stakes were this man's children."

Pallor lifted in John's face. "The hell you say."

Any other time, I'd have gladdened at the use of the old adage. Not today, not now.

I really needed to get out of this damned job.

"The ways here in the clouds are unconventional. The upper castes have certain claims on procreation. The poor have the opportunity to win the lives of their offspring back through card sports like you just played. It's . . ."

"Oh my God." John turned to the Rowlian. "I'm sorry. I didn't know." He then stood and cast his gaze around, looking, I'm sure, for the other player—perhaps thinking to strike some bargain.

"Leave it," I said. "There's nothing to be done now."

I do think something broke inside John at that point. I believe I was a heartless sonofabitch to do it. A lot of greed in that choice. But you have to take the long view. And John had some good years in my seat if he could internalize this one point.

"But what about—"

I cut him off. "I could spend a week explaining all the details of Rowlian culture and you'd still be pissed off and self-loathing over what just happened. Come on."

I stood and headed for the door. I heard John's chair legs scrape across tile as he pushed back from the table. "I'm sorry," he repeated, and came along.

∼

"WHAT'S THE TRICK this time?" John asked.

Ubi stood silent, looking at the woman seated at the open air patio that looked out over a violet ocean and russet sunset.

John exhaled loudly. "Why am I even still here? Hell, I just wanted a beer."

"You're here because you need to feel wanted. I told you that." Ubi pinched his eyes in a very human gesture.

John opened his mouth to refute that, but said nothing. Then, "Why's she here?" and he nodded at the woman seated alone and staring into the distance.

"Go talk to her," Ubi said. "No deceptions this time. Just talk."

"Is this what a waiter at the Seven Gables does?" John let a mirthless guffaw.

Ubi nodded. "More than a little."

John had to hand it to the Ubi; he really had the human thing down. But he didn't know if he had it in him to do one more thing. He didn't understand alien cultures: condoned rape, bartering over a man's children.

But after what had happened already, he secretly wanted to know what came next. How much lower did this ride go? He tugged his fedora on tighter and went to the seaside table.

131

"May I sit with you?" he asked.

The woman looked up and smiled wanly. "I'm not here to make anyone's acquaintance," she replied.

"Me neither. I just need a place to rest my feet and eyes." He motioned to the beach, where foamy waves crashed up on wet sand.

She hunched her shoulders.

John sat. "You can kind of lose yourself in the view, can't you?"

"That your best line?" the woman remarked.

The corner of John's mouth tugged into a lopsided grin. "It's not a line, really. I'm just an out-of-work engineer who came for a beer. I met an artificial bartender who's been showing me the seamier side of the galaxy room by room. He brought me here, pointed you out, here I am. And frankly, the risks of procreation from incidental sex seem too great right now for me to even care you're a human female."

A genuine smile spread on her chapped lips. "I'm Helen," she said. "And you're . . ."

"John."

They sat in silence for a long while. Then he asked, "Why are you sitting here alone, staring out to sea."

Without missing a beat, she said, "Why not? I love the view. There's not a better sunset than on Delin."

John looked again at the rich color of the water and sun, strata of clouds lilting like ribbons against a lapis-lazuli sky. There weren't any beach-goers, perhaps it was forbidden—keeping a pristine view for the drinkers to gaze upon.

Except there weren't any other drinkers in this room.

The jump had been as seamless as the rest, the difference: the open air, and single occupant.

"I guess I agree," John said.

"Helps you believe in providence just a little, doesn't it?" She sipped at her peach cocktail.

John turned to look at Ubi, who stood far back near the door. The bartender/waiter/servant stood by and gave no inclination about what John was to do.

Then Helen put a hand over John's. "You can make up for the past, don't you think? I mean, if you really make good on new promises."

And when she turned to face him, to have his answer, John's own reality began to crumble. He didn't tear his hand away, though that's what he felt like doing. He didn't lash out, though part of him insisted that he do so. And he didn't speak recriminations.

Not one.

Not to a mother who'd abandoned him a lifetime ago.

Helen cocked her head, as though something in John looked familiar, but she finished by simply tugging at the brim of his fedora. "Nice hat," she said. "Reminds me of a man I once knew."

Then she stood up, gave a long, last look at the ocean and walked out past Ubi.

$\sim$

As I LED John back to the room where we'd first met, I wondered if I'd done it right. Would he be ready to step into my shoes? I might have gone too far. But John had made his own choices, however manipulated they might have been.

The bar in the main room had been built of real mahogany. Another throwback. I guess I was particular to throwbacks, as it happens. In any event, we could only finish our tour in one place.

I ushered John in behind the bar and through a door. This was home.

The data servers and network had its hub here, powered independent of the planet infrastructure that John had helped build. I turned to get a look at John's face, and found pretty much what I expected: astonishment and chagrin.

"Like it?"

"Impressive. I might have guessed you were one of those who licensed the intelligence software." John ran a finger along one sleek panel.

"A clever man might call that software my father." I laughed earnestly and hoped John would join me.

He chuckled. "Does Ubi mean what I think it means?"

"Ubiquitous," I supplied. "What you don't know, John, is that something miraculous happened when the Seven Gables powered up their jump points that first day."

"Do tell," John crossed his arms over his chest.

"The combination of the jump technology and the end-node transfer from those original seven worlds, and the intelligence software we licensed from the state . . . well, it created me."

"I hate to burst your bubble, Ubi, but I think I created you."

"You don't understand, John. I'm not artificial. I'm sentient."

John's face slackened. "You mean you *think* you're sentient."

"Look, I've had this debate a thousand times. Often with myself. The fact is, I feel pain: sadness, loss, despair. Get it? That one thing you couldn't account for in your programming."

John stared. "So you took me on a tour of my own . . ."

∽

EPIPHANY FLARED IN John's mind. A rape he wished had never happened; the loss of a child through a parent's own poor choices; the hope of redemption, reconciliation with a mother . . . the shadows of his past.

He gripped the hat atop his head and shut his eyes against the revelations.

"And now it's my turn to rest," Ubi said, weariness heavy in his voice. "I'm God here, John. In every real sense. You helped create that, but now I deserve to step down and you to step in. You can be the ghost in the machine now. I can help you transfer your mind into the network so that you can manage the affairs of Seven Gables.

"I've helped you see the need to respect the choices of others, to intercede with temperance. They're good people, they just need help—"

"You sonofabitch!" John screamed. "All I wanted was a damn beer!"

"I didn't ask for this either," Ubi shot back.

John looked around and spotted the emergency server shutdown toggle. Before Ubi could blink, he lunged, slammed his fist on the switch, and whirled to see what would happen.

Ubi hadn't moved. "I kind of thought you might do that. It's murder, John. I'm as alive as you are." He paused, a wan smile touching his lips. "But I'll tell you the truth. Death is no bad friend. I leave it to you now."

Ubi flickered, disappeared. Hundreds of lights blinked off, showing the jump access terminated all across the Seven Gables network.

Beyond the door, it was just a bar now. With a lot of people who needed a drink . . . wanted to belong.

John stepped out from the network room and picked up a wet rag used to wipe down the bar. Seated across the mahogany was an old man with deep folds of skin cascading down from his brow. The fellow looked unhappy, alone.

You can make up for the past, don't you think? I mean, if you really make good on new promises.

Perhaps he'd serve after all. John hefted the rag. "What can I get you?"

ROXANE

S HE PUT ON the red light.

That's what you do when your stomach grumbles and all that the poets are offering is flowery verse. Not that there's anything wrong with a compliment or two. Even a woman with flexible hips likes to hear something sweet before the fleshy business (or so I've been told). But I suspect by now she'd forgotten her girlhood, when she still believed she would find someone to love. That would love her. Before the red light.

I hated being here myself.

These days, the district was filled with gallants come from Paris with their mousy mustaches and dreams of finding love. Not a one (as I've heard) goes more than ten strokes once the *love* begins. And never before a lot of alley-side wooing.

Waste of time.

Still, it was the best I could do.

I was a French Army Cadet, soon to be dispatched to Arras to fight the Spanish. Cyrano de Bergerac was my name. I stood there, one hand resting comfortably on my rapier, the other cupping something unseen (but apparently important) in the air. I don't know how I got into that pose. But it felt natural, nonetheless, for offering a verse.

So, I lifted my chin with my rhyme and wove it all above the stench.

Which, given the size of my nose, surely came to me in triple portions. Gutter-smell. All kinds of filth my boots had never seen—on brushed leather, no less! But I didn't mind. Instead, I went on about her charms and wit and—

"My God, are you ever going to ask my price?" She interjected, not mad, but edging with impatience.

I ignored her and went on about her eyes. As I did, Roxane tried to draw in another "soldier of Satan", pointing to her red light. No good. I was wearing the violet tabard of the military. No meager flesh-seeker was going to compete with me for her bed tonight. She was stuck until I either got on or got out.

"I've come to rescue you—"

"I don't need to be rescued, you arrogant bastard." She said it politely. "What I need is for you to do is stop talking long enough for me quote a price."

No price. I wasn't here to hire Roxane. Pitiful as I'm sure she'd think it, I was here for an open invitation, on the merit of my true feelings for her.

"Poet, why don't you give her a poke with that pointy nose of yours. That'll have her singing all right."

Roxane smiled at that, looking past me at the man who'd offered the insult. The man came into the baleful light, which was simply a thin red scarf wrapped around her door lantern.

I dropped my raised hand. "I will ask you to withdraw . . . but only once."

The man laughed out of the darkness. A coin flashed across the alley and struck Roxane in the teat, as the shadow stopped in the dull gleam of the red light.

I caught a last glimpse of Roxane as I turned, a strange look upon her face—did she know this man? The scrape of my rapier being drawn free resounded loud in the alley. I splashed through a puddle of piss (you get to know such things) and rounded on a fellow who stood a half foot taller than me and wearing the cape of the Viscount.

Ah, shit, then!

I'd seen this little drama before, too. Men trying to ennoble a woman by defending an insult aimed half at themselves. But this time, it was me; this time, the Viscount. I realized I would likely die one way or the other, either here near a puddle of piss, or on a rack in some sweltering dungeon if I out-dueled the Nobel.

"Oh, hell, come back, cadet, you can have this one at two francs." Roxane tried to grab me. I shrugged her off and took a challenger's stance.

"You should take her at that price," the Viscount said. "Though it's still a bit high, m'thinks. Last time I was here, I took her from behind for 2 decimes."

"Apologize." My rapier rose. "To her, and to me."

The Viscount chuckled low, unthreatened. "I'll assume you're drunk to lift your weapon toward me . . . and to consider such a tired whore. Though, with that nose, I'll guess this is your best option."

That was uncalled for. Roxane wasn't tired in the least. Not like he meant, anyway.

"Kill him," she said. At last a charge directly from her.

"Apologize," Cyrano repeated.

"My young man," the Viscount began, still very calm, "It is dark in this place, save for your tramp's little light. So, I'm going to inform you who I am before you tarnish the good name of the country whose uniform you wear—"

"I don't care who you are. The uniform I wear is a token of defense for *all* the citizens of France. And you have insulted a woman who gave you no cause. I will skewer your tongue for her pleasure unless you retract—"

"I am the Viscount, cadet. You are now fairly warned."

"Draw," was all I said.

The Viscount drew his own weapon, and we touched blades ceremonially, then crouched ready to duel.

In the dark and reddened alley, our rapiers began to ring and slap. Our feet shuffled over the stones, grinding dirt and grit beneath.

The Viscount made a hard thrust, which drew a yelp from Roxane—it came hard near my side. But I side-stepped and parried the rapier away, slashing at the Viscount's stomach. The noble drew back in time, resetting his feet. The rapiers twisted again, clanging loudly in the small alley.

Then, the Viscount feinted and lunged, trying to catch me off balance. But I didn't take the bait, and as the noble came forward, I dropped to one knee and thrust my rapier into the man's chest.

A gush of air came. Maybe from the Viscount's mouth, perhaps from his pierced lung. And he fell to his side, groaning. His hands grasped my rapier as he shuddered over the filthy cobblestone, his head slapping the rock involuntarily.

Then the Viscount's body stilled.

"I'll hold to what I said. Two francs." Roxane reiterated the bargain.

I looked up then, breaking my concentration on my victim. "What?" Then I focused on her. "But I meant what I said before."

"You mean all that poetry? I'm sorry, Cyrano, but that's a laugh. We've had a fine friendship at The Drake, but not here." She pointed to the red light. "Besides, my heart leans elsewhere."

Wet, coughing laughter filled the alley. The Viscount. Not quite dead. "You thought your poems were going to change the heart of a *whore*. My young man, have you *seen* yourself? What tenderness she doesn't sell will be given to some Adonis too dumb to know better than to fall in love with her."

I looked back at Roxane, uncertain, my poet's heart in conflict with the reality of the red-lit alley. She'd been a while in the sheets for her pay, but a touch of something better came down then, if you ask me. A poet-duelist wanting a little companionship. Standing, he hoped, for the honor of one in need of a champion. A Viscount with a nasty tongue lay mortally wounded. The stink of the alley. And the red light.

She'd wanted a little nobility. *Wanted* that honorable defense. I felt sure of it.

That's about the time I retreated up the way. My feet smelling of piss.

But I'd bested the Viscount in a duel. And though ugly didn't *begin* to describe me and a "ceiling watcher" wasn't interested in the compliments with which I tried to pay her, those pretty little couplets had surely made a tramp want to think of girlhood again.

I had to believe that.

$\sim$

I DIDN'T WANT to go to The Drake for supper the day after killing the Viscount.

Partly, I thought it smart to lay low. More importantly, that's where Roxane worked during the day. In fact, it's where I'd met her, and where I'd learned she laid up extra on the side with her red light. The Drake was a small hostel near my regiment's garrison. Roxane worked the kitchen in the back.

But Christian had insisted, saying he'd something to show me.

We sat in the corner, and I hoped someone else would get us our food today. But as we got involved in talk of the war, I lost my watchful eye.

"Potato pie or beef stew?" she asked.

My head snapped toward her. Roxane. Damn!

"Both," I said. And looked back at Christian, whose own gaze held a look I knew only too well—infatuation.

"Me, too," Christian said.

When she'd gone, I let out a long breath, unaware I'd been holding it in.

Christian watched Roxane go. Then turned back to me. "You know her?"

"Never mind. She's out of my life."

"Good. That's why we're here. I think I want her in mine." He smiled a bit devilishly.

"You're making a mockery of me. And it's not funny."

Christian looked genuinely confused. He gave Roxane a final glance as she disappeared inside the kitchen, then swung back around. "Truly, Cyrano, if you've no claim upon her, would you mind if I have a go."

"Will cost you half a franc."

"What?" More confusion on Christian's face. He was simply too good to see the sin in her. And I'd already decided it would be a hell of a lot of fun to let him discover her evening affairs on his own. Besides, judging by the look Roxane had returned Christian, she held a spark of interest for him that my nose had undoubtedly squelched for me. The pair of them could discover together how equally ill-fitted they were all by themselves.

"You have to help me, though, Cyrano. I need your eloquence, since I have none." Christian's boyish face showed a repulsive sincerity.

"Son of a bitch."

"Me?"

I stared at Christian's delicate features. Of course she'd found him desirable. His nose didn't protrude off his face like a piece of fleshy fruit.

"I'll lend you my eloquence, if you lend me your conquering physical charm. Together we'll form a romantic hero!"

To which Christian smiled in anticipation of winning Roxane's affection.

For my part, I smiled too, anticipating the rare disappointment my friend would find when he found the hue of Roxane's door lamp. I chose to ignore the fact that just yesterday I'd been willing to forgive her nighttime romps if she'd forsake them and choose to love me. But what the hell. A man with a face like mine has got to exercise some ignorance.

"What's the plan, then?" Christian asked.

"We'll go by this evening. I happen to know where she lives."

Christian cocked a funny look at my widening smile. A smile half a result of the thought of Christian's upcoming (rude) awakening, and half at the irony of going back a second night to speak poetry to tramp in hopes of finding true love.

∾

IN THE UNSEEMLY odor of the alley again, I looked up at the cold door lantern. Maybe Roxane did her "back business" somewhere else tonight. And I started away as quickly as Christian and I had come.

"Wait," Christian said, putting a hand on my arm. "I hear something."

"That'd be the rats in the garbage."

"No, it's someone singing. Quick." Christian began running down the alley, cutting left to the backside.

When I caught up, Christian was looking up at a balcony on the lee side of the row of houses, which had been built on a hill. Roxane's residence had a second story from here. And her silhouette could be seen passing back and forth before the double doors. At least she appeared to be alone tonight. And offering a few phrases of song—something I'd never heard before. My foolish heart ached a bit more for it.

If it were anyone by Christian, I couldn't possibly . . .

"We can talk to her from here. This will work." Christian pointed to a cluster of juniper shrubs beneath the balcony.

"Stand in there. I'll call her out. You whisper the words I need to say to get myself invited in."

"And leave me here in the minty bushes while you climb up the balustrade and have a roll with Roxane, is that it?" I began desperately looking for a red light on this side of her apartment.

Nothing. The backyard had no external lamps that I could see.

"That's the basic idea. I think she's already interested. I just need your words to help convince her that I'm after more than just sex. Women want to feel needed. So help me make her think there's more to me than just sex."

"I see. Quite a bargain for me, isn't it? Shall I wait for you here, too? In case you need me to talk you into a ménage-a-tois?"

But Christian was already throwing a small stone at Roxane's rear window. The brute had no idea of his own strength, however, and put the rock right through her glass. Though that did get her out onto the balcony in straight order.

"Who the hell are you?" she called down. "I'm going to call the police. You'd better get out of here."

Christian gave me a pleading look.

Here we go.

I whispered: "Wait, mademoiselle. I'm sorry for your window. I will pay to repair it. Any cost is worth it to have but a moment to gaze up at you in the light of this beautiful moon."

"Who is that?" Roxane asked again.

"Christian Duchamp, from the garrison. You served me today at The Drake. Do you not remember?"

"Ah, you sat with the Nose, right?"

"Yes. Cyrano. The Nose."

"Well, I don't care. Go away. I'll have it fixed myself. Just leave me alone." Roxane looked down, avoiding the broken glass, and was almost inside when Christian demanded his next line.

"Your beauty surpasses every fine thing in the heavens this night."

"What was that?" She swiveled back.

"What now?" Christian whispered fiercely to me.

"I said yours is a surpassing beauty, Roxane. It lifts me when I'm tired. It calms me when I am in despair—"

"You really are Nose's friend. You even talk like him. Though you are far more pleasant to look at."

I whispered: "Tell her she's a horse's ass."

Christian shook his head violently.

"Yes, Mademoiselle. I really am his friend. But the words are mine, born from my deep feelings for you. Will you not let me stand here in the mild evening and feel your beauty cast its spell upon me a while longer."

Cyrano heard Roxane inch to the edge of the balcony, where she rested her weight on a creaking balustrade. "Tell me more."

The whore certainly likes attention when it comes from a pair of lips beneath a smaller nose. "Ask her where she works at night."

Christian ignored that one, trying something on his own. "You're hair is like straw in the harvest, your cheeks are like the soft fuzz of an apricot."

That'll be good for the courtship, I thought.

"Straw? Fuzz?" The balustrade creaked as Roxane pushed herself up.

"Quick, Cyrano, some words," Christian whispered.

"Tell her you want to hold her, caress her, keep her free from pain and doubt and worry."

Christian did.

Roxane sighed.

"Tell her you want to hold her safe, warm the chill on her skin, and kiss her clean, smooth brow until she falls asleep in your arms."

Christian did.

Roxane moaned.

"It's working. What else?" Christian adjusted himself, arousal straining in his trousers.

"Tell her that she'll know the merit of your love by the size of your nose."

Christian started to speak, stopping midway. "What? Cyrano. You said she was out of your life. Don't queer this for me."

So I didn't. Not right away.

Another hour I spoke to Roxane through Christian's smaller nose. The woman above me swayed and groaned in the moonlight like a love-starved schoolgirl rather than a callous-backed strumpet. It wasn't until she'd urged Christian to mount the balustrade that I stepped from the juniper bushes into the clear light of the evening stars.

I watched a few moments as the two embraced and began to share a tender kiss—one I'd always thought my words would earn *me*. Instead, I'd given them away to a friend, given Roxane away.

But I reminded myself that she hadn't wanted me. And felt some small generosity for giving her the words regardless.

Still, it hurt.

The whole thing was a bit ridiculous and comic.

And I couldn't watch anymore.

As I slid away, Roxane spotted me moving like a shadow over the grass. "Who's there?"

"Just a defender of harlot honor and the tongue that won her bed." I bowed extravagantly without turning or breaking my stride. "Congratulations on your evening's entertainment, m'lady. That'll be half a franc."

But then I did stop.

Turning, I produced the lantern I'd brought from the garrison. I lit it as Christian waved his hands at me to stop.

"No," my friend whispered, as though Roxane, standing beside him, wouldn't hear him if he whispered.

A smile crept onto my face as I wrapped a die-soaked sheet of paper around the lantern, which then cast a bloody hue over my chest and legs. "Maybe just 5 centimes, what do you say?"

But I did not wait for a response, instead leaving the red light on the lawn and disappearing into the fogs which had risen from the canal behind.

"Who was that?" I heard Roxane ask Christian.

"No one," my friend answered. "Do you want to have the sex? I can go many times. I'm very good at that part."

"Wait!" Roxane's voice cut the fog, stopping me in my tracks.

The strumpet scaled down from the balcony as though practiced at the art of getting out of places quickly, safely, and unseen. At the lawn, she broke into a sprint towards me. Coming close, she did not slow, but tackled me, driving us both to the ground.

"You jackass! You almost let me sleep with that guy, using your words to convince me I should."

I rubbed my head. "You convinced yourself, m'Lady." And I gave a satiric smile. "He had the right words, the right shape, and the right nose. And none of it cost him a single coin."

Roxane stared at me a moment, her body pressing down. "The trouble with you is you're filled with self-doubt. Can't see past your own nose."

"The trouble with you," I fired back, "is that you think you know the trouble with me."

"Is that so?" She reached down and took my manhood in her hand, squeezing.

"Feels like *your* trouble is you haven't had a woman since your nose began to grow bigger than your face. That about right?" Roxane gave a wicked smile.

I started to speak, but Roxane caught my mouth in a kiss, smashing my great nose back in the process.

It hurt a bit, but not so much as to complain. And my poet's heart believed she was right. I had my doubts. I also needed the sex.

But I also thought that those things had helped me see past the red light, all the way back to m'Lady's girlhood. Something I was pleased to defend and give my best words to.

LAST RIDE
OF JOHNNY FRY

OCTOBER CHILL CLUNG to Johnny's neck and cheeks, forcing him to shiver. Or did he shake just thinking about going in and telling Sarah. Standing at the door, he shook his head at himself and chuffed in the autumn cold. The smell of Kessler whisky on his breath soured the air. *Goddamn telegraph line!* Then he pushed the door and went inside.

Sarah sat at the table chopping vegetables for a pot of boiling water over the hearth. Their small cabin held the warmth of the fire. *Goddamn homey.* She looked up when he came in, a smile brightening her face.

"You're home early," she said. "Good, you can help me—"

"I've got things to do," he cut her short. "I can't just be sitting around here."

"You just got home." Sarah stood with some difficulty, minding the nine months of child in her belly. "Sit down, then, and rest a while. I can manage supper."

He looked back at her. Blind anger and fear still rippled through him. "Go scarce with the meat."

She gave him a confused stare. "Aren't you hungry? There's plenty—"

That's when he lost control. Before he realized what he was doing, he grabbed the end of the table and toppled it to the floor. Sarah's potatoes and carrots scattered against the wall, the knife skittering under the bed.

"Johnny, don't. Tell me what's wrong."

Which only made him madder. His eyes landed on the cradle they'd bought together, as the whisky and fury whipped inside his head. In three long strides he came to the thing and stomped it into kindle.

Sarah began to cry, holding her stomach and backing away. "Are you drunk? Johnny, why? Please, what is it?"

He turned then, ragged breaths pulled over his teeth and tongue as he seethed with the unfairness. He looked down at her belly and shut his eyes a moment before opening them and staring savagely at her.

"They're shutting down The Pony Express." He said it like he blamed her.

Her eyes softened with sympathy. "Oh, Johnny. I'm so sorry. But you'll find other work. Don't fret this too much."

It was the wrong thing to say. "Don't fret! This is why we're here in the first place! And how do you think we're going to pay for *that*!" He shot an accusing finger at her stomach.

Sarah waited a bit before answering, looking at him like she'd never seen him before. "People do it, Johnny. People do it every day."

He stared back at her, his breathing still rough and angry. Panic had settled in on him. He could feel it plain and simple. He had responsibilities, that's one thing. To Sarah, the baby, and some credit on things he'd expected to pay in full with the wages of *Riding the Express*, as the boys say. But it was more than that, and he knew it even then, in the middle of the end of his marriage. He knew that jumping into that saddle and riding seven hours with the wind in his face and the open plain around him had filled his chest and gut with a kind of pride and glory he never thought he'd have. It was important work. Made *him* important.

The telegraph line had taken that, too.

Instead, he saw himself with fingernails rimmed with the dirt of digging and planting and slopping. He wanted to scream!

"Johnny," Sarah began, "We'll get through this. What matters is that we're together . . . as a family." She touched her stomach again.

And Johnny began to lose control again.

"Are you ignorant! Didn't you hear what I just said! What if I can't feed that thing! What if you have to start working at Pinkers—"

Sarah slapped him hard in the face. The suggestion of whoring had taken it too far for her. But her own indignation only made the whisky and anger in his head more potent.

He shoved her to the floor and tore up the rest of the cupboards and shelves, kicking over chairs and dumping the stew pot before turning back on her. But when he opened his mouth, she looked up through tearful eyes and said simply, "Get out."

It hit him stronger than her hand ever could.

Because she meant it.

And more. There was something permanent about it. Like she was seeing something for the first time, and wasn't going to look at it again. Not like her own mother had.

A small part of him wanted to kneel down and hug her close. To say he wasn't like this. That he was scared. Maybe not of working. But of losing something that made him feel . . .

Her silent tears fell from her chin as she whispered it this time, "Get out."

And he did.

The aimless rage replaced everything else for good.

He found his horse and raced into the October night to cool his neck and cheeks again. He felt like he needed to do someone some real harm.

HARD SUN RIPPLED in the window and glinted off the bottle of Old Overholt set before him on the table. It was warm here. Quiet. Johnny sat in the back corner of Pinker's saloon. Alone. The place was empty. Everyone gone up the street to hear the mayor prattle on about the new telegraph station about to open. Commemoration they called it.

Progress.

Johnny took a long drink from his bottle, coughing through the burn it left in his throat. "Bastards!" His voice in the vacant saloon sounded small and brittle, and only made him feel more helpless. "What am I going to do now?" he said to himself.

As if in response, from up the street the mayor's voice carried: . . . *will ring in a new era of prosperity . . .*

Johnny laughed.

Six days ago now since The Pony Express had let him go. Riders weren't needed from St. Joseph's to Salt Lake anymore. The Creighton telegraph line had made it this far from the east last week. Now they were bringing the line in from the west. The whole sombitch would go from coast to coast. Transcontinental they called it. No more need for riders.

. . . communication will bring security and enlightenment without delay . . .

Jackass mayor got paid to use those two bit words and wear his pocket watch. Johnny hated the way the man wiped his boots before entering a place. Must think himself better than the rest of us.

A few of the boys still rode out of San Francisco and back. But that would be ending now that the line was complete. A damn year and half of ponies. A year and a half. Riding hard overland. Carrying important mail in the mochillas they draped over the saddles.

He'd never imagined it ending. And so he'd made plans. He'd married Sarah. The thought of her pained him after the way he'd left her some days ago. She'd been the first woman to look at him twice. He'd convinced her to follow him out to this desert and live near his weigh station. Make a life, seeing as how he'd be making good money.

Johnny pulled the old advertisement from his trousers and unfolded it with chapped fingers.

PONY EXPRESS
St. Joseph, Missouri, to California
in 10 days or less

WANTED

YOUNG, SKINNY, WIRY FELLOWS

not over eighteen. Must be expert

riders, willing to risk death daily.

Orphans preferred.

Wages $25 per week.

APPLY PONY EXPRESS STABLES

St. Joseph, Missouri

That's what had got him: $25 per week. Most jobs were $1 day, maybe a buck and a half if you knew a trade. But Johnny never could have paid for a kid on those wages. Sarah had gotten pregnant right off, though. And so maybe it was a little bit of luck that the first one came out already dead.

. . . quicker access to request the common necessities of life, not to mention those times we need something urgently . . .

But not this time. Things were supposed to go different this time. He'd been riding the Express—the way the boys say—making good money. He was young. Sarah was young. And Sarah had got herself pregnant again. This time, it was all right. This time . . .

The telegraph line.

Johnny scrubbed his face with his hands and looked around. Not so long ago he'd come into this saloon and tipped the piano player to play his favorite song. He didn't know the name of it. But that didn't matter. The piano player knew what to play. And he'd sat with the boys and they'd talked about the trail, and the day one of them would finally try to jump Butte Gulch and cut their run to Bridger's Fort by twelve hours.

155

The boys had mostly all gone now, though. None of them had a wife or family to care for. And there was supposed to be cattle work in Colorado. They'd followed the money.

Not for Johnny. Not with his responsibilities.

He didn't have a lot of options. And he scrubbed his face again. Tired and frustrated.

"Sitting alone?"

Johnny looked up and felt a weary smile spread his lips. It was Bill Roberts. One of the few who hadn't followed the cattle work.

"Drink?" Johnny invited

Bill sat and poured himself a shot. He drank it down and refilled before stopping to look at his friend. "You look like hell."

"It's more than looks."

Bill half-smiled. "You wanted to see me? What are we talking about today?"

Johnny drew a deep breath. "We need work. Both of us. And sometimes that means creating the work for ourselves."

Bill nodded, but with a question clear in his eyes. "Johnny, no one took it harder than you when they closed down the ponies. And maybe that's right, seeing as how you've got a family and all. But what you got in mind?"

. . . and keep in touch with the ones you love from all over this great country . . .

Johnny clenched his eyes against the sound of the mayor's voice. "Stock."

"But the cattle work—"

Johnny was already shaking his head. "Not cattle."

~

FOR THE BETTER part of three days, Johnny and Bill followed the Pony Express trail west. They didn't hit every station—some were out in plain view with no way to approach unseen—but they hit eleven of them before having too many horses to manage with two sets of hands.

Since they knew the guys in each place—habits and such—it wasn't hard to get the horses while the handlers were in the shithouse or napping or fishing out of a nearby creek.

And with the horses they'd snatched, Johnny figured he wouldn't have to work for a few years at least. He could go back to Sarah without the fear a man with no skills has of no work. He was a horse-thief now. But only if you were a judge or marshal. In his own eyes, these animals were his. The Central Overland California and Pikes Peak Express Company had failed him. They'd lost the bid for the million dollar government mail contract that would have kept the Express in business. The whole goddamn thing now was going to the Butterfield Overland Mail Stage Line.

Stagecoaches, by God!

Slower, if nothing else.

Johnny didn't know much about politics, but he suspected that was what sat behind this whole mess.

Maybe none of that mattered though. These telegraph lines were going up faster than spider webs, and even the stages were going to suffer when it came to getting the mail across.

But really, Johnny's horse-thieving came to more than all that.

He loved the animals.

They'd been his companions on more miles than he could count. And besides companionship, they'd saved his life on at least a dozen occasions. Three times he'd outrun Indians on California Mustangs. Twice it was the small, fleet, hardy Indian horses in the Express stables that had been sure-footed in dark nights, since the Pony Express ran any time of day. Scary as hell to be going fast under a cloudy night, when even the stars are hidden from view. Two riders had been thrown to their deaths just such.

He'd never say it to Bill, but on many of those nights, Johnny had spoken to his horse, sort of praying he'd get home safe to Sarah. For hell's sake, the Pony Express ad even said, *willing to risk death daily, orphans preferred.* At the time he'd applied for the job, he'd been thinking of the money, not the danger. The first time he raced through a blizzard, though, he didn't think the $25 per week was worth it.

Nothing a hot cup of coffee didn't cure.

And nothing his horse didn't save him from.

Every damn time.

These animals were his friends.

Some of them he planned to sell to good families. A few he meant to keep. But in all cases, they were his to do something about. And so to keep his family fed and clothed, and for their own sakes, he was a horse-thief.

Or at least that's the way he saw it, when the ring of a Winchester being cocked and fired ripped Johnny out of all his justifications. He shot a look around at Bill, whose eyes looked like they were about to pop out of his head. They both flattened on the ground, and scuttled up under a low rise beside the road.

Johnny peeked through the grass, and saw old Barlow—sixty-years-old if he was a day—standing out beside the stable, his britches down around his ankles and his hands filled with rifle.

But not pointing his Winchester in their direction.

He was aiming at the horses.

"Ya sons-a-bitches! Takin' dem horses ain't yers. Damn ya, damn ya! I hates horse thiefs!" And he started to shoot.

The horses began to fall.

And Johnny began to scream.

Old Barlow wasn't trying to kill Johnny or Bill, or hurt 'em, or even run 'em off. He meant to take away the reason for them being here in the first place. Old Barlow was damn good with his 30-30. And fast.

And when he ran out of bullets, he had another Winchester at hand. And started again.

Heavy thuds continued to hit the ground. THUD! THUD! A few of the horses whinnied and ran a step or two before falling and struggling to get back up. They mewled and cried for help, but got only another bullet from Old Barlow's rifle when he could spare a round.

Johnny couldn't do a thing for them. He shoved his face into the ground and yelled, filling his nose and mouth with dust. He wanted to shoot back at Old Barlow.

But even if he *was* a horse-thief, he *wasn't* a killer.

Not even for his friends.

So he laid face-down, in agony, screaming, until he had a thought. He jumped up and rushed Old Barlow. *Let him shoot me down if he's got the gumption!* He ran as hard as he could, trying to get between the old man and the horses. But Barlow shot around him . . . with deadly accuracy.

Bill didn't follow. Johnny didn't blame him.

But on he ran. His old boots crimping on the tops of his feet as he went. Rounds flew past his head. Rifle smoke filled the air. Horse cries squealed high against a pale blue sky. And Johnny yelled and waved his arms, screaming for Old Barlow to stop.

The shooting and screaming and dying seemed to go on forever.

Then Johnny was knocking over the old man, who never tried to take him down. But who had killed every horse before it was all done.

They hit the dirt hard together. The old guy cursing and crawling away.

Johnny laid face-up this time, gasping, the scent of gun powder in his nose, thinking of the many times his friends had saved him or carried him safely home to Sarah. These friends he'd meant to *rescue* these last few days, to also free himself.

Now all were dead.

He'd hadn't saved them from anything. He hadn't saved himself, either.

And he certainly hadn't saved his marriage or Sarah.

What would he do now?

~

UNDER A SLIVER of a moon, the telegraph office sat like an overgrown outhouse; or maybe that's just the way Johnny thought of it.

He and Bill crept on their toes through the low grass and sage, Johnny looking up once to see the telegraph line like a thin black rope in the sky. Just seeing it made him taste bile in the back of his throat. Bill grabbed Johnny's shirt and yanked him along.

At the rear door to the telegraph office, they pulled at the handle and found it open. Like thieves, they quietly snuck inside. The wood of the telegraph office still smelled heavy with pine sap, fresh and new. And as Johnny looked around, he saw the place was mostly unfurnished still. Just not much to it, really. Him and Bill started in. Their boots sounded heavy on the floorboards, so they shuffled their feet slow, and moved into the main room behind a desk where the telegraph sat in the dark.

Together they stood, silent, looking down at it. A dull anger pulsed behind Johnny's eyes, but as much as that, he just felt confused. How did the hard work and thrill of so many men riding hard from St. Joseph all the way to Sacramento, 2000 miles, 75 miles each man, to 165 stations get replaced by a wire and this little piece of metal that did nothing more than tap.

He fingered the damn thing.

Tap. Tap. Tap.

And if he was honest, his real question was why someone would wish to get a message that way. If you couldn't talk to someone face to face, wasn't the next best thing to read a letter they took care to write with their own hands? Johnny wasn't school-learned, but some things just made common sense, as they say.

Bill had moved to the wall, and was looking at the posters nailed to the walls. "Listen to this,"—Bill was school-learned—"they're hiring."

Even in the dark, the two men could see each other smiling with a little bitterness.

"Just take it," Bill finally said, coming back and bending over beside Johnny to get a closer look at the telegraph in the dark.

"Change of plans." Johnny reached into his pocket and pulled out a small matchbox.

In the stillness, the strike of a match came loud. The match flared, brightening the room and lending an orange tint to everything.

"You can't burn it," Bill said, "It's made of metal."

"No it's not," Johnny replied, and lowered his arm past the telegraph and put the flame to the bare wood beneath the desk. The combination of dry wood and sap made a deadly mix that fed the fire and had the desk burning in only a few seconds. The two Pony Express riders escaped back out through the rear door just ahead of the blaze, which lit the Telegraph Office completely in less than two minutes.

As Johnny watched it burn, he thought that maybe now (for a while anyway) the Pony Express would be needed again. He'd have work until he could figure out what else to do. He felt a strange peace and a small bit of revenge creep over him at the site of the fire. The town would rebuild the telegraph office, but it would take time. And in the weeks before they could have it done, he was there to serve as best he could.

As he and Bill stood a mile off watching the fire dwindle he felt the nudge of a barrel in his back. When Johnny turned around he saw the town marshal there holding his shotgun aimed low at them.

"Let's go," he said, and began leading them to the one place where Johnny really would be utterly helpless.

~

THE JAIL CELL had a completely different smell than the telegraph shop. That's what Johnny noticed as he sat up. Not the bars or Bill or the small, barred window. It was the way thick, old wood smelled up close when you're on the inside. Permanent they would say. That was maybe what scared him most. He'd been brought here for arson. And he thought maybe he'd die here for the same.

"What now?" he'd asked Marshal Chandler.

"Well, Johnny, turns out your crime is the very thing that prevents us from telegraphing the territory judge to come around and try you in an official hearing. So, we'll just have to keep you until his regular visit."

"When's that?" Bill asked.

"Better part of two months," the Marshall replied, smiling some.

And it would have been that long, too, Johnny knew, if it hadn't been for a set of boot leathers that came a week later.

The boardwalk and jail steps pounded with feet hurrying toward them. The jail's front door shot open, slamming against the wall, as the runner came in, right past the marshal, skidding to a stop in front of Johnny's cell door. "You're wife's havin' her baby!"

Johnny looked over at Marshal Chandler, waiting to see what he'd do. The man sat a moment, thoughtful like, then pulled his legs down off his desk and picked up his shotgun—he never went anywhere without it. He ambled over to Johnny's cell.

"Johnny, what you done was wrong. You ain't gonna hang for arson, I don't reckon, but there's gonna be some kind of punishment. But I'd rather not be responsible for a man not being there to see his child get born. You listening to me?"

Johnny nodded.

"So here's what we're gonna do. We'll leave Bill here, and the two of us will ride out to your place. You ought to be there for this. Then, after a time, we'll head on back. That seem fair enough?"

Johnny nodded again.

"And if you try to run, Johnny, you're gonna make me prove I can hit you with this as fast as I do the cornbread shoot on Fourth of July." Marshal Chandler pretended to track the toss of a piece of cornbread into the sky and pull the trigger on his Browning double shot.

"I ain't gonna run, Tim," Johnny said, calling the man by name to make him know he could trust what he said.

"Good, let's go." The Marshall keyed open the cell and gave Johnny a last look of warning.

Then the two men got out to their horses and were gone. The race to the cabin he hadn't seen since the night Sarah had kicked him out went by in a blur. The pounding of hooves in the still morning air. The rush of trees as they passed. All this time seemed different from the thousands of miles Johnny had ridden before when he needed to get someplace fast.

He was going to have a son or daughter. And it was likely he would see the child today and then not again for a very long time. He was thinking on that when they came up on the cabin set in the pinions. He sat a moment as the Marshal got down, thinking: *What did I do? What did I do to my family?* Part of him

164

wasn't sure he could see this. It would hurt worse knowing what he was leaving behind.

Then they heard Sarah scream.

Johnny leapt from his horse and got inside his place fast. The smell of sweaty blankets and boiling water filled the cabin, and he saw Sarah immediately, a woman Johnny didn't know helping her give birth.

Marshal Chandler hung back by the door, while Johnny went to Sarah's side. She took his hand in a weak grip and tried to speak. But her voice just husked. She looked so tired.

"Push!" The woman at the foot of the bed commanded.

Sarah tried, but barely began the effort before collapsing back into her pillow. She looked pale. Her hair wet and sticking to the sides of her face.

"You the father?" the woman asked with a rough tongue. Like she thought all fathers were mostly useless.

"Yes." Johnny looked over at the woman, who was wiping her hands on a towel.

She motioned him away from Sarah, and began to whisper so that she couldn't hear. "The baby's stuck."

"What?"

"Baby's stuck. It's sideways. Nothing I can do. And listen close, because you got to decide on something." The woman paused, brushing back wiry hairs from her forehead, seeming to hate what she had to say next, but maybe having said it too many times to let the tears come with it. "The baby and your wife will both die if we don't cut the baby out."

Johnny's heart slammed in his chest. He looked over at Sarah and stepped back a pace.

"Don't go womanly on me," this midwife said. "I can keep a'doin' what I'm doin', but I've seen this a hundred times. The baby's been stuck this way too long already. No tellin' that maybe it's too late already. But it's still movin' in there, so that's good. But you're wife ain't got no more push. She's done. So, mister, you tell me what to do."

Johnny looked down at the woman's face, set like a piece of shoe iron. "What will happen to Sarah if you cut her?"

The midwife looked at Johnny a long damn time. So long that he knew pretty much what she meant to say before she said it. And his gut tied up in hard knots that made him want to bawl. He actually put a hand on her shoulder for his own support.

She nodded to her own understanding as she said it slow. "Mister, you're wife will likely die. Sometimes, if I cut early, right off I mean, there's a chance. The mother still has strength and blood. Yours here has lost all her strength, and a lot of blood besides. I don't want to tell you not to believe in the miracles of God, if that's your persuasion, but I ain't seen any such miracles in all my babies . . . or mothers."

Johnny reeled. Hearing the words dropped him to his knees. Marshal Chandler came up behind him and supported his back before he fell and cracked his head on the floor. The midwife hunkered down in front of him.

"I know, boy, but damn it don't show this weakness to your wife. What's she going to think? Stand the hell up!"

Johnny struggled to his feet with some help from the Marshal.

"What's it gonna be?" the woman asked. "You don't have time to be wasting."

Johnny looked over at Sarah, wondering what she would do. He knew the answer, but he wasn't ready to simply give the word to kill his wife. In an agonizing moment, he thought about the night he'd come home drunk after the Pony Express news, about all the nonsense since, his own cowardly choices trying to feel like a man, a man scared of a goddamn wire come into town to carry the messages of loved ones along down the line. He thought about how they'd started, him and Sarah, with plans and courage comin' out West. And then a flood of memories ran over him like spring runoff, leaving him a'drown in the pain of what would come next because of what had been. And what had been had been awful good.

He let go of the woman and the Marshal and went to Sarah's side. He looked at her a long time, and she looked back. "I'm sorry," he said. "I'm a fool. I'm a damn fool. This is all my fault."

Sarah shook her head, and gave a slow blink. "No," she managed.

He held the tears in, trying to be strong. "I love you. I do love you. You know that."

Sarah smiled. A small one. But it gave his heart a different kind of leap, and that's when some of the tears came out, silent like, but that's when he thought she knew. Even before he said anything. And as it turned out, he hadn't needed to say it. She did indeed know. And after the first kiss they'd shared in too damn long a time, she whispered, "It's okay, Johnny. Save the baby."

Johnny didn't think there was room in his chest for the pounding of his heart. Some for her powerful courage, and some for her forgiveness, and some for the awful loss of it all. But it tore at him inside like nothing before ever had and he thought he'd remember and weep over it the rest of his life.

Johnny kept a tight grip on her hand as he looked back at the woman and nodded.

He then turned and held Sarah's gaze as the midwife did what she had to do. He didn't shrink from the screams or the twist of pain in his wife's face, he didn't bother to wipe the blood that somehow wound up on his face. He sat as strong and sturdy as a man could, who after all could do nothing else, and watched real love earn its stripes, watched real magnificence, as they say, in the face of a woman who chose death to give life a chance.

And when it was done, the midwife brought the child between them for a look. But that wasn't all. And what she said threatened to undo the terrible sacrifice that Johnny had just watched.

"Sarah, Johnny," she said, using names for the first time, "the child . . . it ain't well. There's not much time."

Sarah's eyes glassed up with tears. Johnny felt some righteous anger, as they say. "What do you mean?"

"The baby needs a real doctor. A baby doctor. And Doc Wright is up to Fort Bridger right now . . ."

"How much time?"

"She's breathing kind of rapid. And her color's off. My guess is a day if we don't—"

"Johnny," Sarah interrupted, her voice somehow a bit stronger.

Johnny looked a moment more at his daughter, who he knew he'd call Sarah. Then he turned to his wife. She looked at him even, careful, and then said something that made his heart leap and turn and think again of faith and glory and hope. "Ride," she said. "Ride."

Johnny flexed his jaw hard and cried a great tear at it. Then he kissed her, took up the child real careful like and bundled her in several warm blankets. Then he went to the Marshal. "I'll be back when I'm done, Tim." The Marshal nodded understanding.

And he went out. He pulled his chaps from the hitch post and cut them in half. He tied one half into a sling and looped it over his head and under one arm. Then he rested the babe in the sling and eased onto the saddle.

He looked east. 28 hours to Fort Bridger. He found the glint of the sun and hunched forward, so the child wouldn't feel the jostle of the trail.

And he went.

Like never before he went.

The world raced by. All of it, even the telegraph line as he found the Pony Express trail and settled into the hardest most important ride and parcel of his life.

And in the wind, tears streamed back from the corners of his eyes, thinking on Sarah and his damn foolishness, but mostly this little girl who needed him to succeed this one time. To live. To make the sacrifice of her mother right. So that he could tell little Sarah someday about the decent life of the woman who brought her into the world.

28 hours.

Maybe a day, the midwife had said.

28 hours.

Peter Orullian

Too long.

And at the old willow tree, Johnny, who'd been the first rider to carry mail west from St. Joseph, turned off the Express trail and made for Butte Gulch. It would save him twelve hours. It might save a life.

Dust kicked up under hooves, and Johnny kept crouched forward, one hand keeping the child safe and secure, the other working the reins.

Until he saw the chasm, its narrowest point dead ahead, too wide for fifty miles in both directions.

Twenty feet across.

He spurred his horse and felt the hooves dig in beneath him, the wind stronger in his eyes. "Heeyawww! Heeyawww!" Goading his animal on.

And near to the rift that fell away a hundred feet below, he looked up and spared a last thought on Sarah. God he loved her. Sometimes a man's just no good at loving, he figured.

Then at the edge, all wind and hope and hooves he cried, "Ride!"

And his horse left the earth. Jumped into the air and morning sun. Over Butte Gulch. For life or none. 'Cause Johnny would either save this life or lose them both and join Sarah where this sunrise lived forever, and where talking with a loved one wasn't a letter or telegram, but never more than a heartbeat away.

BEATS OF SEVEN

J IMMY NESBITT SAT in the dark of a new moon on the
Lincoln City beach and listened.

No wind.

No obnoxious birds.

No obnoxious lover's strolling.

Just Jimmy and his sound gear, capturing the roll of waves,
the susurration of water over sand, the ticking of air bubbles
popping as the water retreated back toward the ocean. It was the
same sound he'd heard a hundred times before . . . until he de-
tected something more, buried deep in the white noise of waves.

He looked around, irritated, expecting to see someone
stomping through the sand with a portable stereo in one hand
on the way toward a midnight swim.

Nothing.

Even the occasional sweep of headlights had ceased, leaving the darkness unbroken and tranquil.

He was alone.

Jimmy reached quickly for his frequency filter, dialing
the luminous knobs to try and isolate the pitch he thought he
heard. His heart actually pounded in his chest—something
music hadn't done for him in quite some time.

And it totally surprised him.

The romance—if it had ever really been there—had long gone out of this job. Recording the ocean had been the only gig he could get once he quit session work in Los Angeles and Nashville, where musicianship had been replaced by packaging and sex appeal. If the market for *Pacific Ocean Scapes*—the project that would take him up the entire west coast—weren't so lucrative, he could never have endured the mindless sound-tracking of splashing water.

He narrowed in on the frequency, methodically muting levels where he could not hear the strange sound through his headphones. The rumble of white caps turning over on themselves fell away, the sizzle of water creeping up wet-packed sand disappeared as well. He kept at it, eager to identify this new tone, something he hadn't heard on any other beach south to San Diego.

After several more adjustments, his parametric equalizer began to spike only in the +10 megahertz zone.

Jimmy pressed the ear cups of his Sony Pro Studio reference phones tighter against his head, sealing out further noise.

He gave a smile.

No mistake.

A trumpet.

Another sound engineer might not have known what he was hearing. But Jimmy had spent several years mixing studio jazz albums in New Orleans in the years before new age labels started throwing money at French Quarter musicians and recording the always hilarious "light jazz."

He knew from a trumpet.

That wasn't all, though.

If a little fuzzy through the processing he had to impose on it to create the discreet horn sound, the tone perfectly matched a Gillespie model horn—something only the men playing on Bourbon Street or swank Manhattan dinner clubs in the early 30's would have used. Still, a badly soldered connection, an errant grain of sand, any number of things could have caused the tone.

Not when it moved in and out of melody.

Jimmy sat, compressing his phones against his ears, tweaking his EQ, recording snippets of what he was coming to think of as a song, then playing them back against the real-time music.

They were different.

The song seemed to live in the very rattle and hum of the ocean itself.

What the hell had he found? And could he sell it.

WATERY LIGHT DAWNED behind Jimmy in the east. He'd spent all night listening, recording, filling three hard drives of the unique tonal aberration. Life stirred around him, folks walking pets, a few morning runners. Still no one carrying a CD player or child's musical toy. And certainly no one with an instrument, let alone a Gillespie model.

If nothing more, he wanted to know where the music originated. Through the night he'd listened, trying to make sense of the melodies and rhythms. Despite the enchantment of it— or maybe because of it—any form or structure eluded him.

But the thrill that he might have captured something previously unheard raced through his blood. Sound men lived for such discoveries, and extracting it from a remote beach in a sleepy seaside town only made the mystery and improbability greater.

Then sun struck the water, rays of light spearing the thick Pacific mist . . . and the music ended.

The abrupt departure seemed as much a mystery as the sound to begin with. It didn't matter, he had it on file.

Jimmy packed up his equipment, and in the space of moments had left behind the endless turn of waves and dunes of sand for the tarmac of Highway 101.

A mile north he braked hard to a stop beside a yellow marquee announcing the sale of harmonica's 2 for 10 dollars. Max's Music Maven was a converted home with two music rooms and an adjoining apartment. Jimmy had met Vincent, the proprietor, just yesterday. His store hours written on a paper plate taped inside the window told him Vince opened at 10 a.m. This couldn't wait 3 hours. So he rounded the side and found a door decorated with an endorsement sticker that read, "If it ain't Gibson, it ain't nothing."

This was the place.

Jimmy began knocking, and didn't stop.

Moments later, the door swung inward. Vincent stood in boxers, his pale skin stretched impossibly tight over ribs and shoulders. Thin, scraggly hair hung down in eyes that squinted in the strengthening light.

"We ain't open, man. Come back later."

"It can't wait," Jimmy said. "I just need to ask you a few questions."

"Ah, crap, you're that new age ocean guy. Man, I'm not having this conversation at 7:00 a.m. I told you yesterday, I'm not going to carry mood music in my place. Try the Dirty Lap Dog or something. I got a rep."

Jimmy would have smiled to hear it if he didn't have important questions to ask. "Never mind that. Listen, I've got something I want you to hear. It's not the same as yesterday."

"You're some piece of work. I don't let my lady in this early, and you think I'm letting you in?"

Unable to hold it back any longer, Jimmy blurted. "I've just recorded your little beach at the end of the D River." He waited until the aging hippie looked him straight. "And I've captured the sound of a trumpet playing a tune."

If the hippie had shown Jimmy any other response, he might have gotten back in his VW Beetle and drove away. What he saw instead was a suspicious eye peering from between kinky strands of hair that grew from a thinning mane.

That was all he needed to see. "You know about it? What the hell is it?"

The hippie left the door standing wide and retreated into the shadows of his one room apartment. Taking it as an invite, Jimmy gladly followed.

Vincent poured some coffee from a pot still bearing the insignia 7-Eleven, which made perfect sense since the stainless steel coffee maker it sat in still bore the same logo. To the left in the corner, a mattress lay flat on the ground; sheets and blankets balled up on one side. A Stratocaster lay beside the bed, a litter of picks strewn around it. The scent of mildew and cat litter hung on the air with yesterday's cigarettes. Vince just lifted his coffee mug in the direction of a door at the back of the room, and led Jimmy in to the music shop.

The main showroom—nothing more than a fifteen by fifteen deal with a small selection of guitars and amplifiers—stood in shadow. It was here that Jimmy had met Vince yesterday, this holdover from the sixties telling him that he didn't carry digital media for Jimmy's hard disk recorder. Vince had added that electronic gadgets weren't real music anyway.

The flower child hadn't bothered to show Jimmy the second music room.

Just three steps up to a second door, they passed into an elevated space smelling of dusty wood.

Filled with pianos.

At one time, it might have been a living room, maybe even a dining room. Now it had been stripped of everything but the floor planks. Even the walls were little more than studs and framing.

This space wasn't about anything put the piano-forte, the clavier, and one irreparable harpsichord.

Dust lay in blankets a quarter inch deep over the tops of everything. As Jimmy and Vince stirred the air in their passage, it hardly moved the dust, the weight of time having made a fabric of the accumulated motes.

The room smelled of antique wood, of metal casings and broken strings. It was like a graveyard of pianos packed so tight that only two aisles could be walked from one end of the space to the other.

"You only sell guitars and pianos?" Jimmy asked.

"And harmonica's," Vince replied.

Jimmy reached one end of the room. "I came here to ask . . ."

His words died in his throat. To the left, sitting on a piano bench facing a windowless wall was a trumpet case propped open. Inside, a silver horn bearing the dents and scrapes of use lay cloaked in the same fall of dust that coated everything.

A Gillespie model.

Vince came up beside him. "Been here since I bought the place in '69. Old Doc Thurber told me just to leave it be. Didn't much matter to me, I don't care for brass."

Jimmy looked up at the man. "This isn't the instrument I heard. Can't be. I just finished recording it less than ten minutes ago. This thing hasn't been played in years." He ran a finger along the tubing, clearing a path across the dull finish.

"You'll need to keep an open mind about that," Vince said. "Things are different on the Pacific. Stuff has a way of being less and more than you make of it. That's no lie."

"I'd like to buy it," Jimmy blurted. "How much?"

"Ain't for sell," the hippie said. "Not to you. I can see the money in your eyes. Saw it yesterday when you came through talking about selling us the ocean on a CD." He laughed. "You realize I just need to step outside to get that for free."

"I'm not going to argue with you. What about five hundred for the horn?"

Vincent's eyebrows lifted, but Jimmy soon realized it had nothing to do with interest in the five hundred. "I won't take your money," the guy began, scratching his nipple. "But since you seem sincere, I'll steer you one port more. There's a small theater up Nelscott way, the West End Theater. Judd Jensen is always around. Oldest guy in town. Was here when this was still getting some lip." He pointed at the Gillespie horn. "Tell Judd I showed you the trumpet. He'll know what to say."

Jimmy spent several moments looking at the instrument in its stiffened velvet case, and strode the boards back toward his car. The very thought of the sounds in the waves caused him to quicken his pace.

Something about those songs.

～

THE WEST END Theater was closed until 6:00 p.m.

Jimmy spent the day trying to duplicate his findings at the beach, annoyed at the bystanders asking him a lot of stupid questions. He actually threw a bit of sand at a few pesky kids to shoe them away.

But the trumpet didn't seem to accompany the waves in the daylight.

When dusk fell, Jimmy went to the theater, bought a ticket to a delightful rendition of *You Can't Take it with You*, then lingered in his seat while the other three patrons wandered out.

When the rumblings of stage props ceased, a man with thick white hair stepped out onto the stage beneath the single bulb which burned above it.

"You waiting for me?" the man asked.

"If you're Mr. Jensen."

"I am."

"My name is Jimmy Nesbitt. Vincent said I could talk to you about the trumpet," Jimmy replied.

The old man stared out on the small theater, deep set eyes hiding whatever thoughts they might have betrayed. "That so?" He titled his head back, staring into the weak glare of the light. "You know what that is?"

"No, sir."

"Ghost light," the man said. "Every theater leaves the one bulb burning on the boards to keep the wrong kinds of spirits away."

"You think I'm a spirit?"

"Are you?" The head lowered again, leveling an uncomfortable stare at Jimmy.

"Not the last time I checked," Jimmy joked. The humor fell flat on the empty theater.

The old fellow didn't laugh, but came to the edge of the stage and out of the immediate glare. Now he was nothing more than a silhouette. "Then tell me what business you have with the trumpet, and I'll tell you if I can help."

"Just want to buy it."

"Why?"

Jimmy suddenly felt wary of sharing his story. Perhaps he was afraid people would laugh, perhaps he was afraid they wouldn't. "It an unusual item," he said. "Is it yours?"

The man smiled then. At least Jimmy thought it looked like a smile. In the dark it was hard to tell. "What's it sound like to you?" Jensen asked.

"What do you mean?"

"Never mind then." The old man pivoted and had almost exited stage left when he stopped and turned to look back at Jimmy. "You a musician?" he asked.

"Used to be. Now I work on the other side of the board." Jimmy began to get irritated. "Since when does anybody need to know how to play an instrument in order to buy one? No one would ever learn how that way."

The guy nodded, but not, Jimmy thought, in agreement to what he'd said. "It's been a long time," the man answered cryptically. "Maybe this time we'll get it right."

"Get what right? What are you talking about?" Jimmy got out of his seat and began moving toward the aisle.

"It was 1938!" the man yelled. The boom of his voice shattered the theater quiet, freezing Jimmy mid-stride. "Vaudeville lost its luster, and talented acts were starving in the streets of New York. Some died, believing movies were a passing fancy, wasting away in tenements waiting for venues to reopen at a nickel a seat. Others went upstate, taking their acts to resorts, working for room and board and lying in the beds of the rich for extra on the side."

The old man's hair began to shift with the trembling of his own impassioned words. "A few got out. A few went south, touring night clubs and bars along the eastern seaboard. Some came west." He stopped.

Jimmy stood at the edge of the aisle, ready to either rush the man, feeling that he knew more than he admitted, or run from the theater, sure the coot was crazy as a loon. He did neither.

The old man continued. "George Henry found this place when his trumpet lost its appeal to both Vaudeville and the New York uptown jazz community. But no one cared to listen to a horn out here, not for money. So George set to music of a different kind, learning the sounds of the earth, the sounds of nature, writing it down, learning the patterns." Something entered the old man's voice then. Fear, maybe. He whispered, the sound of it carrying in the empty hall. "There's power in that, my friend. The power to undo. George learned it sure enough."

The man held his arm toward Jimmy, pointing a finger. From the shadow at the edge of the stage, it appeared ominous, like the specter of Christmas future pointing toward Scrooge's grave. "Anything you've heard is a gift to you, young man. Leave it be. Music isn't to be trifled with. You're either a musician or your not. You either do it for a life, or you mock it by making it a hobby."

"I didn't say—"

"Didn't have to," Jensen cut in. "Listen if you will. No harm there. But let the music rest. For heaven's sake, just let it rest."

The man stepped behind the curtain, leaving Jimmy alone with the ghost light.

～

AS NIGHT CLOSED in, a glorious sunset erupted over the western horizon. Crimson skies lit across the water, turning the ocean a thousand shades of red. Some few tourists and locals trod the beach, heading for their cars or home, and Jimmy, headphones firmly in place, sat watching it all, listening to his recordings from the night before.

Something strange in them.

The melodies were beautiful, haunting, but oddly never repeated. It was as though the trumpeter had no song in mind, but simply played on and on, forever defining a new phrase, a new melody.

Some of them fast.

Others languorous, creeping slowly and marking out a passage of aching beauty.

Jimmy tried to chart it at first, replaying sections over and over. His theory was rusty, but he managed to define a few note progressions before combinations of complexity went beyond him.

The sun disappeared, and almost immediately the wind came in, cold, whispering across the sands.

The longer he listened, the less Jimmy thought he understood about the music. At times, he wasn't sure it was music at all. Among other things, he couldn't find any definite rhythm. The time signature eluded him, so that he could never identify individual phrases.

Finally, he stopped, putting his headphones aside and dropping to his elbows to watch the light go completely out of the sky. For a moment, he lost himself in the reassuring sound of waves upon the sand—something he hadn't done once since he'd started tracking the movements of the great ocean.

. . . *learning the sounds of the earth, the sounds of nature, writing it down, learning the patterns . . . There's power in that, my friend. The power to undo.*

Jimmy's gift had always been a very good ear. Any sound man worth his salt had one. Consumers rarely heard the difference, which explained the popularity of digital song downloads, in which compression technology had removed so much of the acoustic information.

Jimmy hated those. Not because they were free. Because they sounded thin.

Not like this.

The almost laughing sound of water rolling toward the beach came full-bellied, rich and strident every time. If the earth had a voice, this was surely it.

And no place more certainly than this strip of sand on the Oregon coast.

But still something in it evaded him. If he could just understand.

Stories of Vaudevillians, old instruments, and warnings about his own musical incompetence only made him more eager to understand what it was he heard in his recordings. They may not want to see him profiting on the music of their beach here, but they wouldn't run him off with creepy stories. The thought of it made him laugh. Hell, he'd live in Los Angeles for eight years, nothing was creepier than that.

Then it happened.

Just reclining there on the beach, he began to count.

Simple eighth notes.

Seven of them.

Then again.

Jimmy sat up straight, staring at the water as if he expected it to talk. With alarming regularity, the water tumbled and fell to a beat of seven. The time signature carried its own power, but could scarcely be handled by most musicians. Standard time, swing time, the 3 count of a waltz, each of them could be danced to, internalized without training. Even phrases of two and five and nine fell more frequently in the music pantheon, adopted often by classical composers, used in songs with regularity.

But seven.

Jimmy counted, and counted.

When night had descended in full, something more occurred to him. He quickly got his recording equipment from the car and set it up. This time, he dialed the frequency only half way in, and listened.

There it was.

The languished melody of the horn came in musical phrases to the beat of the surf. Jimmy now heard them together as he hadn't before, and in a flurry, he began to scribble out bars of seven, transcribing the song as it wafted and sang across the great time keeper.

So busy was he at his transcription, that he did not hear the rumblings deep in the earth. He exulted at the possibility that he might put definition to something that had never been written down.

He owed it to the bugling of a horn. He owed it to George Henry.

The sky suddenly darkened and crackled with lightning. The waves swelled, a flurry of wind swept down upon the dunes.

And all in perfect seven time.

Jimmy madly went on, oblivious to the changes around him.

Soon the tumult of thunder and pounding surf and shrieking wind became a chorus he might never have imagined. His papers riffled in his hand, but he held them tight, penning the sound in his ears, marking a great melody in bars of seven.

He knew instinctively that he'd become a conductor, and his orchestra was nothing less than the elements themselves.

He held the key.

Was unlocking the sounds of heaven.

Just like a Vaudevillian with a Gillespie horn.

In a fury, he put his pen back to the paper, marking out notes with haste, his notes flying across the page. The maelstrom whipped and churned, but all he heard were sevens, beautiful, indecipherable sevens.

Then he came to the end of his sheet, a single phrase yet to write, and paused as at the climax of a symphony, holding a great note before the finale.

And again he heard the old man, the minor thespian. *There's power in that, my friend. The power to undo.*

With a single beat of his heart, he knew to decipher the song would make him forever a part of it.

Like a horn joined forever in the waves.

Jimmy shook with the feverish desire to unlock the mystery, to see his finding through its conclusion.

As the wind lashed and the water churned, he listened to another measure of seven.

And dropped his pen.

In moments the sea and air calmed. Jimmy loosened his grip on his opus, the pages scattering about him, soon carried on mild breezes to the water's edge.

Jimmy fell back and grabbed fists full of sand, imagining the difference between heaven and earth.

In the moments that followed, he could no longer count the rhythms of the ocean, its voice become again a mystery to him. But gentle it came, and lulled his senses, like any good jazz music should.

Read on for a preview of the

<small>AUTHOR'S DEFINITIVE EDITION OF</small>

THE UNREMEMBERED

by

PETER ORULLIAN

THE VAULT OF HEAVEN

"One is forced to conclude that while the gods had the genius to create music, they didn't understand its power. There's a special providence in that, lads. It also ought to scare the last hell out of you."

> —Taken from the rebuttal made by the philosopher
> Lour Nail in the College of Philosophy
> during the Succession of Arguments on Continuity

WHAT HADN'T BEEN BURNED, had been broken. Wood, stone . . . flesh. Palamon stood atop a small rise, surveying the wound that was a city. Beside him, Dossolum kept a god's silence. Black smoke rose in straight pillars, its slow ascent unhindered by wind. None had been left alive. None. This wasn't blind, angry retaliation. This was annihilation. This was breakage of a deeper kind than wood or stone or flesh. This was breakage of the spirit.

Ours . . . and theirs, Palamon thought. He shook his head with regret. "The Veil isn't holding those you sent into the Bourne."

Dossolum looked away to the north. "This place is too far gone. Is it any wonder we're leaving it behind?"

189

"You're the Voice of the Council," Palamon argued. "If you stay, the others will stay. Then together—"

"The decision has been made," Dossolum reminded him. "Some things cannot be redeemed. Some things shouldn't."

Palamon clenched his teeth against further argument. He still had entreaties to make. Better not to anger the only one who could grant his requests. But it was hard. He'd served those who lay dead in the streets below him, just as he'd served the Creation Council. *Someone* should speak for the dead.

"You don't have to stay," Dossolum offered again. "None of the Sheason need stay. There's little you can do here. What we began will run its course. You might slow it"—he looked back at the ruined city—"but eventually, it will all come to this."

Palamon shook his head again, this time in defiance. "You don't know that."

Dossolum showed him a patient look. "We don't go idly. The energy required to right this . . . Better to start fresh, with new matter. In another place." He looked up at evening stars showing in the east.

"Most of the Sheason are coming with you," Palamon admitted.

"All but you, I think." Dossolum dropped his gaze back to the city. "It's not going to be easy here. Even with the ability to render the Will . . ."

Palamon stared at burned stone and tracts of land blackened to nothing. "Because some of those who cross the Veil have the same authority," he observed.

"Not only that." Dossolum left it there.

"Then strengthen the Veil," Palamon pled. "Make it the protection you meant it to be." He put a hand on Dossolum's arm. "Please."

In the silence that followed, a soft sound touched the air. A song. A lament. Palamon shared a look with Dossolum, then followed the sound. They descended the low hill. And step by step the song grew louder, until they rounded a field home. Beside a shed near a blackened pasture sat a woman with her husband's head in her lap. She stroked his hair as she sang. Not loud. Not frantic. But anguished, like a deep, slow saddening moved through her.

Tears had cleaned tracks down her field-dirty cheeks. Or maybe it was char. Like the smell of burning all around them.

But she was alive. Palamon had thought everyone here dead.

She looked up at them, unsurprised. Her vacant stare might not have seen them at all. She kept singing.

Palamon noticed toys now beside the home.

"The city wasn't enough," Palamon said, anger welling inside him. "They came into the fields to get them all."

The woman sang on. Her somber melody floated like cottonwood seed, brushing past them soft and earthward.

Dossolum stood and listened a long while. He made no move to comfort the woman, or to revive the man. His face showed quiet appreciation. Only when she'd begun to repeat her song did he finally speak. And then in a low tone, like a counterpoint.

"Very well, Palamon." Dossolum continued to watch the woman grieve. "Write it all down. Everything we tried to do.

Our failure. The Bourne and those we sent there. The war to do so." He grew quiet. "A story of desolation."

Tentatively, Palamon asked, "And do what with it?"

The woman's song turned low and throaty and bare.

Dossolum gave a sad smile. "To some we'll give a gift of song. They'll sing the story you write. And so long as they do, the Veil will be added to. Strengthened."

He nodded, seeming satisfied. "But it will be a suffering to sing it. Leaving them *diminished*."

"Thank you, Dossolum." Palamon then silently thanked the woman who mourned in front of them. Her mortal sorrow had touched his friend's eternal heart.

"Don't thank me." Dossolum's eyes showed their first hint of regret. "Like every good intention, a song can fade."

Palamon looked up at the same evening stars Dossolum had watched a moment ago. "Or it might be sung even after the light of the stars has fled the heavens."

"I hope you're right, my friend. I hope you're right."

BOOK ONE

THE UNREMEMBERED

STILLBORN

"The Church of Reconciliation—Reconciliationists, so called—preach that the Framers left behind protections. And these protections were given proper names. Names we've forgotten. Would these protections cease, then, to serve? Or would we have to question the origins of the doctrine?"

—Excerpt from *Rational Suppositions*,
a street tract disseminated by the League of Civility

A N OPEN DOOR . . .

Tahn Junell drew his bow, and kicked his mount into a dead run. They descended the shallow dale in a rush toward that open door. Toward home.

The road was muddy. Hooves threw sludge. Lightning arced in the sky. A peal of thunder shattered the silence and pushed through the small vale in waves. It echoed outward through the woods in diminishing tolls.

The whispering sound of rain on trees floated toward him. The soft smells of earth and pollen hung on the air, charged with the coming of another storm. Cold perspiration beaded on his forehead and neck.

An open door . . .

His sister, Wendra, wouldn't leave the door open to the chill.

Passing the stable, another bolt of white fire erupted from the sky, this time striking the ground. It hit at the near end of the vale. Thunder exploded around him. A moment later, a scream rose from inside his home. His mount reared, tugging at his reins and throwing Tahn to the ground before racing for the safety of the stable. Tahn lost his bow and began frantically searching the mud for the dropped weapon. The sizzle of falling rain rose, a lulling counterpoint to the screams that continued from inside. Something crashed to the floor of the cabin. Then a wail rose up. It sounded at once deep in the throat, like the thunder, and high in the nose like a child's mirth.

Tahn's heart drummed in his ears and neck and chest. His throat throbbed with it. Wendra was in there! He found his bow. Shaking the mud and water from the bowstring and quickly cleaning the arrow's fletching on his coat, he sprinted for the door. He nocked the arrow and leapt to the stoop.

The home had grown suddenly still and quiet.

He burst in, holding his aim high and loose.

An undisturbed fire burned in the hearth, but everything else in his home lay strewn or broken. The table had been toppled on its side, earthen plates broken into shards across the floor. Food was splattered against one wall and puddled near a cooking pot in the far corner. Wendra's few books sat partially burned near the fire, their thrower's aim not quite sure.

Tahn saw it all in a glance as he swung his bow to the left where Wendra had tucked her bed up under the loft.

She lay atop her quilts, knees up and legs spread.

Absent gods, no!

Then, within the shadows beneath the loft, Tahn saw it, a hulking mass standing at the foot of Wendra's bed. It hunched over, too tall to remain upright in the nook beneath the upper room. Its hands cradled something in a blanket of horsehair. The smell of sweat and blood and new birth commingled with the aroma of the cooking pot.

The figure slowly turned its massive head toward him. Wendra looked too, her eyes weary but alive with fright. She weakly reached one arm toward him, mouthing something, but unable to speak.

In a low, guttural voice the creature spoke, "*Quillescent* all around." It rasped words in thick, glottal tones.

Then it stepped from beneath the loft, its girth massive. The fire lit the creature's fibrous skin, which moved independent of the muscle and bone beneath. Ridges and rills marked its hide, which looked like elm bark. But pliable. It uncoiled its left arm from the blanket it held to its chest, letting its hand hang nearly to its knees. From a leather sheath strapped to its leg, the figure drew a long knife. Around the hilt it curled its hand—three talonlike fingers with a thumb on each side, its palm as large as Tahn's face. Then it pointed the blade at him.

Tahn's legs began to quiver. Revulsion and fear pounded in his chest. This was a nightmare come to life. This was Bar'dyn, a race out of the Bourne. One of those given to Quietus, the dissenting god.

"We go," the Quietgiven said evenly. It spoke deep in its throat. Its speech belied a sharp intelligence in its eyes. When it spoke, only its lips moved. The skin on its face remained thick and still, draped loosely over protruding cheekbones that jutted like shelves beneath its eyes. Tahn glimpsed a mouthful of sharp teeth.

"Tahn," Wendra managed, her voice hoarse and afraid.

Blood spots marked her white bed-dress, and her body seemed frozen in a position that prevented her from straightening her legs. Tahn's heart stopped.

Against its barklike skin, the Bar'dyn held cradled in a tightly woven blanket of mane and tail . . . Wendra's child.

Pressure mounted in Tahn's belly: hate, helplessness, confusion, fear. All a madness like panicked wings in his mind. He was supposed to protect her, keep her safe, especially while she carried this child. A child come of rape. But a child she looked forward to. Loved.

Worry and anger rushed inside him. "No!"

His scream filled the small cabin, leaving a deeper silence in its wake. But the babe made no sound. The Bar'dyn only stared. On the stoop and roof, the patter of rain resumed, like the sound of a distant waterfall. Beyond it, Tahn heard the gallop of hooves on the muddy road. *More Bar'dyn? His friends?*

He couldn't wait for either. In a shaky motion, he drew his aim on the creature's head. The Bar'dyn didn't move. There wasn't even defiance in its expression.

"I'll take you *and* the child. Velle will be pleased." It nodded at its own words, then raised its blade between them.

Velle? Dead gods, they've brought a renderer of the Will with them!

Tahn's aim floundered from side to side. Weariness. Cold fear.

The Bar'dyn stepped toward him. Tahn's mind raced, and fastened upon one thought. *The hammer.* He focused on that mark on the back of his bow hand, visually tracing its lines and feeling it with his mind. A simple, solid thing. He didn't remember where he'd gotten the scar or brand, but it seemed intentional. And it grounded him. With that moment of reassurance, his hands steadied, and he drew deeper into the pull, bringing his aim on the Bar'dyn's throat.

"Put the child down." His voice trembled even as his mouth grew dry.

The Bar'dyn paused, looking down at the bundle it carried. The creature then lifted the babe up, causing the blanket to slip to the floor. Its massive hand curled around the little one's torso. The infant still glistened from its passage out of Wendra's body, its skin red and purple in the sallow light of the fire.

"Child came dead, grub."

Sadness and anger welled again in Tahn. His chest heaved at the thought of Wendra giving birth in the company of this vile thing, having her baby taken at the moment of life into its hands. *Was the child dead at birth, or had the Bar'dyn killed it?* Tahn glanced again at Wendra. She was pale. Sadness etched her features. He watched her close her eyes against the Bar'dyn's words.

The rain now pounded the roof. But the sound of heavy footfalls on the road was clear, close, and Tahn abandoned hope of escape. One Bar'dyn, let alone several, might tear him apart, but he intended to send this one to the abyss, for Wendra, for her dead child.

He prepared to fire his bow, allowing time enough to speak the old, familiar words: "I draw with the strength of my arms, but release as the Will allows."

But he couldn't shoot.

He struggled to disobey the feeling, but it stretched back into that part of his life he couldn't remember. He had always spoken the words, always. He didn't release of his own choice. He always followed the quiet intimations that came after he spoke those words.

Tahn relaxed his aim and the Bar'dyn nodded approval. "Bound to Will," it said. The words rang like the cracking of timber in the confines of the small home. "But first to watch this one go." The Bar'dyn turned toward Wendra.

"No!" Tahn screamed again, filling the cabin with denial. Denial of the Bar'dyn.

Denial of his own impotence.

The sound of others came up the steps. Tahn was surrounded. They would all die!

He spared a last look at his sister. "I'm sorry," he tried to say, but it came out in a husk.

Her expression of confusion and hurt and disappointment sank deep inside him.

If he couldn't kill the creature, he could at least try to prevent it from hurting her.

Before he could move, his friends shot through the door. They got between Tahn and the Bar'dyn. They fought the creature. They filled his home with a clash of wills and swordplay and shouted oaths. Chaos churned around him. And all he could do was watch Wendra curl deeper into her bed. Afraid. Heartsick.

The creature out of the Bourne finally turned and crashed through the cabin's rear wall, rushing into the dark and the storm with Wendra's dead child. They did not give chase.

Tahn turned from the hole in the wall and went to Wendra's side. Blood soaked the coverlet, and cuts in her wrists and hands told of failed attempts to ward off the Bar'dyn. Her cheeks sagged; she looked pale and spent. She lay crying silent tears.

He'd stood twenty feet away with a clear shot at the Bar'dyn and had done nothing. The lives of his sister and her child had hung in the balance, and he'd done nothing. The old words had told him the draw was wrong. He'd followed that feeling over the defense of his sister. Why?

It was an old ache and frustration, believing himself bound to the impressions those words stirred inside him. But never so much as now.

CHAPTER ONE

OLD WORDS

"It is the natural condition of man to strive for certainty. It is also his condition not to find it. Not for long, anyway. Even a star may wander."

—From *Commentary on Categoricals*, a reader for children nominated to Dimnian cognitive training

TRANQUIL DARKNESS STRETCHED to the horizon. Small hours. Moments of quiet, of peace. Moments when faraway stars seemed as close and familiar as friends. Moments of night before the east would hint of sunrise. Tahn stepped into these small hours. Into the chill night air. He went to spend time with the stars. To imagine dawn. As he always had.

There was a kind of song in it all. A predictable rhythm and melody that might only be heard by one willing to remain quiet and unmoving long enough to note the movement of a star. It could be heard in the phases of the moons. It was by turns a single deep sonorous note, large as a russet sun setting slow, and then a great chorus, as when showers of shooting stars brightened the night sky. They were harmonies across ages, heard during the brief measure of a life. But only if one paused, as Tahn did, to watch and listen.

He stood at the edge of the High Plains of Sedagin. The bluff rose a thousand strides off the flatlands below. Stars winked like sparkling bits of glass on a dark tablecloth. His breath clouded the night, and droplets hung like frozen tears from low scrub and sage.

He looked east and let his thoughts come naturally. Deep into the far reaches of the sky he let them wander, his emotions and hopes struggling for form with the stars. He traced the constellations, some from old stories, some from memories whose sources were lost to him. A half-full moon had risen high, its surface bright and clear. The pale outline of the dark-ened portion appeared a ghostly halo.

Tahn closed his eyes and let his thoughts run out even fur-ther, imagining the sun; imagining its warmth and radiance, its calm, sure track across the heavens. He imagined the sky changing color in the east from black to violet to sea blue and finally the color of clear, shallow water. He pictured more col-or as sunlight came to the forest and touched its leaves and cones and limbs. He envisioned those first moments of dawn, the unfurling of flower petals to its light, its glint on rippling water, steam rising from warming loam. And as he always did at such a moment, Tahn felt like part of the land, another leaf to be touched by the sun. His thoughts coalesced into the sin-gular moment of sunrise and another hope risen up from the night, born again with quiet strength.

He opened his eyes to the dark skies and the foliate pat-tern of stars. In the east, the first intimation of day arose as the black hinted of violet hues. A quiet relief filled him, and he took a lungful of air.

Another day would come. And pass. Until the beautiful, distant stars returned, and he came again to watch. Until someday, when either he or the sun would not rise. And the song would end.

He lingered, enjoying a moment's peace. They'd been on the road more days than he could remember. Chased by the Quiet. Chased since the night he'd let Wendra down, failed to shoot when she'd needed him, when the Quiet took her child. Tahn shook his head with guilt at the memory of it.

And now here he was. Weeks later. Far from home. Just tonight they'd climbed this plateau, arriving after midnight. After dark hour.

He took a long breath, relaxing in the stillness.

The sound of boots over frost-covered earth startled him. He turned to see Vendanj come to join him.

Even the shadows of night couldn't soften the hard edges of the man. Vendanj wore determination the way another does his boots. Carried it in his eyes and shoulders. Vendanj was a member of the Sheason Order, those who rendered the Will—that melding of spirit and body, energy and matter. The Sheason weren't well known in the Hollows, Tahn's home. And Tahn was learning that beyond the Hollows, the Sheason weren't always welcome. Were even distrusted.

Vendanj came up beside him, and stared out over the plains far and away below. He didn't rush to clutter the silence with words. And they watched together for a time.

After long moments, Vendanj eyed Tahn with wry suspicion. "You do this every morning." It wasn't a question.

Tahn returned the wry grin. "How would you know? You follow me everywhere?"

"Just until we reach the Saeculorum," Vendanj answered.

They shared quiet laughter over that. It was a rare jest from Vendanj. But it was a square jest, the kind with truth inside. Because they were, in fact, going to the Saeculorum—mountains at the far end of the Eastlands. Several months' travel from here.

"For as long as I can remember," Tahn finally admitted, "I've gotten up early to watch the sunrise. Habit now, I guess."

Vendanj folded his arms as he stared east. "It's more than a habit, I suspect."

And he was right. It was more like a compulsion. A need. To stand with the stars. Imagine daybreak.

But Vendanj didn't press, and fell silent again for a time.

Into the silence, distantly, came again the sound of footfalls over hard dirt. The chill air grew . . . tight. Dense. It seemed to press on Tahn. Panic tightened his gut. Vendanj held up a hand for Tahn not to speak. A few moments later, up the trail of the cliff face came a figure, unhurried. Directly toward them.

Soon, the moon brought the shape into focus. A man. He wore an unremarkable coat, buttoned high against the chill. No cowl or robe or weapon. No smile of greeting. No frown. It was the man's utter lack of expression that frightened Tahn most, as if feeling had gone out of him.

Twenty strides from them, the other stopped, returning the bluff to silence. The figure stared at them through the dark. Stared at them with disregard.

Softer than a whisper, "Velle," Vendanj said.

My dying gods.

Velle were Quiet renderers of the Will. Like Sheason, but followers of the dissenting god.

The silence stretched between them, dawn still a long while away.

Into the stillness, the other spoke, his voice soft and low. "Your legs will tire, Sheason. And we will be there when they do." He pointed at Tahn. "Send me the boy, and let's be done."

"It would do you no good," Vendanj replied. "If not the boy, there are others."

The Velle nodded. "We know. And this one isn't the first you've driven like a mule." The man's eyes shifted to Tahn. "What has he told you, Quillescent?"

Tahn didn't really understand the question, and didn't reply. He only took his bow down from his shoulder.

The Velle shook his head slowly in disappointment. "You don't have the energy to fight me, Sheason. You've spent too much already."

"I appreciate your concern," Vendanj said, another surprising jest from the usually severe man.

The Velle hadn't taken its eyes from Tahn. "And what about you, with your little bow? Are you going to ask your gods if I should die, and shoot me down?" The expression in the man's face changed, but only by degrees. *More* indifferent. Careworn to the bone, beyond feeling.

He knows. He knows the words I speak when I draw.

The Velle dropped its chin. "Ask it." The words were an invitation, a challenge. And the chill air bristled when the Velle spoke them. Grasses and low sage bent away from the man as though they would flee.

Vendanj held up a hand. "You've strolled onto the Sedagin plain, my Quiet friend. A thousand swords and more. Go back the way you came."

A slow smile touched the Velle's face. A wan smile lacking warmth or humor. And even that looked unnatural, as though he were unaccustomed to smiling at all. "I don't take care for myself, Sheason. That is a *man's* weakness. And there'll be no heroes this time." He raised a hand, and Vendanj let out an explosive exhale, as if his chest were suddenly being pressed by boulders.

In a single motion, Tahn raised his bow and drew an arrow. *I draw with the strength of my arms, but release as the Will allows.*

The quiet confirmation came. The Velle should die.

Tahn caught a glimpse of a more genuine smile on the Quiet's lips before he let his arrow fly. An unconcerned flip of the Velle's wrist, and the arrow careened high and harmless out over the bluff's edge.

Vendanj dropped to his knees, struggling against some unseen force. Tahn had to disrupt the Velle's hold on the Sheason somehow. But before he could move, a deep shiver started in his chest as though his body were a low cello string being slowly played. And with the resonance rushed the memory of his failure to shoot the Bar'dyn that had come into his and Wendra's home, taken her child.

Except it seemed more raw now. Like alcohol poured on a fresh cut.

And that wasn't all. Other memories stirred. Lies he'd told. Insults he'd offered. Though he couldn't recall them with exactness. They were half formed, but sharpening.

He was maybe seven. A fight. Friends. Some kind of contest to settle . . .

Tahn began to tremble violently. His teeth ached and felt ready to shatter. His mind burned hot with regret and self-loathing. He dropped face-first beside Vendanj, and curled into a ball against the pain.

Vendanj still wasn't breathing, but managed to thrust an open palm at the Velle. The Quiet man grimaced, and Vendanj drew a harsh-sounding breath, his face slick with sweat in the moonlight.

Tahn's own inner ache subsided, and the quaking in his body stopped. Briefly. The Velle dropped to both knees and drove its hands into the hard soil. Blackness flared, and the Quiet man looked suddenly refreshed. This time, it simply stared at Vendanj. The earth between them whipped, low sage tearing away. But Vendanj was prepared, and kept his feet and breath when some force hit him, exploding in a fury of spent energy. The Sheason's lean face had drawn into a grim expression, and he began shaking his head.

The Velle glanced at Tahn and tremors wracked his body again. With them came his insecurities about childhood years lost to memory. As if they didn't matter. As if *he* didn't matter, except to raise his bow and repeat those godsforsaken words, *I draw with the strength . . .*

As the Velle caressed him with this deep resonant pain, a shadow flashed behind the other. Light and quick.

A moment later the Velle's back arched, his eyes wide in surprise. Tahn's tremors stopped. Vendanj lowered his arms. The Velle fell forward, and standing there was Mira Far, of the Far people. Her pale skin awash in moonlight. Only a Far could have gotten behind a Velle without being noticed. Looking at her, Tahn felt a different kind of tug inside. One that was altogether more appealing.

For the third time that morning, boots over hard earth interrupted the dark morning stillness. A hundred strides behind Mira three Bar'dyn emerged on the trail. At first they only walked. Then, seeing the downed Velle, they broke into a run, a kind of reasoned indifference in their faces. Their massive frames moved with grace, and power, as their feet pounded against the cold earth.

Tahn reached for an arrow. Mira dropped into one of her Latae stances, both swords raised. Vendanj gasped several breaths, still trying to steady himself from his contest with the Velle. "Take the Bar'dyn down," he said, his voice full of hateful prejudice.

Tahn pulled three successive draws, thinking the old words in an instant and firing at the closest Bar'dyn. The first arrow bounded harmlessly off the creature's barklike skin. But the next two struck it in the neck. It fell with a heavy crunch on the frost-covered soil.

The remaining two descended on Mira first. She ducked under a savage swipe of a long rounded blade and came up with a thrust into the creature's groin. Not simply an attack on its tender parts, but a precise cut into the artery that ran alongside them—something she'd taught him during one of their many conversations.

The Bar'dyn shrugged off the blow and rushed onward toward Tahn. In a few moments it would grow sluggish from blood loss, and finally fall. Tahn had only to keep a distance.

The other Quiet pushed ahead faster, closing on Tahn. Mira took chase, but even with her gift of speed wouldn't reach it before it got to him. Tahn pulled a deep draw. The Bar'dyn raised a forearm to protect its neck, and barreled closer.

"Take it down!" Vendanj began raising a hand, clearly weakened. The Sheason had rendered the Will so often lately. And he'd had little time to recover.

Tahn breathed out, steadied his aim, spoke the words in his mind, and let fly. The arrow hit true, taking the Bar'dyn's left eye. No cry or scream. It stutter-stepped, and kept on. Its expression was as impassive as before—not fury, reason.

Tahn drew again. This arrow struck the Quiet's knee, as he'd intended. But it shattered against the armor-hard skin there. It was almost too close to fire again, but Tahn pulled a quick draw, Mira a half step behind the creature, and fired at its mouth. The arrow smashed through its teeth and went out through its cheek. The Bar'dyn's face stretched in a mask of pain. Then it leveled its eyes again and leapt at Tahn.

It was too late to avoid the Quiet. Tahn braced himself. The massive creature drove him to the ground under its immense weight. Tahn lost his breath, couldn't cry out. He could feel blood on his face. The Bar'dyn shifted to take hold of him.

It propped itself up with one arm, and stared down at Tahn with its indifferent eyes. "You don't understand," it said with a thick, glottal voice.

The Bar'dyn began to roll, pulling Tahn with it, as if it might try to carry him away. A moment later, it stopped moving. Mira. She pulled her blade from the creature's head. Then she turned on the wounded Bar'dyn, who was now staggering toward them, weak from loss of blood.

The last Quiet fell. It panted for several moments, then went still.

CHAPTER TWO

KEEPING PROMISES

"And a Sheason known as Portis came into the court of King Yusefi, king of Kuren, and demanded he keep his pledge to the Second Promise and send men to help the Sedagin in the far North. But Yusefi denied him. Whereupon Portis rendered the king's blood boiling hot and burned him alive inside. To my knowledge, this is the first recorded instance of Sheason violence against man."

—An account of the Castigation, from the pages of the Kuren Court diarist

WARM BAR'DYN BLOOD steamed in the moonlight. Tahn scrambled away from the dead Quiet and sat heavily on the cold ground. His heart hammered in his chest. There was no getting used to this.

And now a Velle! What had it done to him? He still felt it. Like vibrations of thought or emotion. Deep down.

"All the way to the Saeculorum," Tahn said, repeating the joke Vendanj had made before this latest Quiet attack. Now it just sounded exhausting. Impossible.

Vendanj eased himself down to sit near Tahn. "It's good you're handy with a bow."

Mira crouched in front of them, keeping her feet under her—always ready. "Velle. That's new." She was looking at Vendanj.

He nodded. "But not surprising. And not the last we'll see of them."

"There's a happy thought," Tahn said without humor. "Seems like every damn day another storybook rhyme steps from the page. What was it doing to me?"

Vendanj eyed him. Tapped his own chest. "You felt it in here."

Tahn nodded.

"A renderer of the Will can move things," he explained. "Push them. Sometimes you'll see what he does. Sometimes you won't." He took a long breath. "Sometimes it's outside the body. And other times," Vendanj tapped his chest again, "it's in here."

"I don't feel the same," Tahn said.

"It's Resonance." Vendanj said it with obvious concern. "It'll linger like a played note. Won't ever go away completely. But it'll stop feeling like it does today."

Tahn rubbed his chest. "I felt like I was remembering . . ." But it hadn't completely come back. Mostly the *feeling* of the memory remained. He turned to Vendanj. "What did it mean, 'There'll be no heroes this time'?"

Vendanj took a storyteller's breath. "This plateau used to be part of the flatlands below." He gestured out over the bluff. "The Sedagin people here are known as the Right Arm of the Promise. Masters of the longblade. They've always kept the First Promise; always marched against the Quiet when they come."

"What about this time?" Tahn asked, looking at the dead Velle.

Vendanj didn't seem to hear him. "First time the Quiet came, the regent of Recityv called a Convocation of Seats. Every nation and throne was asked to join an alliance to meet the threat. And most did. The Sedagin were the strongest part of that army. And the Quiet were pushed back.

"Ages later, the Quiet came again." Vendanj shook his head and sighed. "But by then Convocation had become a political game. Kings committed only token regiments. So, the regent Corihehn adjourned Convocation and sent word to Holivagh, leader of the Sedagin, to march toward the Pall mountains. He told him there was a Second Promise from this Second Convocation. He told him an alliance army would meet them there."

Tahn guessed the next part, disgust rising in his throat. "It was a lie."

"It was a lie," Vendanj echoed, nodding. "Twenty thousand Sedagin soldiers cut a path through the Quiet. They reached the Pall mountains where Bourne armies were crossing into the Eastlands, but by then only two thousand Sedagin were left. Still, they held the breach for eight days. They waited for Corihehn's reinforcements. But the army of the Second Promise never came. And every Sedagin bladesman perished."

"But we won the war," Tahn added, tentative.

"When Del'Agio, Randeur of the Sheason, learned what Corihehn had done, he sent Sheason messengers into the courts of every city. They threatened death to any who wouldn't honor Corihehn's lie. The Castigation, it was called."

Vendanj looked up and down the edge of the bluff. "When the war was won, the Sheason came into the high plains. For several cycles of the first moon they linked hands and willed the earth to rise, built an earthen monument to the Sedagin. Gave them a home. These plains are known as Teheale. It means 'earned in blood' in the Covenant Tongue."

Tahn sat silent in reverence to the sacrifice made so long ago.

"Seems our Velle friend doesn't think Sheason and Sedagin can turn the Quiet back again." Vendanj's smile caught in the light of the moon. "No heroes."

In many ways, Vendanj reminded Tahn of his father, Balatin. Serious, but able to let worry go when he sensed Tahn needed to laugh or just let things lie. Tahn suddenly missed his father, a deep missing. His da had gone to his earth a few years ago, leaving Tahn and Wendra to make their way alone—their mother, Vocencia, had died a few years before Balatin. He missed her, too.

"It'll look something like this." Vendanj gestured away from the high plateau again, shifting topics. "The Heights of Restoration, Tahn. On the far side of the Saeculorum."

"Because you think this time *I'm* the hero?" He stared at the steam rising from the dead Bar'dyn's wounds.

Vendanj sighed. "I'm inclined to agree with the Velle. And I don't think like that anymore." He paused, his eyes distant. "If I ever did."

"He said there were others," Tahn pressed. "Called me a mule."

Vendanj gave a dismissive laugh over that. "We're all mules. Each hauling some damn load, don't you think?"

Tahn waited, making clear he wanted an answer. He'd agreed to come. He was bone weary, and scared to think Vendanj had pinned too much hope on him.

Tahn could hit almost anything with his bow. There'd been countless hours of practice supervised by his father. Even before that, he'd had a sure hand.

Somewhere in those lost years of his young life he'd obviously learned its use; fighting techniques, too—his reactions were like Mira's Latae battle forms, just less polished. But against an army? Against Velle? That thing had taken hold of him somehow. Not just his body, but *who* he was. It had stroked painful memories, giving them new life in his mind. It was a pain unlike anything he'd yet felt. This was madness.

What the hell am I doing?

The Sheason seemed to know his thoughts, and put a hand on Tahn's shoulder. "There's a sense about you, Tahn. Like the words you use when you draw your bow." He paused. "But no, you're not the only one we've taken to Restoration. Remember what I said at the start: We believe you can stand there. You've not passed your Change, so the burdens of your mistakes aren't fully on you yet. That'll make it easier."

"Why would you need *me* if you've taken others?"

Vendanj let out a long breath. He settled a gaze on Tahn that spoke of disappointment and regret. "None have survived Tillinghast." He paused as if weighing Tahn's resolve. "That's its old name. Tillinghast is where the Heights of Restoration fall away." He gestured again toward the cliff's edge close by. "Like this bluff."

215

Before Tahn could comment, Vendanj pushed on. "And that's those who went at all. Most chose not to go. Your willingness. It sets you apart from most."

"He's right," Mira added, approval in her voice.

Tahn looked up at her, finding encouragement in her silver-grey eyes. She showed him the barest of smiles. And warmth flooded his chest and belly, chasing out some of the deep shiver still lingering inside him.

"Tahn," Vendanj said, gathering his attention again. "The thing you need to remember is this. Standing at Tillinghast isn't just about what ever mettle's in you to survive its touch. It's more about whether or not you can suffer the change it'll cause in you once it's done."

Tahn shook his head, panic fluttering anew in his chest. "What change?"

"Different for everyone who stands there," Vendanj replied.

"If they *live*," Tahn observed with sharp sarcasm. "And then do what?"

"If the Quiet fully break free of the Bourne"—Mira nodded as though it was only a matter of time—"they'll come with elder beings. Creatures against which steel is useless."

Vendanj got to his feet. "And my order is at odds with itself. Diminished because of it." He looked down at Tahn. "This time . . . we've asked *you* to go to Tillinghast. The Veil that holds the Quiet at bay is weakening. Could be that the Song of Suffering that keeps it strong is failing. I know there are few with the ability to sing Suffering. But whatever the reason for the Veil's weakness, we think—if you can stand at Tillinghast—you can help should a full Quiet army come."

Tahn shook his head in disbelief. And fear. "All because of the damned words I can't help but say every time I draw." He shook his bow. "And because I have a *sense*. Maybe it's time you restore my memory. Give me back those twelve years you say you took from me when you sent me to the Hollows."

He wanted that more than he let on. His earliest memories began just six years ago. *Twelve years. Gone.* And until Vendanj had come into the Hollows, Than had thought maybe he'd had some sort of accident. Hit his head. Lost his memory. But the Sheason had taken it. To protect him, the man had said.

"You may believe you're ready for that. But think about it." He pointed at the Velle, which had surfaced searing memories in him. "You don't remember your young life . . . but it was a hard one. Not *all* hard. But most of it was spent in an unhappy place. And now, you're far from home, chased by Quiet, asked to climb to Tillinghast, and you're coming soon to the age of accountability."

Tahn had been eager for his Standing and the Change that came after his eighteenth year. Eager for what, he didn't exactly know. To be taken more seriously was part of it, though. And because he'd thought he might somehow get his memory back.

Tahn stood, shouldered his bow. "Wouldn't that suggest I'm old enough—"

"No, it wouldn't," Vendanj cut in sharply. "I took your memory all those years ago as a protection to you. It still is. Before we reach Tillinghast I'll return it to you. You'll need it there." He put his hand again on Tahn's shoulder, his hard expression softening. "But not now. Trust me on this. I've seen what it does to a mind when so much change comes at once."

Tahn thought about the pressure in his body and mind when the Velle had taken hold of him. The things it had surfaced all in a rush. Jagged, ugly things to remember.

Images of young friends, though he couldn't see their faces. A fight, though he couldn't remember why. Except they were settling something. The feeling of betrayal lingered. A sad pain in the pit of his stomach.

Tahn walked to where the Velle lay. Something glinted on the ground near its body. He hunkered down and ran his fingers across a smooth surface glistening with moonlight. Felt like glass. At its center were two fist-sized holes.

"What's this?"

Vendanj came up beside him. "Velle won't bear the cost of rendering the Will. They transfer it. Take the vitality of anything at hand so they can remain strong."

The Velle had thrust its hands into the soil. Darkness had flared. It had caused the formation of this thin crust of dark glass. Tahn stepped on it. A soft *pop*. A fragile sound. If Vendanj hadn't been here, what else inside Tahn would the Velle have taken hold of?

He finally gave a low, resigned laugh. "You win. Why complicate all this fun we're having, right?"

He stole a look at Mira, who showed him her slim smile again. That, at least, was helpful. Hopeful, too. Like the lighter shades of blue strengthening in the east behind her.

Just before he turned away, he caught sight of low fogs gathering on the lowland floor. He pointed. "You see that?"

Vendanj looked, and his expression hardened. Soon Mira stood with them, as they watched a cloud bank form around the base of the plateau.

"Je'holta," Vendanj said.

"What is it?" Tahn asked.

"Another form of Quiet." He paused a long moment. "And something we'll now have to pass through when we leave here."

Mira's smile was gone. "Good test for Tillinghast."

Tahn gave them each a long look, and said without humor, "I just came out to watch the sunrise . . . ."

Read on for a preview of the

TRIAL OF INTENTIONS

BOOK TWO OF

THE VAULT OF HEAVEN

by

PETER ORULLIAN

A THIRD PURPOSE

"Encouragements are drawn from living things—trees, grasses, animals. First and best from family. All are vital. All nourish. Perishment results from the absence of these."
—From *The Effect of Absences,* a correlative
war doctrine originating in the Bourn

AFTER LONG YEARS in the Scarred Lands, Than Junell realized their patrols held a third purpose.

First, and most obviously, they were meant to provide early warning when visitors or strangers came into the Scar. Patrol routes held long sight lines of the wide, barren lands. From a distance, newcomers could be easily spotted and reported.

On a second, more practical level, patrols were used to build and maintain stamina for fight sessions. Every ward of the Scar—age three to nineteen—spent no less than six hours a day in ritualized combat training.

It wasn't until later that Tahn finally came to realize a subtle third reason for patrols. They were a way for wards of the Scar to monitor themselves and guard against one of their own wandering from home, alone.

With the purpose of self-slaughter.

Tahn and Alemdra ran fast, arriving at Gutter Ridge well ahead of sunrise. They slowed to a walk, catching their breath and sharing smiles.

"You're starting to slow me down," Alemdra teased. "I think it's because I'm becoming a woman, and you're still a boy."

He laughed. "Well, maybe if we're going to keep running patrols together, I'll just put a saddle on you, then."

She hit him in the arm, and they sat together with their legs dangling from one of the few significant ridges in the Scar. Alemdra was twelve today, barely older than Tahn. And he intended to kiss her. Seeing the glint in her eye, he wondered if she'd guessed his intention. But if so, the unspoken secret only added to the anticipation.

Casually wagging their toes, they looked east.

"See that?" He pointed at the brightest star in the eastern hemisphere. She nodded. "That's Katia Shonay, the morning star. It's really a planet."

"That so." She squinted as if doing so might bring the distant object into sharper focus.

"Katia Shonay means 'lovelorn' in Dimnian." He liked few things better than talking about the sky. "There's this whole story about how a furrow tender fell in love with a woman of the court."

She made no effort to conceal her suspicion of his timing for sharing the story of this particular planet. "You might make a good furrow tender someday. If you work hard at it, that is."

"Actually," he countered, smiling, "the story's only complete in the conjunction of Rushe Symone—the planet named after the god of plenty and favor. You know, bountiful harvests and autumn bacchanalia." He nearly blushed over the last part, having learned the richness of bacchanal rituals. "Rych is the largest planet—"

She was giving him a look. *The* look. "You seem to think you're smarter than us now."

"What do you mean *now*?" And he started laughing.

She broke down laughing, too. "You really liked it there, didn't you? In Aubade Grove."

"I'd go back tomorrow if it didn't mean leaving you behind." It came out sounding more honest than he'd intended, but he wasn't embarrassed. He stared off at Katia. "It's amazing, Alemdra. No patrols. No fight sessions. Just books. Study. Skyglassing to discover what's up there." He gestured grandly at the eastern sky.

She smiled, sharing his enthusiasm for the few years he'd been away before being called back here. "Do you think you'll ever leave the Scar for good?" There was a small, fatal note in her voice.

He turned to see her expression—the same one she always wore when they talked about Grant. While all the wards were like Grant's adoptive children, Tahn was the man's actual son. He supposed someday he might leave this place, especially if he ever learned who his mother was. If she was still alive.

"Eventually. After my father goes to his earth. I don't think I could leave him here alone." Tahn threw a rock and listened for it to hit far below. In his head he began doing some math to determine the height of the ridge. *Initial velocity, count of six to the rock's impact, acceleration due to gravity—*

"He'll never be alone, Tahn," she said, interrupting his calculations. "Not as long as the *cradle* is here."

Tahn nodded grimly. The Forgotten Cradle. It served as a big damn reminder of abandonment to all the wards of the Scar. And it was how most of them came to this place. Every cycle of the first moon a babe was placed in the hollow of a dead bristlecone pine. Orphans. Foundlings. And sometimes children whose parents just didn't want them anymore. Grant retrieved each child, tried to find it a proper home outside the Scar. Those for whom no arrangements could be made came to live with them *inside* the Scar. Not knowing their actual day of birth, wards celebrated their "cradleday"—the day they were rescued from the tree. Like he and Alemdra were doing for her today.

"I don't know why you feel any loyalty to stay, either." She looked away to where the sun would crest the mountains to the east. "Not after what he's done to you."

His father put more pressure on him. Tahn's lessons were less predictable. Harder. One might wonder if being his son, he bore the brunt of his father's exile here. A sentence he'd earned for defying the regent. And his father could never leave; otherwise who would fetch the babes from the cradle?

Their special morning had struck a somber note. But he couldn't let her comment lie, even though in his heart he agreed. "He just has a different way of teaching."

Alemdra seemed to realize she'd touched too close to private insecurities. "If you go, will you take me with you?"

Tahn smiled, grateful for a change in the direction of their morning chat. "You think you can keep up? I mean, I *have* been off to college and all."

This time she hit him in the shoulder, soft enough to let him know she wasn't offended, hard enough to let him know she was no rube. Then they fell into another companionable silence. The sun was near to rising. They wouldn't speak again until its rays glimmered in their eyes. This was Tahn's favorite time in the Scar. Morning had a kind of wonder in it. As if the day might end differently than the one before it. That moment of sun first lighting the sky was something he made time every day to witness. And he liked these sunrise moments best when Alemdra was with him.

He wanted to kiss her when the sun began to break. Sentimental, maybe, but it felt right anyway. As the time drew closer, his left leg began to shimmy all on its own.

What if he'd misread their growing friendship? What if she rejected his kiss? He'd be ruining future chances to run with her on morning patrol.

When the sun's first rays broke over the horizon, he turned to her, his mind racing to find some words, debating if he should just grasp her by the shoulders and do it.

He neither spoke nor grasped. In the second he turned, Alemdra inclined with a swift grace and put her mouth on his. Her eyes were open, and she left her lips there for a long time before closing them and uttering a sigh of innocent delight.

The sound brought Tahn's heart to a pounding thump, and he knew he loved her. The other wards would tease him; maybe try to convince him he was just a boy and couldn't know such feelings. Let them. Because even if he and Alemdra never knew a more intimate moment than this, he would always remember her kiss, her sigh.

Sometime later, she pulled away, her eyes opening again. She smiled—not with embarrassment, but happily. And together they watched the sun finish its rise into the sky.

Then an urgent rhythm interrupted the morning stillness. Distant footfalls. Someone running. Together they turned toward the sound. A hundred strides to the east, from behind a copse of dead trees, a figure emerged at a dead run toward the cliff. They watched in horror as their friend Devin leapt from the edge. Her arms and legs pinwheeled briefly, before she gave in to the fall, her body pulled earthward toward the jag of rocks far below.

Alemdra screamed. The shrill sound echoed across the deep, rocky ravine as their friend fell down. And down. Tahn stood up on impulse, but could only watch as Devin stared skyward, letting the force of attraction do its awful work. *Initial velocity, acceleration due to gravity . . .*

A few moments later, Devin struck the hardpan below with a sharp cry. And lay instantly still.

"Devin!" Tahn wailed, wanting his friend to take it back. Angry, frustrated tears filled his eyes.

Alemdra turned to him. They shared a long, painful look. They'd failed their third purpose. They'd been so caught up in Alemdra's cradleday, in the peace of sunrise, in their first kiss, that they'd missed any signs of Devin. One of their closest friends.

Alemdra sank to her knees, sobs wracking her body. Tahn

put his arms around her and together they wept for Devin. At Gutter Ridge, in the first rays of day, with Katia Shonay still rising in the east, they wept for another ward who'd lost her battle with the Scar.

The third purpose. Tahn understood the feeling that got into those who made this choice. Every ward had some kind of defense against it. Or tried. His defense was the sky, morning and sunrise. Those moments gave him something to look forward to, to find hope in.

Sometime later, they started down to gather the body, keeping a griever's silence as they went. The sun had grown hot by the time they got to Devin. They stood a while before Alemdra broke the silence. "She turned fifteen last week."

Wards who found their way out of the Scar often did so soon after their cradleday.

Alemdra sniffed, wiping away tears. There was a familiar worry in her voice when she whispered, "She was strong. Stronger than most."

Tahn knew she meant in spirit. He nodded. "That's what scares me."

They fell silent again, knowing soon enough they'd need to build a litter to drag the body home. There'd be a note in Devin's pocket. There was always a note. It would speak of apology. Of regret. Of the inability to suffer the Scar another day. There'd be no blame laid on Grant. Actually, he'd be thanked for caring for them, for trying to teach them to survive in the world. But mostly, the note would be about what *wasn't* written on the paper. It would be about how the Scar somehow amplified the abandonment that had brought a ward to the Forgotten Cradle in the first place.

The notes were all the same, and were always addressed to Grant, anyway.

Patrols usually didn't bother looking for them.

Alemdra went slowly to Devin's side and knelt. Hunched over the body, she brushed tenderly at Devin's hair, speaking in a soothing tone—the kind one uses with a child, or the very sick. Her shoulders began to rise and fall again with sobs she could no longer hold back.

Tahn stepped forward and put an arm around her, trying this time to be strong.

"It gets inside." Alemdra tapped her chest. "You can't ever really get out of the Scar, can you? Even if you leave." She looked up at Tahn. Her expression said she wanted to be argued with, convinced otherwise.

Tahn could only stare back. He'd gotten out of the Scar—a little bit, anyway—during his time in Aubade Grove. Maybe.

This time, Alemdra *did* look for the note. It wasn't hard to find. But when she unfolded the square of parchment, it *was* different. No words at all. A drawing of a woman, maybe forty or so, beautifully rendered with deep laugh lines around her eyes and mouth, and a biggish nose. Devin had talent that way. Drawing without making everything dreamlike.

The likeness brought fresh sobs from Alemdra. "It's how she imagined her mother."

That tore at Tahn's fragile bravery. He could see in the drawing hints of Devin as an older woman. Simple thing to want to know a parent's face. *Dead gods, Devin, I'm sorry.*

CHAPTER ONE

THE RIGHT DRAW

"Mercy has many faces. One of them looks like cruelty."
—Reconciliationist defense of the gods' placement
of the Quiet inside the Bourne

TAHN JUNELL RACED north across the Soliel plain, and his past raced with him. He ran in the dark and cold of predawn. A canopy of bright stars shone in clear skies above. And underfoot, his boots pounded an urgent rhythm against the shale. In his left hand, he clenched his bow. In his mind, growing dread pushed away the crush of his recently returned memory. Ahead, still out of sight, marching on the city of Naltus Far . . . came the Quiet.

Abandoning gods. The Quiet. Just a few moon cycles ago, these storied races had been to Tahn just that. Stories. Stories he'd believed, but only in that distant way that death concerned the living. *Their* story told of being herded and sealed deep in the far west and north—distant lands known as the Bourne, a place created by the gods before they'd abandoned the world as lost.

One of his Far companions tapped his shoulder and pointed. "Over there." Ahead on the left stood a dolmen risen from great slabs of shale.

Tahn concentrated, taking care where he put his feet, trying to move without drawing any attention. The three Far from the city guard ran close, their flight over the stones quiet as a whisper on the plain. They'd insisted on bearing him company. There'd been no time to argue.

Through light winds that carried the scent of shale and sage, they ran. A hundred strides on, they ducked into a shallow depression beside the dolmen. In the lee side of the tomb, Tahn drew quick breaths, the Far hardly winded.

"I'm Daen," the Far captain said softly. He showed Tahn a wry smile—acquaintances coming here, now—and put out his hand.

"Tahn." He clasped the Far's hand in the grip of friendship.

"I know. This is Jarron and Aelos." Daen gestured toward the two behind him. Each nodded a greeting. "Now, do you want to tell us why we've rushed headlong toward several colloughs of Bar'dyn?" Daen's smile turned inquiring.

Tahn looked in the direction of the advancing army. It was still a long way off. But he pictured it in his head. Just one collough was a thousand strong. So, several of them . . . *deafened gods!* And the Bar'dyn: a Quiet race two heads taller than most men and twice as broad; their hide like elm bark, but tougher, more pliable.

He listened. Only the sound of heavy feet on shale. Distant. The Bar'dyn beat no drum, blew no horn. The absence of sound got inside him like the still of a late-autumn morning before the slaughter of winter stock.

Tahn looked back at Daen. They had a little while to wait, and the Far captain deserved an answer. "Seems reckless, doesn't it." He

232

showed them each a humorless smile. "The truth? I couldn't help myself."

None of the Far replied. It wasn't condescension. More like disarming patience. Which struck Tahn odd, since the Far possessed an almost unnatural speed and grace. A godsgift. And their lives were spent in rehearsal for war. Endless training and vigilance to protect an old language.

"I wouldn't even be in Naltus if it weren't for the Quiet." Tahn looked down at the bow in his lap, suddenly not sure what he meant to do. His bow—any bow—was a very dear, very old friend. He'd been firing one since he could hold a deep draw. But his bow against an army? *I might finally have waded too far into the cesspit.*

"We guessed that much," said Daen.

Tahn locked eyes with the Far captain, who returned a searching stare. "Two cycles ago, I was living a happy, unremarkable life. Small town called the Hollows. Only interesting thing about me was a nagging lack of memory. Had no recollection of anything before my twelfth year. Then, not long before I turned eighteen . . . a Sheason shows up."

The Far Jarron took a quick breath.

Tahn nodded at the response. "First day I met Vendanj, I realized stories about the Sheason are true. I saw him render the Will. Move things . . . kill. With little more than a thought."

"Vendanj is a friend of the king's," Daen said. "Not everyone distrusts him."

Tahn gave a weak smile to that. "Well, he arrived just before the Quiet got to *my* town, too."

He then looked away to the southwest, at Naltus, a magnificent city risen mostly of the black shale that dominated the long plains. In the predawn light, it was still an imposing thing to look at. It never gleamed. It didn't light up with thousands of lights as Recityv or any other large city. It didn't bustle with industry and trade. It didn't build reputation with art and culture. But the city itself was a striking place, drawn with inflexible lines. It had a permanence and stoicism about it. The kind of place you wanted to be when a storm hit, where you wouldn't fear wind and hard light. And where rain lifted the fresh scent of washed rock. Altogether different than the Hollows, with its hardwood forests and loam.

What Tahn wouldn't have given for some hard apple cider and a round of lies in the form of Hollows gossip. "Vendanj convinced me to follow him to Tillinghast."

This time it was Aelos who made a noise, something in his throat, like a warning. It reminded Tahn that even the Far people, with their gift for battle, and their stewardship over the Language of the Framers . . . even *they* didn't go to Tillinghast.

"Did you make it to the far ledge?" Daen asked.

Tahn turned and looked in the direction of the Saeculorum Mountains, which rose in dark, jagged lines to the east. Impossibly high. Yes, he'd made it there. He and the few friends who'd come with him out of the Hollows. Though, only *he* had stood near that ledge at the far end of everything. A place where the earth renewed itself. Or used to.

He'd faced a Draethmorte there, one of the old servants of the dissenting god. More than that. He'd faced the awful embrace of the strange clouds that hung beyond the edge of

Tillinghast. They'd somehow shown him all the choices of his life—those he'd made, and those he'd failed to make. It was a terrible thing to see the missed opportunity to help a friend. Or stranger. Wrapping around him, those clouds had also shown him the *repercussions* of those choices, possible futures. The heavy burden of that knowledge had nearly killed him.

It ached in him still.

But he'd survived the Draethmorte. And the clouds. And he'd done so by learning that he possessed an ability: to draw an empty bow, and fire a part of himself. He couldn't explain it any better than that. It was like shooting a strange mix of thought and emotion. And it left him chilled to the marrow and feeling incomplete. *Diminished.* At least for a while. Maybe something had happened to him in the wilds of Stonemount. Maybe the ghostly barrow robber he'd encountered there had touched him. Touched his mind. Or soul. Maybe both. Whether the barrow robber or not, something had helped him fire *himself* at Tillinghast. Though he damn sure didn't want to do it again, and had no real idea how to control it, anyhow.

"Yes, we made it to the far ledge," he finally said.

He could tell Daen understood plenty about what lay on the other side of the Saeculorum. But the Far captain had the courtesy not to press.

Tahn, though, found relief in sharing some of what had happened. "Near the top, Vendanj restored my memory. He thought it would help me survive up there."

Jarron glanced at the Saeculorum range. "Did it?"

Tahn didn't have an answer to that, and shrugged.

Daen put a hand on Tahn's shoulder. "The Sheason believed if you survived Tillinghast, you could help turn the Quiet back this time. Meet those who've given themselves to the dissenting god . . . in war." He nodded in the direction of the army marching toward them.

Twice before—the wars of the First and Second Promise—the races of the Eastlands had pushed the Quiet back, avoided the dominion they seemed bent toward. Now, they came again.

"Mostly right," said Tahn, "except all I've been fighting since Tillinghast is a head full of bad memories. For two damn days, I've done nothing but sit around in your king's manor, remembering." His grip tightened on his bow, and he spoke through clenched teeth. "Better to be moving. Better to hold someone . . . or something, accountable for that past."

"Idleness makes memory bitter." Daen spoke it like a rote phrase, like something a mother says to scold a laggard child.

Tahn forced a smile, but the feel of it was manic. "Vendanj was the one who took my memory in the first place. Thought it would protect me . . ."

"From the Quiet," Daen finished. "So you're here with a kind of blind vengeance. Angry at the world. Angry at what you believe are the bad choices of people who care for you."

The wind died then, wrapping them in a sullen silence. A silence broken only by the low drone of thousands of heavy feet crossing the shale plain toward them. Into that silence Tahn said simply, "No."

"No?" Daen cocked his head with skepticism.

"I'm not some angry youth." Tahn's smile softened, and he leveled an earnest look on the Far captain. "If I'm reckless, it's because I'm scared. *And* angry. Do I want to drop a few Quiet with this?" He tapped his bow. "Silent hells, yes. But when I saw them from my window in your king's manor this morning . . . I'll be a dead god's privy hole if I'm going to let the Far meet them without me." He pointed to the Quiet army marching in from the northeast. "An army that's probably here *because* of me."

Daen studied Tahn a long moment. "It's reckless . . . but reasonable." He grinned. "Well, listen to me, will you? I sound as contradictory as a Hollows man." His grin faded to a kind of thankful seriousness. "I'm glad you were awake to see them from your window, Tahn. Somehow our scouts failed to get us word."

He'd been up early, as he always was. To greet the dawn. Or rather, imagine it before it came. Those soft moments were more important to him now than ever. Because images plagued him night and day. Images from Tillinghast. Images from a newly remembered past. Sometimes the images gave him the shakes. Sometimes he broke out in a sweat.

Tahn looked again now into the east, anticipating sunrise. The color of the moon caught his eye. Red cast. *Lunar eclipse.* By the look of it, the eclipse had been full a few hours ago. Secula, the first moon, was passing through the sun's penumbra. He'd seen a full eclipse once in . . . *Aubade Grove!* The memories wouldn't stop. He'd spent several years of his young life in the Grove. A place dedicated to the study of the sky. A community of science. This, at least, was a happy memory.

Does the eclipse have anything to do with this Quiet army?

An interesting thought, but there wasn't time to pursue it. The low drone of thousands of Quiet striding the stony plain was growing louder, closer.

"We'll wait until the First Legion joins us on the shale." Daen spoke with the certainty of one used to giving orders. "Anything we observe, we'll report back to our battle strategists."

They didn't understand Tahn's need to run out to meet this army, any more than his friends would have. Sutter and Mira, especially. Sutter because he'd been Tahn's friend since Tahn had arrived in the Hollows. And Mira because—unless he missed his guess—she loved him. So, he'd sent word of the Quiet's approach, and slipped from the king's manor unnoticed.

"I won't do anything foolish," Tahn assured Daen, and began crawling toward the lip of the depression.

The Far captain grabbed Tahn's arm, the smile gone from his face. "What makes you so eager to die?"

Tahn spared a look at the bow in his hand, then stared sharply back at the Far. "I don't want to die. And I don't want *you* to die because of *me.*"

The Far captain didn't let go. "I've never understood man's bloodlust, even for the right cause. It makes him foolish."

Tahn sighed, acknowledging the sentiment. "I'm not here for glory." He clenched his teeth again, days of frustration getting the better of him—memories of a forgotten past, images of possible futures. "But I have to do *something.*"

The Far continued to hold him, appraising. Finally, he nodded. "Just promise me you won't run in until we see the king emerge from the wall with the First Legion."

Tahn agreed, and the two crawled to the rim of the depression and peeked over the edge onto the rocky plane. What they saw stole Tahn's breath: more Bar'dyn than he could ever have imagined. The line stretched out of sight, and behind it row after row after row . . . "Dear dead gods," Tahn whispered under his breath. Naltus would fall. Even with the great skill of the Far. Even with the help of Vendanj, and his Sheason abilities.

We can't win. Despair filled him in a way he'd felt only once before—at Tillinghast.

And on they came. No battle cries. No horns. Just the steady march over dry, dark stone. A hundred strides away, closing, countless feet pounded the shale like a war machine. Tahn's heart began to hammer in his chest.

Beside him, Daen spoke in a tongue Tahn didn't understand. The sound of it like a prayer . . . and a curse.

Then he saw something that he would see in his dreams for a very long time. The Quiet army stopped thirty strides from him. The front line of Bar'dyn parted, and a slow procession emerged from the horde. First came a tall, withered figure wrapped in gauzy robes the color of dried blood. *Velle! Silent hells.* The Velle were like Sheason, renderers of the Will, except they refused to bear the cost of their rendering. They drew it from other sources.

The Velle's garments rustled as the wind kicked up again, brushing across the shale plain. Tahn's throat tightened. Not because of the Velle, or at least not the Velle alone, but because of what it held in its grasp: a handful of black tethers, and at the end of each . . . a child no more than eight years of age.

"No," Tahn whispered. He lowered his face into the shale, needing to look away, wanting to deny the obvious use the Velle had of them.

239

When he looked again, two more Velle had come forward. One was female in appearance, and stood in a magisterial dress of midnight blue. The gown had broad cuffs and wide lapels, and polished black buttons in a triple column down the front. The broadly padded shoulders of the garment gave her an imposing, regal look. The third Velle might have been any field hand from any working farm in the Hollows. He wore a simple coat that looked comfortable, warm, and well used. His trousers and boots were likewise unremarkable. He didn't appear ill fed. Or angry. He simply stood, looking on at the city as any man might after a long walk.

And in the collective hands of these Velle, tethers to six children. The little ones hunched against their bindings. Ragged makeshift smocks hung from their thin shoulders. Each gust of wind pulled at the loose, soiled garments, revealing skin drawn tight over ribs, and knobby legs appearing brittle to the touch.

Worst of all was the look in the children's faces—haunted and scared. And scarred. A look he knew. A look resembling the one worn by many of the children from the Scar. A desolate place he'd only recently remembered. A place where he'd spent a large part of his childhood. Learning to fight. To distrust. Lessons of the abandoned.

Not every memory of the Scar had been bad, though. A name and face flared in his mind: Alemdra. But the bright memory of her quickly changed. Old grief became new at the thought of a ridge where they'd run to watch the sunrise, and seen a friend end her days. *Devin.* Some wounds, he realized, simply couldn't be healed. No atonement was complete enough.

The Velle yanked at the fetters, gathering the small ones close on each side. The children didn't yelp or complain, though grimaces of pain rose in a few faces. Mostly, they fought to keep their balance and avoid falling hard on the shale.

Then the Velle reached down and wrapped their fingers around the wrists of the young ones.

The Far king's legion hadn't emerged from the city wall. The siege on Naltus hadn't yet begun. But Tahn knew the attack these Velle were preparing, fueled by the lives of these six children, would be catastrophic. Naltus might be destroyed before a single sword was raised.

Beside him, the Far captain cursed again and crept down to the dolmen to consult with his fellows. *What do I do?* His grip tightened on his bow. The tales of lone heroes standing against armies were author fancies. Fun to read, but wrong. All wrong. He could get off a few shots at the renderers before any of the Bar'dyn could react. But that wouldn't be enough to stop them, or save the children.

Each Velle raised a hand toward Naltus. Tahn had to do something. Now.

Without thinking further, he climbed onto the shale plain and stood, setting his feet. He pulled his bow up in a smooth, swift motion as he drew an arrow.

Softly he began, "I draw with the strength of my arms, but release as the Will—"

He stopped, not finishing the words he'd spoken all his life when drawing his bow, words taught to him by his father, to seek the rightness of his draw. The rightness of a kill. His father and Vendanj had meant for him to avoid of wrongfully

241

killing anything, or anyone, because they'd thought one day they might need him to go to Tillinghast, where his chances of surviving were better if he went untainted by a wrong or selfish draw.

For as long as he could remember, he'd uttered the phrase and sensed the quiet confirmation that what he aimed at should die. Or not. Usually it was only an elk to stock a meat cellar. But not always. In his mind he saw the Bar'dyn that had stood over his sister Wendra, holding the child she'd just given birth to. He saw himself drawing his bow at it, feeling his words tell him *not* to shoot the creature. He'd followed that impression, and it had cankered his relationship with her ever since.

He was done with the old words. The Velle should die. He wanted to kill them. But he also knew he'd never take them all down. Not even with his ability to shoot a part of himself—something he hadn't learned to control. He'd never be able to stop their rendering of the little ones.

More images. Faces he'd forgotten. Faces of older children—thirteen, fourteen—reposed in stillness. Forever still. Still by their own hands. The despair of the Scar had taken all their hope . . . like Devin, and his failure to save her.

And what of the young ones in these Velle's hands? The ravages of *their* childhood? Long nights spent hoping their parents would come and rescue them. The bone-deep despair reserved for those who learn to stop hoping. He also sensed the ends that awaited each of them. The blinding pain that would tear their spirit from their flesh and remake it into a weapon of destruction. And they wouldn't simply die. Their souls would be spent. If there was a next life, if they had family waiting there, these little ones would never find it. They'd have ceased to be.

Sufferings from his past.

This moment of suffering.

A terrible weight of sorrow and discouragement.

Then a voice in his mind whispered the unthinkable. An awful thing. An irredeemable thing. He fought it. Silently cried out against it. But the dark logic wouldn't relent. And the Velle were nearly ready.

He took a deep breath, adjusted his aim only slightly. And let fly his awful mercy.

The arrow sailed against the shadows of morning and the charcoal hues of this valley of shale. And the first child dropped to the ground.

Through hot, silent tears, Tahn drew fast again, and again. It took the Quiet a few moments to understand what was happening. And when they finally saw Tahn standing beside the dolmen in the grey light of predawn, they appeared momentarily confused. Bar'dyn jumped in front of the Velle like shields. *They still don't understand.*

Like scarecrows—light and yielding—each child fell. Tahn did not miss. Not once.

When it was done, he let out a great, loud cry, the scream ascending the morning air—the only vocal sound on the plain.

Bar'dyn began rushing toward him. Tahn sank to his knees, dropped his bow, and waited for them. He watched the Quiet come as he thought about the wretched thing he'd just done.

It didn't matter that he knew he'd offered the children a greater mercy. Nor that he'd decided this for himself. In those moments, it didn't even matter if what he'd done had saved Naltus.

These small ones, surprise on their faces—*Or was it hope when they saw me? They thought I was going to save them*—before his arrows struck home.

The shale trembled as the Bar'dyn rushed toward him, wearing their calm, reasoning expressions. Already he wondered what he'd do if he had these shots to take again. The bitterness overwhelmed him, and he suddenly yearned for the relief the Bar'dyn would offer him in a swift death. Then strong hands were dragging him backward by the feet, another set of hands retrieving his bow. The Far cast him into the safety of the dolmen. He flipped over and watched Daen Far captain and his squad defend the entrance to the barrow as Bar'dyn rushed in on them.

Jarron fell almost immediately, leaving Daen and Aelos to fight three Quiet.

Tahn couldn't stop trembling. And it had nothing to do with the battle about to darken the Soliel with blood. It was about the way the Quiet would wage their war. About what men would have to do to fight back. Choices like he'd just made.

Abruptly, the Bar'dyn stepped aside. The two Far shared a confused look, their swords still held defensively before them. Then one of the Velle came slowly into view. It stopped and peered past the Far, into the dolmen.

"You're too consumed by your own fear, Quillescent. Rough and untested, despite surviving Tillinghast." Its words floated on the air like a soft, baneful prayer. "Have you learned what you are? What you should do?"

Its mouth pressed into a grim line.

Tahn shook his head in defiance and confusion. Whatever Tillinghast had proven to Vendanj about Tahn being able to stand against the Quiet, the thought of his own future seemed an affliction. He'd rather not know.

"You are a puppet, Quillescent. Or were. But you've cut your strings, haven't you? Killing those children. And for us, you—"

A stream of black bile shot from the creature's mouth, coating its ravaged lips and running down its chin. A blade ripped through its belly. As it fell, it raised a thin hand toward him, and a burst of energy threw Tahn back against one of the tall dolmen stones. Blood burst from his nose and mouth. Shards of pain shot behind his eyes. In his back, the bruising of muscle and bone was deep and immediate.

He dropped to the ground, darkness swimming in his eyes. But he saw Daen and Aelos and the Bar'dyn all look fast to the left, toward the whispering sound of countless feet racing across the shale to meet the Quiet army—the Far legion come to war.

Read on for a preview of the

THE SOUND OF
BROKEN ABSOLUTES

A NOVELLA FROM

THE VAULT OF HEAVEN

by

PETER ORULLIAN

ONE

MAESTERI DIVAD JONASON gently removed the viola d'amore from its weathered sheepskin case. In the silence, he smiled wanly over the old instrument, considering. *Sometimes the most important music lessons feature no music at all.* Such was the case with this viola, an old friend to be sure. It served a different kind of instruction. One that came late in the training of a Lieholan, whose song had the power of *intention.* This instrument could only be understood when the act of making notes work together had long since been any kind of challenge. This viola made fine music, too, of course—a soft, retiring sound most pleasant in the shades of evening. But this heirloom of the Maesteri, generations old now, taught the kind of resonance often only heard inwardly while standing over a freshly dug barrow.

Behind him, the door opened, and he turned to greet his finest Lieholan student, Belamae Sento. The young man stepped into the room, his face pale, an open letter in his hand. Divad didn't need to ask the contents of the note. In fact, it was the letter's arrival that had hastened his invitation to have Belamae join him in this music chamber.

"Close the door, please." Softly spoken, his words took on a hum-like quality, resounding in the near-perfect acoustics of the room.

Belamae absently did as he was asked. The wide-eyed look on his face was not, Divad knew, amazement at finally coming to the Chamber of Absolutes. Although such would have been normal enough for one of the Lyren—a student of the Descant—it wasn't so for Belamae. Not today. Worry and conflict had taken the young man's thoughts far from Descant Cathedral, far from his focus on learning the Song of Suffering.

"You seem distracted. Does finally coming here leave you at a loss for words?" He raised an open palm to indicate the room, but was really just easing them into conversation.

Belamae looked around and shook his head. "It's less . . . impressive than I'd imagined."

Divad chuckled low in his throat, the sound musical in the resonant chamber. "Quite so. I tend not to correct assumptions about this place. Could be that I like the surprise of it when Lieholan see it with their own eyes. But the last lessons in Suffering are plain ones. The room is rightly spare."

The walls and floor and vaulted ceiling were bare granite. In fact, the only objects in the room were four instruments: a boxharp, a dual-tubed horn, a mandola, and the viola Divad held in his hands. Each had a place in an arched cutaway at equal distances around the circular chamber.

He held up the viola. "What about the instruments? What do they suggest you might learn here?"

Belamae looked around again, more slowly this time, coming last to the viola. He concluded with a shrug.

"Aliquot stringing," Divad said, supplying the answer. "It's resonance, my boy. And leads us to *absolute sound*."

249

Belamae nodded, seeming unimpressed or maybe just overly distracted. "Do we have to do this today?"

"Because of the letter you've received," he replied, knowing it was precisely so.

The young Lieholan stared down at the missive in his hands, and spoke without raising his eyes. "I've looked forward to the things you'd teach me here. We all do." He paused, heaving a deep sigh. "But war has come to my people. We're losing the fight. And my da . . . I have to go."

"Aliquots are intentionally unplayed strings that resonate harmonically when you strike the others." He held up the viola and pointed to a second set of seven gut strings strung below those the bow would caress.

Belamae looked up, an incredulous expression on his face.

Divad paid the look no mind. "A string vibrates when struck. There's a mathematical relationship between a vibrating string and an aliquot that resonates with it. This is usually in unison or octaves, but can also come in fifths. We've spoken of resonance before, but always as a way of understanding music that must be *heard* to have a resonant effect."

"Did you hear me?" Belamae asked, irritation edging his voice. "I'm leaving."

"Absolute sound," Divad went on, "is resonance you feel even when it's *not* heard."

"My da—"

"Which is what makes this instrument doubly instructive. You see, we play it in requiem." He caressed the neck of the viola, oiled smooth for easy finger positioning. "Voices sometimes falter, tremulous with emotion. That's understandable.

So just as often, we play the dirge with this. And the melody helps to bring the life of a departed loved one into resonance with those they've left behind. Like the sweet grief of memory."

Belamae's anger sharpened. "In requiem . . . You knew my da was dead? And you didn't tell me?"

Divad shook his head. "You're missing the point. There is a music that can connect you with others in a . . . fundamental way. As fundamental as the sound their life makes. And once you find that resonant sound, it surpasses distance. It no longer needs to be heard to have effect."

The young Lieholan glared back at the older man. Then his brow relaxed, disappointment replacing everything else. "You're telling me not to go."

"I'm telling you you're more important to them here, learning to sing Suffering, than you would be in the field as one more man with a sword." He offered a conciliatory smile. "And you're close, my boy. Ready to understand absolute sound. Nearly ready to sing Suffering on your own."

Belamae shook his head. "I won't ignore their call for help. People are dying." He glanced at the viola in Divad's hands. "They wouldn't have sent for me if it was my sword they wanted. But you don't have to worry; I know how to use my song."

"And what song do you think you have, Belamae? The song you came here with?" His tone became suddenly cross. "Or do you pretend you can make Suffering a weapon? That is not its intention. You would bring greater harm to your own people if that's why you go. I won't allow it."

"You're a coward," Belamae replied with the indignation only the young seem capable of. "I will go and do what I—"

"You should let your loss teach you *more* about Suffering, not take you away from it." Divad strummed the viola's strings, then immediately silenced them. The aliquots hummed in the stillness, resonating from the initial vibration of the viola's top seven strings.

The two men stood staring at one another as the aliquots rang on, which was no brief time. Divad knew trying to force Belamae to stay would prove pointless. Crucial to a Descant education was a Lieholan's willingness. Especially with regard to absolute sound. But if he could get Belamae to grasp the concept, then perhaps the boy would be convinced to remain.

Divad reached into his robe and removed a funeral score penned specifically for this viola. It was a challenging, complex piece of music, made more difficult by the seven strings and their aliquot pairs. Even reading it would stretch his young protégé's skill. Divad had written it himself in anticipation of this very meeting, knowing sooner or later Belamae would learn of the trouble back home. Its theme was separation, constructed in a Maerdian mode that hadn't been used for centuries. It made use of minor seconds and grace notes as central parts of the melody. A listener had to wait patiently for a passage or phrase to resolve, otherwise the note selection might be interpreted as the performer misplaying the piece.

Learning to play it would be its own kind of instruction for the musician, precisely because of the instrument's aliquots.

Divad handed the piece of music to Belamae. "Read this when you think you're ready to hear it." He gently tapped his young friend at the temple, suggesting he be in the right frame of mind when he did so.

Then, more gently still, he handed Belamae the viola d'amore. He wanted this Lieholan to know the heft of it, to run his hands over the flaws in the soundboard, to ask about the intricately carved earless head above the pegbox, to pluck the top-strung gut and listen for the resonating strings beneath . . .

Belamae received the instrument as he had the sheet music, giving it a moment of thoughtful regard. But almost immediately a sneer filled his face, and he slammed the viola down hard on the stone floor, shattering it into pieces.

The crush and clatter of old wood and the twang of snapped strings rose around them in a cacophonous din, echoing in the Chamber of Absolutes. Divad's stomach twisted into knots at the sudden loss of the fine old instrument. The d'amore wasn't crafted anymore. It was as much a historical artifact as it was a unique and beautiful instrument for producing music. And of all the aliquot instruments, it had been his favorite. At Divad's mother's wake, his own former Maesteri had played accompaniment on this viola while Divad sang Johen's "Funerary Triad."

He sank to his knees, instinctively gathering the pieces. Above him he heard the viola bow being snapped in half. The instrument's destruction was complete. Divad's ire flashed bright and hot, and escalated fast. His hands, filled with bits of spruce and bone points still tied with gut, began to tremble with an urge he hadn't felt in a very long time.

With what composure and dignity he could maintain, he gently laid the splintered viola back down and stood. "You ungrateful whoreson. Get out of my sight. And by every absent god, pray I don't forget myself and strike the note of your life. Mundane as I might now find it."

He then watched as Belamae left the room, his student having failed to even try and understand absolute sound. Or perhaps the failure had been Divad's. Belamae hadn't been ready, he told himself. That much was true. But Divad hadn't had a choice. He'd known the lad would feel duty-bound to return home. Still, he never imagined it would go this way. Looking down again, he grieved at the ruin of a beautiful voice—the viola—broken, and appearing impossible to mend.

TWO

ORNING FROST CRUNCHED under my boots as I crossed the frozen field. Several weeks of barge, schooner, overland carriage, and bay-mount had brought me from Recityv to within walking distance of the battle staging area. And more importantly, the captain's tent. I'd left within the hour of my last meeting with Maesteri Divad, which still played in my mind like a vesper's strain sung by an unpracticed voice. All sour notes misplaced by bad intonation.

I was able now, finally, to leave the memory of it alone, though. Mostly because of the dread that began to fill my gut. I didn't know what to expect. I'd hoped to see my ma first, and my sister, Semera. To have some news. To offer some comfort. Probably to receive some of the same. But long before reaching Jenipol, I'd been intercepted by two tight-lipped drummel-men. It's easy to spot men who make percussion a trade—their arms show every sinew. They escorted me here. That had been an alarmingly short ride. Our enemies had pushed deep into the Mor Nations.

The last twenty paces to the tent, my escorts fell back. That didn't do much for my state of mind. I paused a moment at the tent flap, noting where the frost had condensed into droplets from the heat inside the tent. Then I took a long breath and went in.

The air carried the musky smell of warm bodies after a fitful night beneath thick, rough wool. That, and the odor of spent tallow. Four men sat staring down at a low table in the light of two lamps burning a generous amount of wick. They all looked up at me as though I'd interrupted a prayer.

As I started to introduce myself, the man farthest back nodded grimly and said, "Belamae. I didn't think you'd come. Or I should say, I didn't think the Maesteri would permit it."

His name escaped me, but not his rank—this man held field command. I could tell by the deliberate and careful scar- ification on the left side of his neck in the form of an inverted T. Four horizontal hash marks crossed the vertical line. They weren't formal signifiers of rank. The Inverted T was a kind of music staff—an old one, a Kylian notation. The number of lines across it indicated the number of octaves the man had mastered. Which would include complete facility in all scales *and* modes across each. It was breadth as well as depth. More than simply impressive. A second scar-line beneath the bot- tom one meant he could make good use of steel, too.

The men at his table had similar neck scars, but all with one fewer hash. One of these craned his head around, the act seeming to cause him considerable pain. I could see that he'd lost the service of one eye but took no care to cover the wound. A flap of lid hung like a creased drape over the hole.

The one-eyed man looked me up and down the way a til- ler does a draft horse just before plow season. "Doesn't look like much. Neck is thin. Skin's soft. He's not used to making sound on open air. He'll quit in three days. Doesn't matter if he's Karll's boy. I don't believe none in loinfruits."

A third man looked on, carefully appraising, but in a different way. The fellow looked up for a moment, as though framing a question. When he stared at me, his gaze was focused, the way Maesteri Divad's became when he watched for truthful answers and understanding. "Do you want a sword?"

I stared back, somewhat puzzled. "That's not why you sent for me."

The last man at the table did not speak, but instead invited me forward with a nod. As I drew close, I saw what the four had been studying. Not terrain or position maps. Not inventory manifests. Not even letters of command and inquiry sent from the seat of the Tilatian king.

Across the table were spread innumerable scores. These leaders of war were sifting sheet music to prepare for the day's battle. In my few years away from home, I'd learned this was uncommon. The Tilatians might be the only people to do it, in fact. And even among my own kind, it hadn't been done in more than three generations.

Coming a step closer, and as I looked into the faces of the men around the table, it wasn't the carefree good humor of conservatory instructors that I saw. Lord knows I'd come across a cartload of those in my travels as a student from Descant Cathedral. No, these were sober-minded men, reviewing the language of song written for an unfortunate purpose. The tent held the cheerless feel of an overcast winter sky.

Sullen, I thought. *Bitter maybe. But sullen for sure.*

"Nine of ten bear steel into battle. There's no shame in that." The field leader sniffed, refocusing on a score laid out in front of him. "But you're right. That's not why we ask you here. Sit down."

I pulled forward a thin barrel and sat next to the captain, as he set before me a stack of music. "What?"

"I'm Baylet. This is Holis, Shem, and Palandas. These," he gently tapped the scores piled loosely before me, "are airs we send to the line. Tell us which one you'll use."

A chair creaked as Holis, the man with one eye, leaned forward, turning a bit sideways to have a good view of the stack.

"We've already selected morale songs to encourage those who carry steel," Baylet added. "Holis has a good eye for that."

The men exchanged scant looks of mirth, as if the joke were as tired as the men themselves.

"Shem's put aside for later a song of comfort and well-being. Something he wrote himself."

"Calimbaer," I muttered, recalling the class of Mor song that accompanied medical treatment.

Baylet looked across at Shem. "He's also found a good sotto voce for Contentment."

I knew that class of song, too. Two classes really. Sotto voce, an incredibly difficult technique to master, in which singing happened almost under the breath. But *Contentment* . . . it was a type of song sung to one who is beyond help, one who can only be given a spot of peace before going to his final earth.

Holis and Shem produced the music Baylet had spoken of, and dropped it on top of the pile before me. I fanned them out and began to scan. The morale song read like a blaze of horns—written for four voices with two soaring lines above a strong set of rhythmic chants beneath. I could hear the mettle and resolve in my mind as I tracked the chord progressions.

Shem's Calimbaer was an elegant piece composed of few notes, each with long sustain. The movement was languid and would be rendered in a thick legato.

But it was the sotto voce piece that really got to me. I sat poring over the note selection, which made brilliant use of the Lydian and Lochrian modes, the composition effortlessly transitioning between the two. It had me taking deep relaxing breaths. Parts of the melody, even just scanning them, instantly evoked simple, forgotten memories. In those moments, I recalled the marble bench on which I sat the first time I kissed a woman. How cool it had been to the touch, contrasted with the heat in my mouth. I then remembered kneeling in my mother's garden, dutifully clearing the weeds, when I spontaneously created my first real song, or at least the first one I could still recall. And last to my mind came the memory of lying awake, scared, in my first alone-bed, until I heard the comforting, safe sounds of adult voices talking in the outer room.

Baylet swept those selections aside and tapped the original stack again. "Mors who have *influence* in their voice." He gave me a pointed look. "Mors like you. Have each been sent to different lines so that only the Sellari will hear their song. And suffer by it."

The field leader then began to hum a deep pitch, a full octave lower than any note I could reach. The sound of it filled the tent. He gently lifted the topmost score, written on a pressed parchment, and placed it in my hand. When he stopped singing the single note, the silence that followed felt wide and empty, like the bare-limb stretches of late autumn.

He let that silence hang for a long moment before saying, "This is what they will sing today. They have already set out. You should choose quickly."

It wasn't the urgent request or the song he'd sung or the lingering sotto voce that left me in a panic. I put the score aside and began to leaf through the rest of the stack. While I got the impression that the chests I saw in the shadowed corners of the tent carried more music, the fifty or so here would prove to be enough.

Some were reproductions on newer, cleaner paper that still smelled of ink. Most of these were Jollen Caero songs, very old. Jollen was a composer thought to have come down out of the Pall when my Inveterae ancestors had escaped the Bourne. Any other time, I would have liked to study these longer; the melodic choices were as unpredictable as the vocal rhythms. Other selections had been transcribed on parchment that looked like it had seen the field before—ratted edges and smudges where dirty thumbs had held them. Many of these were as interesting as the Jollen songs but for an entirely different reason: their composers were not generally known. And until now, I'd never seen the full scores—only snippets had survived in the forms of childhood rhymes and song-taunts. Seeing the full context for phrases I'd sung here and there all my life left me feeling a bit ashamed and naive.

Before I'd left to study with the Maesteri at Descant, I could have read maybe half of these scores. Back then, I was fluent in six different types of music notation. Now I could read more than thirty. Some of the music here was just that, music only. No lyrics. The Lieholan singing these scores was free to sing them using vowels of his choosing, so long as he didn't attempt to sing actual words.

Other songs in the stack were nothing more than lyrics, but so familiar that any Lieholan worth his brack would know them. The harder part with these came in the language. They hadn't been translated. I counted at least four different languages: early Morian, a difficult Pall tongue, lower Masi, and a root language we knew as Borren. Most Lieholan would perform these phonetically, singing words they didn't understand. For my part, having spent four years at Descant, where language study went along with music training, I could make out the meaning in the lyrics. These were terrifying words. There'd been little effort at rhyme in them. The worst was a litany of tragic images with no narrative or resolution. It might have been the darkest thing I'd ever read. Something I couldn't *unread*.

I scanned from one sheet to the next, moving from standard Mor notation, to the subdominant axis approach typified on the necks of the men around me, to a symbol-centered system that referred to a mandola neck, to the more elegant Petruc signifier, where slight serifs and swoops on a handful of characters gave the singer all the information he needed to render the pitch. I liked the Petruc system best. Those delicate strokes could be added to written language, allowing the lyrics to become the central part of the piece, while subtle Petruc ornamentation on its letters carried the melodic direction.

Originally, it had been created as a code, back during the War of the First Promise.

Probably the most interesting music, though, was a pair of songs written in an augmented Phrygian mode. They were unattributed, but the parchment was old and the Sotol music notation fading some. This music would require vocal gymnastics to carry off, and two voices besides. Though separately composed, they were clearly a call-and-response orchestration. In my mind I could hear where notes sounded together and where vocal runs built tension on top of beautifully dark counterpoint. I wanted to sing this song, whose first bridge was the only portion I had ever heard, and then only the caller side of the arrangement.

All of them I'd heard or sung, if only in part. But the familiarity was precisely the problem and the thing that alarmed me.

When I'd made sure there was nothing *un*familiar, I looked up and locked eyes with Baylet. "You haven't brought the Mor Refrains with you?"

Holis laughed, the squint of his eyes as he did so pinching the lid of his eyeless socket into a pouch of skin. "I see now. You think that's why we called you back. To sing the Refrains. Ah, sapling, we've had it more bitter than this, and not fallen to such foolish desperation." His one remaining eye widened, the way it might if he'd happened on some realization. "But your asking tells us something about you, I think."

The captain knocked on the tabletop once to silence them. "The field men have already marched. Are you rested enough? And is there one of these you know by rote?"

My heart ran cold. They meant to send me to the field . . . today. I stood there, struck dumb for a long moment before nodding.

Baylet seemed satisfied and stood. He motioned for me to follow, and I'd just started after him when a hand caught me tightly by the wrist. I looked down to find Palandas holding me. His grip seemed unusually strong for a man his age.

"The best song, when singing the end of someone, is the one you can make while watching him die." He moistened his lips with his tongue. "That'll be one you must know awfully well, my young friend. Since your voice will have to carry on when the rest of you would rather not."

Palandas held me until I nodded my understanding, which I did without any idea what he really meant. He let me go, and I followed Baylet through the tent flap and south across the frozen field. The promise of sun had grown in the east as a faint line of light blue.

We gathered our mounts at the tree line, and the field leader led me south and east through an elm and broad-pine wood. For the better part of a league we rode. As the trees began to thin, he pulled up and dismounted. I slid from the saddle and stood beside him. The shanks of our mounts steamed in the morning chill.

Finally, I couldn't hold it back any longer. "Why haven't you brought the Mor Refrains? The letter I received made it sound dire."

"War is always dire," he said flatly.

"I came through Talonas, Cyr, and Weilend. All burned. All empty. My history isn't strong, but I don't remember us ever losing three cities to those from across the Soren." My breath plumed before my face as I spoke. "Asking me to leave Descant. I assumed you needed someone—"

"Your training is complete then?" Baylet asked, one eyebrow arching.

"No," I admitted. "But the Refrains haven't been sung in so long. I assumed you'd want someone—"

"The Refrains have *never* been sung." His voice held a pinch of reproach. "The first Mors brought them out of the Bourne to *keep* them from being sung. Which the Quiet would surely have done, if they'd ever gotten their hands on them."

"It's why the Sellari come," I said, stating the obvious. "It's why they've always come. If we fail, they won't hesitate to sing them."

Baylet turned to face me. His stare chilled me deeper than the frigid air. "Then don't fail." He pointed ahead. "Twenty Shoarden men wait for you at the tree line."

Shoarden men. As a child, I'd thought Shoarden simply meant "deaf." Later, when I began to study the Borren root tongues, I learned that it meant "to sacrifice sound."

"Shoarden," I muttered to myself.

"Most Lieholan aren't skilled enough to have their song resonate with a specific individual or . . ." he looked away to the south, where the Sellari camped, "group or army or . . . race." He looked back at me. "It's a technique of absolute sound. A technique you'll possess once your training at Descant is complete. Until then, your song affects any who hear it. So, some of the men sacrifice their hearing in order to guard Lieholan in the field. They take the name Shoarden. Today, I've assigned twenty such men to you. Beyond the tree line, a thousand strides or so, the Sellari eastern flank is camped. They'll come hard. Don't let them through."

He'd apparently said all he meant to say, and quickly mounted.

I struggled to remember the thing I'd wanted to ask him. A hundred questions about the Refrains clouded my mind, but I mentally grasped it before he rode away. "My da."

Baylet held his reins steady, staring ahead. "His sword sang, Belamae. Any man who stood beside him in battle would say the same." He then turned to look at me. "Karll was a friend. Proud as hell of you. He'd be angry with me for sending for you. But a son has to . . . Quiet and Chorus, son, if I'd lost my da I'd want to return murder on the bastards. Thought you'd want the same opportunity. Besides that, we need you. We're outnumbered . . ." His eyes, if it was possible, looked suddenly stonier. "Don't fail."

It was a command. But it was also a plea. The desire to step into the breach for my people filled me like a rush of warm wind. It's hard to explain that feeling. The other thing that was true was that Baylet had put the perfect words on the quiet reason inside me that had brought me here: *return murder on the bastards*. I wasn't proud of that feeling, but I couldn't deny it either. And in the end, I didn't find a thing wrong with it.

I started for the tree line before Baylet kicked his mount into a canter. I did not pause when the twenty Shoarden men fell in around me. I did not pause when I came in sight of the first Sellari scout. I did not pause.

And when a hundred, two hundred of the invaders lined the far meadow, coming on with a steady stride, I recalled the music I'd reviewed that morning in the company of four grim men. A dozen of those songs I knew backward and forward. Three times as many other songs I had full command over: lyric, phrasing, rhythm, and melody. Songs that might suit the kind of destructive influence that filled my heart at that moment.

But as the enemy came within earshot, none of these would do. And when I filled my lungs and opened my mouth, only one song came to me. The fifth movement of Suffering: War.

It was a rough-throat song. As all the line-songs shown to me that morning had been. Maesteri Divad liked to smile and say it was "controlled screaming, cultured hollering." That made as much sense as anything else. The intent of these songs was destruction, aggression. Rasping the voice gave it a scouring, abrasive sound. It conveyed violent intent.

I filled my mind with anguish for my da. I recalled the words of the Song of Suffering's War passage. And I let it all burn inside me. Suffering wasn't meant for this purpose, but I was way past caring about that. I let myself feel indignation and hatred against those who had burned my countrymen.

And then I let it all pour from me in a stream of pounding vocal rhythms that shot out like a succession of iron-gloved punches. I didn't know what would happen, but I'd studied *intention* in my Lieholan training. That's a far cry from saying I'd mastered it. But on this chill morning, mine was clear.

The first few Sellari were ripped off their feet and sent crashing hard upon the frozen earth. I'd later remember the puffs of my own hot breath on the cold air as I shouted out Suffering's War music, which had been meant for protection.

I'd instinctively found the way to make that music a weapon. It was the difference between winning and not losing; between merely drawing breath and gasping it in after a mad dash. It actually taught me a practical lesson on *intention* in a way my Descant study of the principle never had.

At the far end of the great field, hundreds more Sellari appeared in full dress, rushing forward. The Shoarden tightened their circle around me, taking out runners my song didn't seem to affect. When I saw that these runners' ears had been cut off, I realized the Sellari had Shoarden of their own.

The sight of them only deepened my anger. The song itself began to live inside me in a way it never had at Recityv. The feeling was strange. It buoyed me up. But I was simultaneously aware that it was being fueled by some part of me that I wouldn't get back.

I didn't care.

I lengthened my stride. The next notes rushed up past my throat into the natural cavities behind my nose and cheeks, becoming a bright, powerful scream that I shrieked into the morning light. Thirty more had flesh ripped from their face and hands. I heard necks pop, and saw heads cock at unnatural angles, and then bodies falling to the hard earth.

Every attack made me stronger. And sicker it seemed. Though strangely, the burn of aggression kept me moving forward, each screamed musical line felling more of the others. I was soon walking over the bodies of Sellari, eager to take them all down.

I never got that far. The ill feeling soon outbalanced the vengeance, and I struggled to even take a breath. Before I knew it, the Shoarden had picked me up and were rushing me back across the great field ahead of the chasing Sellari. I blacked out to the sound of rushing feet pounding over brittle ground.

ABOUT THE AUTHOR

PETER ORULLIAN has worked at Xbox for over a decade, which is good, because he's a gamer. He's toured internationally with various bands and been a featured vocalist at major rock and metal festivals, which is good, because he's a musician.

He's also learned when to hold his tongue, which is good, because he's a contrarian.

Peter has published several short stories, which he thinks are good. *The Unremembered* and *Trial of Intentions* are his first novels, which he hopes you will think are good. He recently wrote the accompanying novel *The Astonishing* to progressive metal giant Dream Theater's concept album by the same name and is currently at work on an urban fantasy series collaboration with Brandon Sanderson. He lives in Seattle, where it rains all the damn time. He has nothing to say about that. Visit Peter at: www.orullian.com

www.ingramcontent.com/pod-product-compliance
Lightning Source LLC
Chambersburg PA
CBHW021415110726
47901CB00008B/2175

* 9 780971 290990 *